seven days in madrid

eliana vazquez

also by eliana vazquez

Fated Lovers Series

The Muse

The Vow

The Melody

Standalones

7 Days in Madrid

Poetry

The Evolution of Love

7 Days in Madrid

To all the women who have been told that it's too late to do the things they want in life once they hit thirty.

Don't believe a myth that's never come to fruition.

Your life is just starting as an adult. Have fun, fall in love, and enjoy life. Maybe just maybe book a trip to Madrid.

playlist

Algo Que Sirva Como Luz — Supersubmarina
telepatía— Kali Uchis
TUS GAFITAS — KAROL G
Otro Atardecer — Bad Bunny, feat. The Marias
Dime — Kimberly Tell
LA CANCIÓN — maye
LA NOCHE DE ANOCHE — Bad Bunny, feat. ROSALÍA
Eres para Mí — Julieta Venegas, feat. Ana Tijoux
AMOR DE CINE — HUMBE
Abrazado a Ti — Kevin Kaarl
Contigo — Carla Morrison
Amapolas — Leo Rizzi
Fuentes de Ortiz — Ed Maverick
Hasta la Piel — Carla Morrison
BESO — ROSALÍA, feat. Rauw Alejandro
Causa Perdida — Morat
Te Imaginaba — Alvaro Soler

CHAPTER ONE
Sylvie

"I DON'T THINK this is working out," Peter says, packing his clothes into his suitcase.

"What do you mean?" I ask, even though I knew exactly what he meant.

He was breaking up with me.

Peter doesn't make much effort to look up at me as he continues rummaging through his things in the apartment. It's not like he would be able to grab everything tonight. Most of the stuff in the apartment, especially the furniture, was his.

Peter sighs before finally having the guts to look me in the eye. "I just think we've kind of been stuck in the same spot for a while," he flails his arms, gesturing to the apartment.

"But we only moved in three months ago; what did you expect? That'd we move out every three months?" If the apartment was his most significant issue, then we could still work things out. I made enough money to afford this apartment on my own; I'd just have to sacrifice a few meals a day... or all of them. And no more coffee runs in the middle of my workday.

I wasn't going to lie and say it didn't suck having your boyfriend admit he wasn't ready to commit to living together, especially after having already moved in, and it was his idea in the first place. But if he was getting cold feet, I wasn't going to make him feel worse by begging him to stick around.

"No, Sylvie, it's not the apartment; it's you." Peter pushes his luggage over to the side and sits on the bed, patting his hand on the comforter for me to take a seat.

I take a few steps toward the bed before plopping right down beside him. Peter runs his hands through his auburn hair. He always maintained the same length so that he could comfortably pull the strands behind his ears.

"Sylvie, I love— like—." Peter pauses, furrowing his eyebrows and gathering his thoughts before speaking again.

"I really care about you." He finally says, reaching his hand over to my clammy ones that are settled on top of my lap.

"In the beginning, I was completely infatuated with all your beauty and your quirkiness, but after being with you for a while, after living with you... I just think I like those things in a friend." Peter's eyes soften as he lays the news onto me that I'm being friend-zoned.

"Friends don't fuck, Peter." I stand back up as I pace around the room, questioning every moment of our relationship.

Peter and I hadn't been together for very long, but the moment we met, it felt as if he were the one; it felt like we had known each other forever. We had bumped into each other at Pandora, a bar my co-workers and I frequented for happy hour. Funnily enough, Peter and his colleagues were there for the same reason. A bit of flirting had led us into three months of dating, which quickly led to the big move-in, and now, after a total of six months, he was ending it.

I quit pacing to stare back at Peter, who remains in the same position on the bed, waiting for my response.

"And friends certainly don't move in together after three months of dating and talk about getting married to one another and someday having kids." I stand there, pissed and blindsided by this fucking asshole of a man.

Peter sighs and stands back up to continue his packing.

"I can give you another month's worth of rent." He offers.

"Just get the fuck out already, Peter! I'd like to fucking wallow in peace."

Gentleman, let it be known that the last thing a woman wants after you break up with them is to see your damn face.

Peter gives a slight nod and puts the last of his things in the duffel bag before standing there awkwardly before me.

"What?" I snarl.

"Should we... You know?" Peter extends his arms out wide awkwardly, asking for a hug.

You've got to be fucking kidding me.

"Out!" I growl, pointing my finger towards the door,

Peter gives me one of his other awkward nods and makes his way out of the bedroom.

It's not until I finally hear the apartment door click that I let myself fall onto the mattress and let out a scream.

CHAPTER TWO
Sylvie

I BLOW my nose even harder and try my best to control the sobs that are bursting out of me. This hurts so much more than I thought it would. And it wasn't like this was my first time. In fact, this may be the eightieth time.

"Can you please get a fucking grip? You've watched this movie exactly seventy-eight times. You know they're going to end up together." My younger sister, Marlene, scowls as she pulls the Ben & Jerry's brownie batter ice cream away from my grasp. Probably afraid that I'll shoot my snot into it.

"I can't help it. She should've just stayed in Ireland with him."

"Then that would defeat the perfect ending of the movie as well as the reasoning as to why it's called Leap Year to begin with." Marlene reasons as she brings another spoonful of brownie batter into her mouth.

"Do you think I'm lovable?" I ask.

Marlene sighs and looks over at me with a look that simultaneously holds concern and annoyance in her stare.

"Of course, you're lovable, Sylvie." She mutters.

"Then why do I have such bad luck when it comes to love?" I groan, stretching myself over to her. I grab the ice cream from her hand and begin stuffing my face with it.

I never did have it easy when it came to love. It just never seemed to work. Whether it was a woman or a man, it seemed like no one could ever stay after the six-month mark. I was starting to think I was cursed.

What was it about me that scared people away?

Growing up, I often thought that my weight was the issue in my relationships. But Marlene shot that idea down immediately. In her words: "They're not blind, Sylvie. They know exactly what they're attracted to, and odds are they've imagined you naked in their fantasies, and they liked what they saw. So don't ever think that's the issue in the relationship."

And her affirming words did make me feel beautiful. But it didn't take away that there was some issue about me that scared all these men and women away.

Was I too overwhelming?

I didn't think I was that messy.

It's not like the people I was with were the most organized anyway.

And I never received any closure from them either.

It was always an "it's me, not you situation."

But that's just another way of saying, "You're definitely the problem, but I'm not sure how to admit that to you without hurting your feelings and making you defensive."

What the fuck is wrong with me?

"You know what your problem is?" Marlene speaks up with concern after a minute of just staring at my face, which probably has chocolate all over it.

"What's that?" I ask a little hesitantly.

"You just fall in love too quickly."

Eureka.

"What do you mean?" I ask defensively.

"Actually, scratch that, I don't think you've actually ever been in love, but rather overly infatuated with all the lovers in your life."

Double Eureka.

"Are you saying that I don't care about the people I date?" I scoff, not wanting to admit something I hadn't even admitted to in therapy.

"Sylvie, I think that's your issue right there." She points out.

"You just confuse caring for someone with love. It's okay to love someone and care for them without having to maintain a romantic relationship." Marlene scoots a bit closer and extends her hand out to pat my back, which for her is like giving a whole-ass hug because she hates physical touch.

"I mean, think about it, Sylvie. Have you ever really cried after a break-up? And I'm not talking about crying at a rom-com. I mean, have you ever had an actual break-up that hurt you so much that you felt a pain in your chest so strong that you thought you could never live without them?"

Marlene looks at me with those identical dark chocolate eyes that we share, and I know she knows the answer without me having to say a thing.

I let out a sigh and face the TV again, trying my best to ignore her stare.

Was she right?

Did I really not love any of these people?

Did I not love Peter?

"Hey, don't think too hard about this. I'm not saying you didn't love them. I'm just saying that you weren't in love with them." Marlene adds, as if she's reading my mind.

Actually, I'm convinced that she can read it.

"And no, I can't read your mind. I just know you. And the person who is head over heels for you, the person who truly loves you, will know you too"

I look back at Marlene and watch as she gives me a look of sympathy. I wish I had been more like her. She didn't need a partner's assurance to make her feel worthy. And she sure as hell didn't care for it. If the opportunity arose to be in a relationship, she took it if she really felt like it could be the one.

But I guess that's why she was married with twins. She didn't distract herself with anyone along the way. She just focused on herself until one day, Yousef came along and swept her off her feet.

"Well, I'm about to be thirty-one, and I've got nothing going for me because I've dated idiots for such a long time. I've let them distract me from the real person I'm meant to be with." I probably passed them by on the street while holding hands with fucking Peter.

Marlene's fist finds my shoulder, and I yelp out an "ouch" before grabbing my arm and soothing the pain.

"What was that for, you bitch?"

"First of all, thirty is the new twenty. And you have a lot of things going for you." She argues.

I lift a brow to question her argument.

"Like what?" I mutter.

"Sylvie, you're a phenomenal software engineer. And an amazing aunt, sister, and daughter. Don't look at this part of your life and think about what you haven't accomplished, but rather what you have accomplished and can still accomplish."

I scoff and roll my eyes. "That's one way to look at it, Mar."

"I'm being serious, Sylvie." She reiterates.

"Sylvie, I used to want to skydive, backpack across Europe, and maybe even try being a hoe. Actually, that's too much physical touch for my liking, so maybe not the last one."

"Where is this going, Marlene?" I cut her off before the girl goes on a whole other tangent.

"I mean that even though I wouldn't change being a wife and mom for anything in this world, there are still a lot of things that I've put a pause on or have decided I will never do because now I have a family to prioritize. So, don't think about the things you haven't done. Think of all the things you can do and take advantage of them." I lean back on the couch and take her declaration in.

Maybe she was right. This didn't have to be a bad thing. It could actually be a very good thing. As time went by, I constantly felt I had to be in a certain position in life, and in the midst of this, I threw myself into these relationships to try to speed up the marriage and family process.

"Come on, what's something you'd like to do that a family might stop you from doing?" Marlene asks.

I sit back and ponder that question for a bit. I guess I had never really thought about it, because I've always imagined living a life where I would get married and have kids, rather than thinking about one without them.

And maybe that was the issue.

I've spent so much of my time chasing a future that might not even be met for me that I've forgotten about other dreams I'd had for myself.

Like finally learning how to cook, getting into a niche hobby, or traveling.

It's not like it even mattered because all of those things took time. Time I'm too busy throwing away at my corporate job.

But maybe that was the problem.

"I haven't taken any time for myself, you know?" I can't remember the last time I used my PTO to go on a vacation.

"That's a start!" Marlene straightens up in excitement.

"I'm going to live vicariously through you. Where are we going first?" She chirps.

"I'm not sure, Lisbon? Madrid? Paris?" I question.

"I would've started with Rome, but to each their own," Marlene says, lifting her hands in surrender.

"Well, who cares. I have unlimited PTO. And I don't necessarily need to be in the office per se. I can work from anywhere." I add.

Marlene hops off the couch in excitement.

"Oh my god, you're going to Europe." She chirps excitedly.

"Oh my god, I'm going to Europe!" I join her and jump into her arms.

I hold her tighter, taking advantage of her hug.

"Okay, that's enough." She murmurs, tapping my back to release her.

But my arms remain tight around her, taking up as much of this hug as I can.

"Sylvie, off now!" She barks like a sergeant.

I release her and bring my hands to my side instantly.

"Thank you." She mumbles, patting her clothes down as if I ruffled her up with my hug.

"Now, let's look at plane tickets." She chirps back up in excitement and walks over to my room to grab my laptop.

Oh my god, this was really happening.

I'm going to Europe.

CHAPTER THREE
Sylvie

AARON WASN'T A BAD MANAGER, but he had a way of making you feel guilty for wanting to take time off, which is why I had never asked for any. And doing so made it even tougher. I knock on his office door, hoping he isn't in there, so I don't have to ask him about this in person.

Maybe an email would suffice.

"Come in." His voice echoes from the other side of the door.

Or not. Fuck, here goes nothing.

I open the door to his office and step inside, leaving the door ajar out of habit. It's a habit I built after some uncomfortable experiences in the corporate world. Not that Aaron has ever made me feel uncomfortable, I often wondered how he got the position as a manager with his airheadedness. Aaron lies back in his desk chair with a tiny basketball in hand and throws it at the basketball hoop hung up on the wall, missing it completely by a long shot. Just like the other balls seemed to have. All scattered in the same corner of the room.

"Sylvie! What's up?! How's that project coming along?" Aaron asks, wildly tapping on his desk in an un-rhythmic beat.

In some ways, Aaron reminded me of a man who never left his Kappa Sig life behind.

"It's coming along great; the team hopes to have it all done by the end of this week."

Aaron leans back in his chair and signals for me to take a seat in front of him. He interlocks his hands and places them below his chest, but right above his gut as he stares at me, nodding his head so often, almost as if he's evaluating me.

"How long have you been working for this company, Sylvie?" He asks, probably already knowing the answer since he took part in my hiring.

"Six years," I answer.

"Six years of hard work, not one PTO, excellent work, and a master's degree in the mix as well," Aaron adds, remaining in the same laid-back position before standing up straight and slamming his hand against the desk and pointing at me.

"And I see all that hard work, Sylvs, I really do. Which is why I've been thinking about giving you this big project coming up." Guilt rises from my gut and towards my chest. This could not be happening. The one fucking time I'm cashing in my PTO, I'm being pushed into a new big project.

Aaron walks around his desk and stops right in front of me, taking a seat right on top of his desk, his feet dangling like some toddler, and it gives me more of an ick than Aaron already had.

"See, I want you to do something bigger. I want you to oversee these teams' upcoming projects. Make sure that everything is coming together. I want you to take charge."

Wait a damn minute.

Was this bigheaded, blonde, frat boy trying to get me to do his fucking job?

I grip the sides of my seat, trying my best to control the sudden urge to beat my own boss.

"You mean, you want me to manage?" I spit.

Aaron brings his hands up in defense.

"Well, you see, I might take some time off for family issues, and I'd need someone to run the ship while I'm gone." He utters, as if this were a totally normal task.

But what Aaron doesn't realize is that I don't fucking play when it comes to being manipulated into doing things. And I sure as hell was going to use his stupidity against him. This wasn't my first rodeo with corporate men trying to take advantage of me for being a woman. I was a woman in STEM, and they still thought that it meant that I had no brain cells. Well, Sylvie Jane Rosenthal has a bunch of brain cells, actually, and they're fucking amazing.

"You know, Aaron, that's too bad because I was going to need some PTO myself, for the same reason, believe it or not. But if you're okay with being demoted, and the job position is open, my family issues can wait. As a matter of fact, I'll head over to HR right now and speak with them." I shoot up from my chair to make my way toward the door, but I don't even need to take one more step before Aaron is already calling out my name.

"How long would your PTO be, exactly?" He asks, obviously aware that I have the upper hand.

I hum in thought and look around the room, really enjoying this beautiful moment where I have this man cornered.

"A month, or two, actually maybe three." I shrug.

Aaron grinds his teeth together and mutters a curse under his breath.

"You know how family issues can sometimes escalate. And this family issue is looking complex." I sigh, as if this PTO will be more of a hassle rather than a well-needed vacation.

Aaron glares at me as if his stare will make me cower into stepping down. When he takes too long to agree, I turn towards the door, "but it's okay, HR will just have to–"

"Fine." He growls, standing back up and walking over to his seat behind his desk.

I give him an award-winning smile that must fuel the fire inside him right now as I turn to take a step out of his office.

"Don't worry, Aaron. I'm actually a great team player and don't mind helping out my team here and there when I get the time." I send him a wink, take a step out of his office, and make my way straight to my desk.

Checkmate, Aaron.

"Three months?" Marlene asks, setting down the lasagna she made in the center of the table. Yousef walks in with both twins in his arms. As much as it frustrated Marlene, the twin girls were an exact image of their father, from the dark curls to their big dark eyes. They had gotten every bit of their father's Moroccan features.

I walk over and take Safia out of his arms so he can put Samira down in her high chair. The girls were two years old, but they were already getting so big. I can only imagine how Marlene and Yousef must feel to see their little girls growing up so fast.

"I missed when all they did was cry, poop, and sleep. Now they smoosh their food when they're not in the mood to put it in their mouth and scream very loudly for attention."

"My kids are cute. " Marlene states defensively.

I pass Safia over to Yousef so he can put her in the other high chair and scowl over at Marlene.

"I know they're cute. But I also know that the toddler phase is hell sometimes." That's why they call it the terrible twos.

Marlene shrugs and cuts up their food into tiny pieces so that they don't choke when they start swallowing their food whole.

"You're telling me," Yousef mutters as Safia begins to cry over having to sit in her high chair.

I give Marlene an "I told you so" look, and she only sighs and brings Safia onto her lap.

"Anty, Anty." Safia screeches, bringing her hands up towards me

Marlene sighs and brings her over to me.

"Here, obviously, she got her need for physical touch from you. So, now you can deal with it." I roll my eyes, but take little Safia into my hands.

"We just can't help it; we love hugs and cuddles, don't we, Safia?" I squeal at her.

Safia giggles and calms down in my embrace, and Marlene sets up our plates while Yousef helps feed Samira.

"So, you were saying you got three months off from work with PTO?" Yousef asks, bringing a piece of noodle to Samira's lips. Who, in return, spits it out.

"Yes, I did. Of course, I did offer to help when I'm needed. Honestly, I don't mind working; I actually love my job. And being able to do it while eating gelato, drinking sangria, or eating croissants does not bother me one bit."

"You hear that, babies? Aunty Sylvie is going to travel through Europe." Marlene chirps, trying to get the children, who barely have any consciousness, to join the conversation. In her defense, they do chime in with their own twin language.

"So, where does this trip take you first?" Yousef asks, giving up with Samira and deciding to feed himself instead.

"Well, the cheapest ticket I found was for Madrid, so I guess I'll start there first, and then I'll probably make my way to Paris or Lisbon by train," I say, taking a bite of Marlene's lasagna.

"Oh my god, I can't believe this is actually happening. You're going to have so much fun. But remember you're there to make friends, not lovers." Marlene lectures yet again.

"Damn, I get it. I won't get into any committed relationships while I'm there." I mutter.

"Where will you be staying?" Yousef asks, derailing the conversation away from my love life.

"There's this beautiful apartment that I found on AirB&B, it's near the Prado Museum, which isn't far from the Retiro Park. It might be one of the first places I go to. I'm not too sure, though. I still have to plan the itinerary out."

I had bought a bunch of different stickers and vintage postcards on Etsy to bring my traveling bullet journal to life. I was going to make a notebook full of memories for myself. I had even purchased extra Polaroid film to keep on hand.

"Well, you're going to have a lot of fun, Syl. This is going to be fun for you." Yousef encourages.

But that's normal when it comes to Yousef; it's what Marlene loves about him the most. He's always so supportive, and I think some of that encouraging personality rubbed off on Marlene, too.

"When do you leave?" Marlene asks.

"A week from now, which gives me just enough time to plan everything out."

I was about to spend three months alone in Europe. And although it's a bit scary to think of being somewhere far from home. It also feels quite liberating, and I'm more than excited about this new change.

Fuck Peter and fuck all the exes that came before him. They don't define me, and I sure as hell don't need a partner in my life to help me feel seen or worthy.

I don't need them to be happy.

And I'm going to prove myself just that.

CHAPTER FOUR
Santi

JAVIER WAS GETTING on my last nerve. Nothing could ever be normal with this man.

"Javi, I told you I wasn't covering half of your rent anymore. You have to pay your part, or I'm finding a new roommate." I mumble, throwing out the empty orange juice container that, for some reason, he likes to hoard in the fridge.

Javi pokes his head out from his bedroom and lets out a scoff.

"You wouldn't do that to your best friend." He challenges.

He was right; I wouldn't, but something had to be done.

Javier walks out of his bedroom with his luggage in hand, sets it by the apartment door, and then walks back to the kitchen, where he sits on one of the stools.

"C'mon, Santi, this is huge. My band is finally getting the recognition that we deserve. This could really work out for me."

I sigh and continue cleaning out our fridge, really thinking this situation through. Javier depended on his bartending job to support himself, let alone his dream. And even though this three-month tour across Europe was amazing for his band, the money he'd be making on it would be divided amongst the members, and whatever's left would be invested right back into the band.

"I get it, Javi. And I'm extremely proud of you. You're my best friend, and I want to see this all come true." As I lecture my friend, who seems bored out of his mind, I take a whiff of the milk that's been sitting in the back of our fridge and visibly gag, sending Javi into a fit of laughter.

"That's actually hilarious; that milk has been there for about six months."

Of course, it has. Neither of us drinks milk, except Carol, who always needed it in her coffee or when she felt the need to bake something sweet.

Six months is precisely the amount of time that she's been gone from my life, which makes this interaction awkward and this milk even grosser.

"Hey, Santi, forget about her. Bigger and better things are coming our way." Javier makes his way around the counter and puts his hands on my shoulders, shaking me out of my misery.

"Think about it, in three months, my band will be signed to a label and making millions. And you will…" Javier lingers in thought for a while before finally concluding as to what awaits me in three months.

"You will have a new painting to talk about at work." He pats my back and moves away awkwardly, obviously not having any good updates for my life besides adding one more painting I'll have to discuss at my job.

"Thanks, Javi, that's some great motivation."

If all I had to look forward to in my future was my job, then something was definitely wrong in my life, which meant that Carol was right.

"It will be three months, I'll figure out a way to pay you back, Santi, I promise."

I lift a brow at him and shake my head.

Was I really going to cover this man's half of the rent for three months?

Javi's eyes hold hope and determination, and they remind me of how much we thought we could accomplish as kids before realizing that life is sometimes too tough for us to reach our dreams. And fuck I didn't want to be the one to ruin that little flame of hope that Javi still had lit.

He had wanted to be a musician his whole life; music wasn't just his passion, it was his entire soul. He made it his priority, and that's why he has this opportunity and a small but growing fandom.

"Don't forget about me when you're rich and famous," I mutter as I tie up the full bag of garbage.

Javi jumps from his stool and brings himself back around to give me an aggressive hug.

"Fuck yeah, thanks, Santi. I'll make this up to you. I promise." I give Javi a pat on the back and untangle myself from the guy.

His love language was definitely physical touch, and mine was whatever the opposite of physical touch was. I wasn't too sure about how many love languages there were to begin with.

"I really appreciate it, Santi." He repeats.

I shrug and move past him to go throw out the trash.

"I think at least one of us should have a much better outcome in the next three months, don't you?"

CHAPTER FIVE
Sylvie

MY EYES SCAN the crowd of people sitting around the airport.

Blonde guy in the corner with the Nike cap on.

Yes.

Redhead with an oversized band t-shirt and biker shorts.

Yes.

A forty-year-old man who looks pretty good for his age, sitting there with his readers on and still squinting at the book in front of him.

Possibly… actually, yes.

What is it about an airport that makes everyone so damn attractive? I mean, I don't even like blondes like that.

Hmm, there should be a reality show about something like that.

Love at first flight?

Love on a High?

Mile High Love?

Hm, whatever they'd call it, I would still rot my brain with it the same way I have with all the other shows.

The buzzing of my phone breaks me away from the brainstorming of my upcoming reality TV show.

Peter's name flashes on the screen, and I let out a groan, making heads turn to look at me immediately.

"Hello?" I answer.

"Sylvie?" He asks, as if he weren't the one calling me.

"Who's Sylvie? You've obviously got the wrong contact name saved to this number."

Peter scoffs into the receiver. I guess he's not a fan of my sarcastic commentary.

"I'm outside of the apartment building; buzz me in."

Buzz him in? The fucker has some nerve.

"No." I could've just said that I wasn't home. But I wanted him to know that even if I were home, I'd have his ass waiting outside the whole time.

"Don't be like this, Sylvie. I forgot something in there. Plus, I was thinking maybe we could still talk about being together somehow." Peter pleads through the receiver, almost sounding apologetic about his decision. But I knew exactly what he wanted.

The iPad that I had bought him for his birthday last year, which I was currently using to play Candy Crush on, and a blowjob that I wouldn't have given him regardless of me being at home right now or not.

"Goodbye, Peter." I sigh into the receiver one last time before ending his call and blocking his number.

I guess this guy had been more of a dick than I thought. Marlene had a point about me being blinded by love. Or better yet, infatuated.

Because, despite living with the guy, I never really loved him the way Marlene loved Yousef or the way my parents loved each other.

And despite how quickly our relationship moved, it definitely wasn't a love like Anna and Declan's from Leap Year.

But love like Anna and Declan only existed in films.

And maybe that had been the problem. I wanted this fantasy version of love that didn't exist.

"You've got a lemon drop on the right bottom corner that you can match up."

I turn to my right and look at the older man with a receding hairline, bushy mustache, beer belly, and missing teeth.

Hard no.

I wouldn't say my plane ride was horrendous, but it wasn't the best travel experience. Honestly, no curvy woman should ever be forced to sit in the middle seat, especially when you've got an older gentleman on the right of you snoring the whole way through the flight and another man smacking his gum on the other side.

When I exit the gate, I pull out my phone that had begun chiming the minute we landed. I look through my messages and see the texts from my mom and Marlene.

MARLENE

Hey, let me know when you've arrived. Just want to make sure you're safe.

MOM

Your father and I just tried our hand at making paella in the spirit of you traveling to Spain. And we may have forgotten your father's shellfish allergy. Nothing that a quick trip to the ER can't fix.

Be careful! Allergies can be genetic!

I text Marlene to let her know I've made it and to keep an eye on our unhinged parents. Then I shoot a text over to mom, making sure she keeps me updated on dad's trip to the emergency room.

I open up the Airbnb app and look for the location of my stay. It was already three in the afternoon, and all I wanted to do was get to my Airbnb as soon as possible and rest for a bit.

The host was sweet and let me know where everything was and even said I could check in earlier if needed, since the place was ready. And that was just what I needed.

Being plus-size in the cramped middle seat was criminal for my body. I didn't even bother eating on the flight. Not that I enjoyed the airplane food, regardless. But it was much less enjoyable when you barely have any room to move your arms.

I make my way around the maze that is this airport before exiting and ordering my Uber.

I lean against one of the airport's concrete pillars and wait for my Uber, which is only twelve minutes away, before an aggravated screech makes me peer over to the right, where a slender woman with straight blonde hair stands regally to the side with her phone pressed against her ear.

"I'm not going to tell him I'm pregnant." She growls into her receiver, her British accent more pronounced than it was when I first heard her speak.

"We will work things out; we always have. This was all just a big mistake, and he will understand, " she murmurs.

"We've been together for years. He will understand that it was just some–"

I incline toward my suitcase a bit more to stretch and hear what she's saying. But wheels have never been friendly with me. Which is why, somehow, I end up with my face on the floor and my suitcase flat on the ground.

The girl looks over, her eyes wide as she finds me flat on the ground.

"Hey, something just came up, so I'll call you back." She says before shoving the phone into her pocket and walking over to me.

"Vaya caída te has dado, tía! Estás bien?" * She hovers over me, blocking the sun from my eyes, and man, she looks like an angel, and I definitely look like roadkill spread on the concrete floor.

---

* "What a fall you took, girl! Are you okay?"

"English, por favor?" I state, though it comes out more like a question.

"Are you alright?" She asks, switching so effortlessly from one language to the other. And hell, she sounds posh in both languages too.

"Um, yeah." I managed to say before forcing myself up with her help.

The blonde stranger walks over to my suitcase, lifts it for me, and rolls it over to my side. And honestly, I'm too fucking scared to touch it.

Louis would never treat Anna this way.

"Love, are you sure you're okay? Should I call the paramedics?" The stranger asks, bringing her phone back out to make a call.

I bring my hand out and stop her, not wanting to create anymore of a commotion than I already have. People were already staring, which is what I get for being nosy myself.

"No, I'm fine, I swear. I must've just leaned too much on my suitcase, and it slipped right out of my grasp. I'm sorry."

"Why are you apologizing to me?" She asks.

Because the only reason I fell on my face is because I was being nosy and wanted to know more about your situation.

"I'm not sure," I say instead, and luckily, the constant beeping of a car saves me from having to say anything else to her.

"Are you, Sylvie?!" The driver shouts, his car's trunk already fully opened for my suitcase.

I nod and make my way over to him. He comes out of the car and mumbles something in Spanish I don't understand, but I know it's probably not anything good since he didn't intend for me to understand it in the first place.

My driver makes his way back to the front, and I'm about to enter the car, but I turn around to thank the blonde stranger who's on the phone once again, probably adding how she met a crazy American into her story.

It's alright, Sylvie. The first official day of vacation starts tomorrow, so technically, this isn't a rough start to the vacation at all.

Now I'll be on my way to the comforts of my stay, and I can put together my itinerary for tomorrow. There would be no distractions or complications. Just me and a nice cozy bed, my itinerary plans, and my Kindle.

Nothing could mess this up.

CHAPTER SIX
Santi

"DID you at least get tipped well today?" Luisa asks, shutting her locker as she waits for me to gather my things.

I close my locker shut and give her a shrug.

"It could've been better, especially when dealing with huge groups all day."

"Tell me about it." Luisa scoffs, following me out of the staff area.

Both Luisa and I started working at the Prado Museum around the same time, and as people came and went to pursue different careers, we seemed to stay.

But I didn't see that as a bad thing, at least not until it ended my relationship.

I loved working at the museum.

I know every art piece and its history.

It was never something I doubted doing until my ex said something about it.

"What are you doing tonight?" Luisa asks.

She usually walked me home. I know it's usually the other way around, but she only ever walked my way because she lived two blocks down from me with her girlfriend. So she always passed my apartment on the way to hers.

"Well, Javi is gone, so I'm looking forward to having the apartment clean and all to myself."

"Oh yeah! His band is on tour, right?" Luisa asks, as she undoes her braid while we walk. Luisa had a darker complexion than I did, but that was mainly because she was born and raised in southern Spain, and her grandparents on her father's side were also Moroccan. And with her darker complexion came her dark black hair, which she constantly wore in a braid or ponytail at work.

"Yeah, they are. I'm excited for him, but I'm also excited not to have to deal with his messiness. He even asked me to clean up his room before he left. Which I was more than gracious of doing because it was starting to reek in there." I say, scrunching my nose at the mere memory of the stench that was coming from that room. Honestly, I wasn't sure how he could fucking breathe in there.

"Yuck, that's disgusting."

"You're telling me? I'm the one who cleaned it." I say, turning the block toward my apartment.

For a split second, as I'm turning, I swear I see her from the corner of my eye, and I can't help but stop and search for her.

But it isn't her.

Instead, it's just another blonde woman who has an uncanny resemblance to Carol. Luisa follows my gaze towards the doppelganger and pulls at my arm.

"Come on, buddy. Let's go, it's not her."

I look down at Luisa, who isn't much shorter than I am. She was a tall, slender woman, and must be at least 5'9. And at this very moment, she's looking at me with pity in her eyes.

"Don't look at me like that," I growl, doing my best to shove her touch off gently and walk ahead. But my speed walking does nothing for her because her long legs help her catch up with no problem.

"I'm not looking at you in any type of way." She argues.

"Yes, you are."

"How was I looking at you?" She challenges.

"With that pity look, the same way you looked at me on that day."

Luisa grabs me by the elbow, halting my step and turning me to look at her.

"In order for me to feel pity for you, I'd have to feel bad for a misfortune that happened to you. And as embarrassing as that day was, I wouldn't say that losing her was a misfortune at all." She tightens her hold on my arms and then pulls me into a hug, knowing damn well that I'm not the biggest fan of them, but that I also wouldn't mind one right now.

"Thanks, Lu."

Luisa pulls away from our embrace and gives me a bright smile.

"Besides, I'd say it's more of a blessing. I had gotten out of a five-year relationship before I met Clara."

I roll my eyes and turn away to continue our walk back home, and Luisa follows right behind me.

"I doubt I'm going to run into anyone that's suddenly the love of my life, and frankly, it's not something I'm that much interested in finding right now." I had done the love thing to the point that marriage had become the next big step that we were making. So the last thing I want is to go through all that again.

I was more than happy to be single for a while. Besides, I was only twenty-eight; there was absolutely no rush.

Maybe the one good thing Carol gave me before breaking things off was the advice to find something more in life than work.

"You never know what life has in store for you. Maybe God has set up a new roommate for you right now. Maybe all of a sudden you have a girl in your apartment just waiting for you to fall head over heels in love with her." Luisa teases.

"One, I don't believe in God," I say, bringing my index finger up to count.

"Two," I state, lifting a second finger. "The fantasies you have involving my love life are quite concerning.

"And three," I say, lifting a third finger and stopping in front of my apartment building's door. "If there is a random woman in my apartment, then I am calling the police immediately."

Luisa only chuckles and shakes her head in disbelief as she stretches up a bit to kiss me goodbye on the cheek.

"I'll see you tomorrow?" She asks.

"No, it's my honeymoon. And I'll be spending the week alone and at home." I assure her.

Luisa cringes at the reminder that this would've been the day that I'd come home after my long shift to finish getting ready to head out for my planned honeymoon with Carol. Though our plan was to get married on our anniversary, we had mutually agreed to go on our honeymoon in the summer so we could enjoy the warm weather in Rome.

I could've kept working rather than set aside these dates for a staycation, but ever since the breakup, I had found it hard to even want to work, which was a setback because I truly loved what I did for a living.

So, I thought it was best to take these days to ground myself and figure out what's next for me.

"Well, just let me know if you want to hang out." Luisa offers, as she begins to walk away backwards.

"Will do, Lu, thank you."

Luisa's lips lift into a grin as she sends me a wink and turns to walk home. I stay there for a moment, soaking in the night's crisp air, before inserting my keys into the lock and opening the heavy set door.

I live up on the third floor, which can honestly be killer some-times when hauling up groceries, but the view is totally worth it. I love everything about living in Madrid, which is why I was ready to settle down here. But the breakup somehow distorted my vision of the future here, and now I'm stuck in limbo, wondering what should come next.

I get up to the apartment and see the light peeking through the bottom of the door. I was sure I had turned off all the lights before leaving the apartment today. Now that I think of it, I don't recall having turned them on in the first place. But maybe I had, and didn't realize.

I insert my key and unlock the door. I enter it slowly and take a look around the front entrance. But nothing seems out of place.

If there were a burglar, I'm sure some things would be ransacked already. Plus, I unlocked my door, and a burglar would have no intention of locking the door if he's here to make a quick entrance and exit.

I lock the door and take my shoes off to leave them by the entrance. I walk over to the kitchen and place my keys and wallet on the counter, like I usually do, before stepping into my bedroom. My room used to be more homey and decorative; hell, my whole apartment used to be. But when Carol moved, she took all her things with her, leaving the apartment mostly vacant and unlived in.

I strip off my clothes, toss them into the hamper, walk out of the room, and go to the bathroom I usually have to share with Javier, and clean after him, too. But now I can enjoy a nice, warm shower without him taking up all the hot water and steaming up the whole bathroom.

I'm about to open the door when I see Javi's room open and the lights on in his room.

What the hell?

Had Javier come home?

I walk over to his room and take a peek inside. Nothing seems out of order, but I do notice the suitcase that's lying in the corner of the room.

"Javi, are you back?" I call out, but I'm met with silence.

If he wasn't in our living space or in his bedroom, then he had to be in the bathroom. I walk over to the bathroom door and give it a knock before turning the handle, finding it unlocked.

"Javi, what happen–" I'm entirely at a loss for words when I'm met with a voluptuous woman whose towel barely covers the creamy smoothness of her skin. Her chestnut brown eyes look at me with horror, and a scream escapes her plump lips.

And suddenly I'm on my knees grasping onto my member that's been hit, and I'm not quite sure if it's the heavens or the brightness of the bathroom light that I'm looking at, but what I do know is that the first thought that comes to my head is:

I believe in God.

CHAPTER SEVEN
Sylvie

MY UBER DRIVER, Rafael, is friendly and asked me if I was okay back there when he was rudely beeping at me while I was trying my best to regain consciousness, some self-respect, and some courage to act like I hadn't just busted my face on the concrete.

I let him know that everything was just fine and that I had tripped over something. I open up the camera app on my phone and take a quick look at my face to make sure there's no scrape or bruise left behind. Not that it would've mattered, but I prefer not to look like I just got beaten and bruised.

Rafael, or Rafa as he prefers to be called, lets me in on all the best restaurants in the city and the best places to visit. He tells me the best days and times to visit the museum, and which restaurants and places to avoid. He also instructed me on where I could find the nearest Dunkin' Donuts and McDonald's in the city.

Because every American needs their Dunkin' and McDonald's.

"Here you are," Rafa says, parking the car over to the side in the narrow street that shouldn't allow two cars to drive on either side simultaneously but somehow does.

Rafa steps out of the car, and I do too, following him to the trunk, where I meet him and take my suitcase from his grasp.

"Gracias," I say, pulling my suitcase onto the steps of the building.

Rafa murmurs, "You're welcome," before getting back into his car and driving off. I guess, despite the rough start and the incoherent mumbling in Spanish, he wasn't too bad a person. I take out my phone and look at the instructions the host gave me on where I can find the key to the building.

I look at the instructions for the key inside the lock box by the door and grab it to open the building's door. I drag my suitcase inside and follow the instructions that lead me up to the third floor, stopping at door 301.

I knew that I would be walking and exercising a lot on this trip, but I didn't think it would start right away. I take a moment to catch my breath before using the other key on the keychain to open the door to the apartment.

I step inside and lock the door behind me, and take in the apartment. It's nice and spacious. And for the most part, it looks like it's curated for IKEA. Sure, there's furniture, but there's not much interior design to it. Everything's very basic and seems to include essentials for a person to live in for a while. I walk around the apartment and take a look at the first room, which seems untouched and holds only art history books on the nightstand.

I walk over to the other room and set my suitcase down in it. I figure I'll choose this room since it's right next to the bathroom and smells fresh and clean, as if it were cleaned fairly recently. I settle down on the edge of the bed and take out my phone to catch up on how everyone's doing back home.

MARLENE

Glad to hear you got there safely.

How does someone forget they have an allergy?

Sometimes I'm unsure of whether we're the parents or the children.

SYLVIE

I just arrived at the place I'm staying at.

I think our own parents forget, too, sometimes.

They are the reason why YOU'RE my emergency contact.

MARLENE

Same.

Facetime?

I press the FaceTime call icon in the top-right corner of the screen, and it only takes two rings for Marlene to pick up. I'm immediately met with the outline of her face as she sits in a dark room.

"Hey! I only have a few minutes before the girls get bored of being with Yousef and begin crying for me." Marlene whispers.

I squint and try to make sense of where she is.

"Are you in the closet?" I ask, catching one of the clothes hangers in the background.

"Yes, it's the most soundproof place in this damn house where the girls won't hear me and immediately begin to cry for me." She groans.

I nod my head as I take a moment to process her explanation.

"How did you find out that the closet was soundproof?" I ask.

"Don't worry about it. Now, let me see where you're staying." She demands.

I let out an exaggerated sigh and lift myself from the bed to show her around the apartment. I even open the French balcony doors and show her the beautiful view.

"This place is so nice. I can't believe it was so cheap, too." Marlene says as I flip the camera away from the view and back to me.

"I know, it's all so pretty. I can't wait to head out tomorrow and spend my day out in the city. I haven't gotten to sit down and look at the itinerary yet, but I will later tonight once I'm snuggled up in bed."

A yawn escapes my mouth immediately after finishing my sentence, and Marlene is quick to say goodbye so I can shower and rest. I'm sure she was being nice, but I'm also just as sure that I heard one of the girls crying in the background. I guess the closet isn't as soundproof as she thought.

I walk back to my room and open my suitcase to grab my shower necessities. I had forgotten to pack one of my own towels, which I usually bring, because the average towel never fully wraps around my body.

Whatever towels they had would have to do for this week. I would try to deliver the towel to the next location I'd be staying at instead.

I walk over to the bathroom and set up the shower. As I wait for the water to heat up, I tie my dark strands into a messy bun at the top of my head, then peel off my clothes and let them fall onto the bathroom's white-tiled floor.

I bring my hand into the shower and let the water run over my skin to gauge the temperature. I wait a second longer before stepping inside, enjoying the way the water warms my skin. God, I needed this after a long day. If I hadn't washed my hair before coming here, I would've thoroughly enjoyed immersing myself in the water.

I lather my body with soap and take my time until I hear a voice.

What the fuck?

"Javi, has vuelto?"* I hear the deep voice loud and clear near the bathroom, and I quickly shut off the water, unsure of what to do. I grab the towel, wrapping it around my body as tightly as I can, just to be sure it doesn't fall off the minute I start running for my life.

The door handle turns, and my hands begin to shake at the thought of these being my last moments.

------

* "Javi, are you back?"

Oh fuck, I should've just stayed home.

Mom was right, no woman is ever safe when traveling alone.

"Javi que ha–"[*]

The bathroom door opens, and a tall man stands there, completely shocked and completely fucking naked.

Oh my fucking god.

I stay there frozen for a second, and before I can think about anything, I bring my leg up and kick the intruder in the balls. He falls onto his knees, holding on to his member in pain. And by the looks of it, you'd think this guy had just seen the heavens.

"Joder!"[†] He groans onto the floor.

Before I can think, I push him over and scream for help.

"Fuck how do you say help in Spanish?" I yell, zipping my suitcase and running out of the bedroom, where the intruder is currently lifting himself slowly. One hand is on his crotch, and the other hand is up in the air in surrender.

"Ayúdame."[‡] He groans.

"Huh?" I ask, my eyes peering over to the kitchen, where I can probably still outrun him around the counter and head straight for the door to get out of the apartment.

"Ayúdame is how you say help me in Spanish." He says, his Spanish accent not going unnoticed as he speaks to me in English.

"You speak English?" I ask, confused about whether I should run or hear this guy out.

"Yes, and you kick like a professional soccer player." He mutters.

I take him in, making sure I have a clear look at what this guy looks like. No more than six feet tall, white, green eyes, buzzcut hair, toned muscles, several tattoos spread out across his body, and a great ass. Though I'm sure the police won't care about that last tidbit.

"What's your name?" He asks, looking annoyed as if I were the intruder.

---

[*] "Javi what has–"

[†] "Fuck!"

[‡] "Help me."

I scoff at his audacity to ask me for personal information.

"What's your name?" I parrot back.

He rolls his eyes, obviously not fond of my reply.

"Santi, my name is Santi, and you're in my apartment." He barks, obviously aggravated by the whole situation.

Well, I am too, buddy, and you–

Wait a minute.

Did he say his apartment?

"Your apartment?" I ask.

"Yes, my apartment. The apartment that has my name on the lease, the one I sleep in every night and clean every day." He reiterates.

I shake my head and search for my phone, which I realize I left in the bathroom. Santi follows my gaze over to the bathroom and nods his head, telling me to go ahead and get it.

"I'm going to put on some clothes and possibly a shield to protect myself. I think there seems to be a misunderstanding, and I'm sure I know who it is." He growls, walking over to the other vacant room in the apartment and shutting the door.

This is the chance a sane person would take to escape a really confusing and dangerous situation. But for some reason, I grab my phone and open up my booked nights for the apartment and begin reading the description, and there it is at the very bottom:

Room in an apartment, with shared bathroom and space available.

I was so fucked.

CHAPTER EIGHT
Santi

I WAS GOING to kill him, and this time, I meant it. It only takes a couple of rings for Javi to pick up the phone with his cheerful fucking attitude that he could shove right up his ass.

"Hey, Santi! I'm so excited we're about–"

"Javi, what the fuck?" I snarl into the receiver.

"Whoa, what's with the hostility?" He asks.

"What's with the hostility?" I mimic, pissed out of my fucking mind.

"Maybe I just so happen to have a stranger in my apartment swearing up and down that it's hers for the time being as well."

Javi takes a moment before sighing into the receiver, "Oh, fuck. Did I forget to tell you?" He asks ever so calmly, as if there's not a fucking beautiful, crazed American woman inside my apartment, clinging to life with the towel around her body.

"You didn't just forget to tell me, Javi. You forgot to discuss this with me. You don't just decide to bring random strangers into our shared home." I reprimand.

With Javi, you always had to explain things to him as a parent would to a child. He lacked common sense and the ability to see the dangers of things. Though at times that was what made him fun to hang out with, it also made him irritating.

"I'm sorry, bro. I should've mentioned it to you. But with all the things going on, it must've slipped my mind. I thought it would just be a great way to make some income to help with my side of the rent until I can get back." Javi's voice is mellow, and I hate being the one to make him feel that way, especially when he's usually a boisterous person.

"It's alright," I say, and I know I've just let him off easy, but what else could I make him do? It's not like he was going to march back over to Madrid and remove the girl from the apartment.

"Please cancel any future rentals of the apartment."

"Done," Javi affirms. "But what about the girl that's there now?"

"Don't worry about her. I'll deal with it."

"Thanks, Santi. You're the best. I'm sorry about this, and I'll definitely make it up to you." I roll my eyes and chuckle at his boisterous self coming back now that he's free from the reprimand.

"Yeah, yeah, just go break a leg," I mumble and end the call.

I hear the yapping of the American on the other side of the door; she's probably on a call with the rental service. Great, now I have to pacify this woman who just kicked my balls out of my body.

I open the door to my bedroom and come out, this time fully dressed and peer over to the woman who is still by Javi's bedroom door, but this time in sweats and an oversized t-shirt, shouting into the phone.

She stops her yapping immediately when her eyes lock with mine from across the room. I motion to the kitchen counter where the stools are set up behind it and encourage her to take a seat while I walk over to the fridge.

"Marlene, I'll have to let you go." She squeaks into the phone. "No, I'm sure he won't kill me. Plus, I think I can take him on. I'm starting to realize why God gave me these broad shoulders." She says, her tone sounding as threatening as it can probably get coming from her.

I hear the pitter-patter of her feet as she walks over to the counter and takes a seat on one of the stools. I remove some items from the fridge to make a sandwich because, honestly, after the loss of my prostate, I don't feel like standing for an extended period of time to cook a gourmet meal for either my new roommate or me.

"Hungry?" I ask.

Before she says anything, the growling of her stomach answers for me.

"You like ham?"

"Prosciutto?" She asks, looking at the package in my hand.

"Jamón Ibérico." I correct; of course, she'd think they're the same thing.

"What's the difference?" She asks.

"This one's better." I don't bother to explain the difference between the two because I doubt she would even care to hear about the process of how the meats are prepared very differently.

"Okay, I guess I do like it then." She replies.

I grab the roll of bread I keep in one of the cabinets and take it out of the bag.

"So, I guess you're my new roommate, unless you plan on finding a new place to stay." I start, concentrating on building our sandwiches rather than on her. One of the reasons being that I wanted this sandwich to come out amazing, but I also didn't want to make her feel uncomfortable with me just staring at her.

"I guess. I tried reaching out to customer service, but haven't received a reply. But, it's also very much my fault, seeing as I didn't realize that I was renting a shared place and not a two-bedroom apartment all to myself." I look up and meet her eyes.

"So you flew to a country all alone and didn't bother to look at who or where you were staying?" I ask, my annoyance at her carelessness showing.

"I just didn't see it." She replies with a shrug.

Great, I have the female version of Javier rooming with me now.

"How long are you here for?" I ask, sliding the plate to her.

"Seven days." She replies, taking a bite out of the sandwich I've made for her and moaning into it like it's the best thing she's ever had.

"Good?" I ask, this time allowing a chuckle to escape my lips.

"Yes, but I can't tell the difference between the prosciutto I know and this one." She opens the sandwich to inspect the meat, then shrugs and closes it back up to take another bite.

Definitely another version of Javier.

"Okay, here are some ground rules," I mutter.

"You do your own thing, and I do mine. Our shared space stays clean, including the bathroom. You're free to have any of the food in the fridge and cabinets, but as I said, keep it tidy." I murmur.

"Got it, Danny Tanner." She murmurs.

"What?"

"Sorry, it's a show. You probably–"

"I've watched Full House." I cut her off, grabbing my plate and walking away.

"Wait!"

I turn to meet her, her cheeks holding the tiniest bit of pink in them.

"What did you say your name was?" She asks.

I stand there for a minute, just looking at her steadiness. She just found out she's sharing an apartment with a stranger, and not a single hint of worry is shown.

"Santi." I finally answer.

Her lips pull into a grin as she introduces herself.

"Nice to meet you, Santi. I'm Sylvie."

"Likewise," I mumble, walking away into the comfort of my bedroom.

But once the door shuts, I can't help but roll the name right off my tongue.

And damn it sounds good.

Day 1

CHAPTER NINE
Sylvie

IT'S my first day in Madrid, and I am alive. I'm a dumb bitch. But most importantly, I am alive. I sit up in my bed and look around the room that I had decided to feng shui last night. Just to find harmony in my new environment. Not at all to barricade the door for any intruder.

But as I stare down the dresser, nightstands, and bookshelf blocking my entrance, I realize how long it's going to take for me to move everything back just so that I can get to the bathroom.

Ugh, for fucksake, Sylvie.

How did you get yourself into this mess?

I'm sure Santi was still sleeping, too, or maybe he had gone to work.

I look over at the clock that reads 9:00 am.

He had to be at work by now, right? I wondered what he did for work. He had a few tattoos scattered around his body, but nothing that would ever be too revealing. He was a bit mean and assertive last night, but that might just be because a random stranger is living in his house for the time being. And the stranger also hit him in the balls.

I remove the bed sheets and walk over to my door, and begin moving the furniture back to its original place. Except for the dresser, that shit was too heavy to move all the way back into place. Instead, I scoot it over just enough for me to open the door and slide through it.

There's no sign of Santi anywhere, so he must be gone. I blow out a breath of relief before feeling a presence near me.

"You're up." A rough voice says to my right.

I jolt in shock and peer over to see Santi leaning against the wall.

"Were you just sitting there waiting for me to get out of my room?" I ask, stepping back towards the bathroom, just in case the fucker decided to change his mind and attack me instead of rooming with me.

"No, I was enjoying my morning coffee until I heard what sounded like a life-size, real game of Tetris coming from your room. Did you build a barricade in there?" He asks, a sly grin appearing on his face.

Did he find this funny?

"No, I just like changing the space up. It helps me sleep better." I mumble, unable to come up with another excuse.

Santi hums and brings the mug of coffee up to his lips, but stops to look at me before taking a sip.

"Those bags under your eyes beg to differ." He mutters before taking a sip of his coffee and walking away into his room.

Bags? I didn't have bags under my eyes.

I close the bathroom door and turn on the light to take a good look at the mirror. And if it wasn't the bags that made it clear I had a rough night, the crazy bed head surely was.

I bring my face into my hands and let out a groan of mortification.

A knock on the door makes me freeze, and it takes me a while to realize that he's probably still waiting outside the door.

"Yes?" I call out.

"I need to get ready. Do you mind rolling in your misery in the bedroom rather than the shared bathroom?" He mumbles.

I want to call him a dick and force him to wait, but instead I only mutter the words, "just a minute." I finish up in the bathroom and head back into my bedroom to get ready.

I pull out my phone and look at the Google Doc that I had set up with Marlene last night. Today would really be focused on sightseeing. I was going to enjoy my walk around the Retiro Park. The park itself was 350 acres, and I doubt I could see it all in one day, but I was going to try my best to see as much as I could.

But first, I needed coffee and some breakfast. It doesn't take long for me to find a cafe with a menu of my interests. I didn't mind trying new things, but Madrid had already brought on too much change for my liking, and it was just my first day. All I wanted right now was an avocado toast and a good cup of coffee.

I enter the cafe and am shocked to find it so full. A waiter passes by me and mumbles something incoherent to me. But I assume he's telling me to take a seat by the way he waves his hand over to the vacant seat and table in the corner of the cafe.

Next to it, a man sits with his MacBook open. The computer's light illuminates his olive-toned skin and bright green eyes. He must feel my stare because his eyes rise to meet mine from across the cafe. I clear my throat and look away instantly, hoping he just thinks I was looking at the vacant seat rather than at him. But the grin on his face as I sit in the seat beside him says otherwise.

His eyes meet mine as I take a seat and clear my throat before practicing my Spanish. "Hola, buenos días." *

____

* "Hello, good morning."

"Buenas,"[*] He murmurs, looking back at his computer and continuing to type.

I scan the QR code that's on the small stand on the table and look through the menu, and every so often feel his stare on me.

I can't help but let out a yawn as I wait for my server. I guess Santi was right: no amount of makeup that I smacked on my face would disguise my exhaustion.

"If you're tired, you picked the best place to get coffee that will actually wake you up." Green eyes murmurs next to me.

I turned my head over to him, shocked at his perfect English.

"Does everyone in Madrid speak English?" I ask, curious about why everyone I've come into contact with so far has spoken my language more than they have theirs.

Green eyes shrugs and closes his laptop before stuffing it in his bag. "It's almost a mandatory thing now. If you work in a city filled with tourists whose main language tends to be English, then you should know enough to be able to defend yourself."

Green eyes peers over to the left and calls over the waiter, "But somehow you found your way into a cafe that speaks little to no English."

Of course I did.

"Do you like milk in your coffee?" He asks.

"Yes," I answered instantly, black coffee just wasn't for me.

"Do you know what you want to eat?"

My eyes skim the menu again, knowing I'm going to ask for the most basic thing on it.

"Is avocado toast too American of me to order?" I ask, hoping there'd be no judgment for my morning cravings.

"Yes, but I will order a side of churros to balance it out." He grins and faces the waiter who's standing in front of us, and relays our order to him. Green eyes lifts up from his chair, and I'm sad to see him go so quickly. I was enjoying his presence.

But he doesn't go far. Instead, he pulls out the chair in front of me and takes a seat.

---

[*] Casual and friendly way of saying "hello."

"You don't mind, right?" He asks.

"Not at all." I can't help the smile that plays on my lips at this guy's forwardness.

"My name is Emilio, by the way. Yours?" He asks, bringing his hand forward for me to take.

"Sylvie. My name is Sylvie." I say, though it comes out almost like a whisper.

How did this man make his smile reach his eyes like this?

He was mesmerizing to look at.

"So, Sylvie, are you staying in Madrid all alone?" He asks, and though he seems like a sensible, normal, attractive man, my mind still wanders to that third-grade seminar in the school's auditorium on stranger danger.

"Um, no, actually."

Emilio raises an eyebrow and nods for me to continue.

But shit, that's all I got.

What else should I say?

That I was here with Marlene? Or I could say I was here with a boyfriend, a six-foot, beefy one at that, who could toss him around if needed.

"I'm actually here visiting a friend." The lie spews out of my mouth before I can think it through.

"A friend? And you're here alone?" He asks,

Damn, was this guy part of the special victims unit or something?

What's with all the questions?

"He's working right now. We agreed to meet in a few, after he was done with work."

Emilio leans back in his chair and nods. "What is it that your friend does?" He asks.

The waiter comes and serves us our coffee and my breakfast, giving me some time to think of a response as we both mumble our thank-yous in Spanish to him.

What was it that Santi did? I mean, I met the guy a few hours ago, and it's not like he wanted to establish some roomie bonding. So this left me with no other choice.

I was going to have to flirt my way out of this lie.

"I don't think you'd switch seats and order us coffee if you were interested in knowing what it is my friend does for a living." The words slide past my lips so easily, but that's because there really was no harm in flirting.

Just as long as I didn't end up in their bed and in a committed relationship afterward.

"You got me there." He says.

Emilio inclines forward to get closer to me, and I let a challenging look play on my face to show him that I'm interested in his banter.

"So, Sylvie, what is it that you do?" He asks.

I bring the cup of coffee to my lips and let out a moan at its warm, creamy deliciousness.

"I told you it was good."

"I guess you're a trustworthy person then." I tease, setting the coffee cup down.

"Trustworthy enough to tell me what you do for a living?" He asks again.

"I'm a software engineer," I answer, taking a bite of one of the churros he had ordered for us.

Wow, that was good too.

"So you're smart?" He asks, a sly grin appearing on his lips again.

I shrug. "I like riddles."

That, and my parents had sent me to a coding bootcamp as a child, and I enjoyed it enough to pursue coding as a career.

"What about you?" I ask.

"What about me?" He asks, with a shrug.

"What do you do for a living?" I ask, waving my churro around before taking another bite of it.

"I own several businesses." He says.

"What type of businesses?" I ask, curious as to what he does for a living.

How come I was an open book, but he was all shy and reserved now?

Emilio shrugs, grabs a churro from the basket, and takes a bite. He chews slowly and continues to stare at me, and I can't help but blush.

"I own a couple of restaurants and clubs in the city." He finally says.

Hm, that sounded fun, or at least fun to be in, not sure about how much fun it'd be to run a restaurant or club.

"Funny, I was just going to ask if there were any places you'd recommend." I take my shot at a chance for free booze and a good time out, and I seem to get that when Emilio stretches out his hand and shoots his eyes over to my phone.

I take my phone and open it up to the contacts before handing it over to him. He types in his info and hands it right back to me.

"I've got to get going, but I sent myself a message through What-sApp. And come here as much as you want. I let my workers know it's free for you." He says, getting up and sending me a wink before leaving, not even giving me a chance to say thank you.

I make a mental note to send him a message later to thank him. I take another bite of my churro, not bothering even to touch my avocado toast yet.

Hm, I guess Madrid isn't too bad so far.

CHAPTER TEN
Sylvie

I COMPLETELY UNDERESTIMATED HOW big 350 acres is. I also underestimated my ability with Google Maps and walking around this park. I have made my way around this a billion times and still no glass palace. There's no way I've passed it.

I sit down on one of the benches at the park and open the maps app, which is struggling to locate exactly where I am.

Great.

I decide to give the maps a break and exit the app completely.

Besides, while I tried my best to look around for this glass palace, my phone buzzed nonstop. It was mostly messages from Marlene asking for an update after I texted her about Emilio.

MARLENE

So, you're telling me the minute you get to Madrid, you're met with a six-foot, grumpy, naked man that you're now rooming with.

And then this morning, you met Hercules's reincarnation?

This is looking like spiritual warfare, Sylvie.

The devil is tempting you.

Stay strong.

SYLVIE

I'm not having sex with either of these men, and I'm definitely not starting a relationship with either one of them.

I blow out a puff of air and look up at the gardens. It was really something beautiful. Everything here was so fresh and clean, definitely better than being back in the city where you're choking on air pollution. I look over to my right, where I see two peacocks walking over to me.

Huh, peacocks.

Better than the City's pigeons that have dedicated themselves to my work blazer more than a handful of times. The birds walk over with calm before stopping right in front of me.

"You guys are kind of cute, aren't you?" I ask them.

One of them walks over to another peacock at the other side of the park while the other continues to look at me.

Suddenly, the bird begins to do what I can only describe as a mating call and spreads its feathers out to me.

"Oh, I'm not sure if I like that." I scoot over the bench and walk away slowly. But the peacock only begins to squawk louder and follow me.

"No! Go away!" I shout, trying my best to shoo the bird away with my hands.

The peacock, on the other hand, seems to have some other ideas when he begins trying his best to jump at me.

"Oh my god, oh my god, oh my god!" I screech, trying my best to push away this giant, colorful turkey.

I try my best to run away from the peacock, but it's too fast, and the last thing I want is to get arrested because I'm beating the crap out of the bird. I push the feathered beast away with my foot, but somehow he ends up holding himself to my pants and moving in a hump-like way.

Ew, gross!

"Get off of me!" I push him off as hard as I can, but he continues to walk back towards me. Marlene was right. This was spiritual warfare.

It's not until something tall blocks my frame that I'm aware that a guy is scaring the bird away.

Not just a random guy.

It's Santi.

CHAPTER ELEVEN
Santi

THE MINUTE SYLVIE LEAVES, I make a call to Luisa, who I hadn't spoken to since she dropped me off at my door last night. I had a few questions for her, but after the shit show that was last night and staying up to watch Carolina's Instagram feed under an anonymous account, it completely slipped my mind to text her.

"Good morning, must be nice not having to be at work." She answers sarcastically.

"Oh, crap, are you at work already?" I rub my face with my hands and look over at my microwave to check the time. It's ten minutes until nine thirty, so she must be on her way there.

"Not yet, I'm just messing with you." She says.

I rub my eyes and try to make sense of my whole night before finally asking Luisa straight up.

"Are you a witch?" I ask, curious but also a bit worrisome.

"What?" She asks, a chuckle escaping her as she asks the question.

"Are you a witch? Because some things happened last night that would definitely point to you being a witch." I groan at how crazy I must sound. But there was no way that Luisa could have guessed that there was a woman in my home.

"Santi, are you okay? Do you need me to stop by and check on you?" Luisa asks, the concern entangled in her voice.

"Luisa, last night you mentioned something about a girl in my apartment." I begin to explain.

"Yes, I did. It was a joke." She defends.

I shake my head, even though I know she can't see me, and sigh into the phone. "No, Lu. That's the thing, when I got upstairs and entered my apartment, there was a woman who was dead set on stating that it was her apartment."

"What?!" Luisa exclaims, and I instinctively pull back the phone to protect my eardrum.

"What do you mean, there was a girl? Did you call the police?" She asks.

"No, actually, I didn't," I mumble.

"What? Santi! Are you insane?" She shrieks.

"There's a random woman in your home stating that it's hers, and you don't call the police? What the hell is wrong with you?" She asks.

"Would you just listen?" I grumble out.

Luisa sighs and mumbles out, "I'm listening."

"Javier seems to have rented out his room along with our shared amenities to this American woman, who also has no idea she would be having to share a space with anyone other than herself."

Luisa grumbles out a jumble of curses towards Javier before letting out a sigh.

I wasn't sure if the sigh was due to what I had just told her or because she was trying to catch her breath on her walk.

"Well, Javier isn't your problem. He should have consulted you about something like this before bringing a total stranger into your home." Luisa reasons.

"Yeah, well, we'll just have to add it to the list of things that Javier should've spoken to me about before making a decision that involves both of us," I mutter, rummaging through my drawers to grab my running shorts.

"Hm, well, maybe this isn't a bad thing." Luisa hums into the receiver.

"Yes, it is," I grumble, as I undress myself to change into my running clothes.

"Is she nice or is she prissy?" She asks.

"I don't know her."

"You don't have to know her completely to know if she's prissy. That would've shown the minute she first spoke."

I roll my eyes and sigh into the phone.

"She seems nice, I guess," I grunt, shoving my foot into my shoe.

"Is she… cute?" Luisa teases.

"Luisa," I warn.

"What? That's a normal question. I'm trying to picture her in my head." She defends.

"I'm sure you are." I tease, which makes her laugh.

There's a pregnant pause after she's finished laughing, and I sit here on my bed for a while before gathering the image of Sylvie perfectly in my mind.

"She's not short, but she isn't tall either."

"So she's a woman's average height?" Luisa asks.

"I wouldn't say there's anything average about her."

"Oh, no?" She asked.

"She's beautiful. She's got the curtain bangs that every woman talks about, and I'm not the biggest fan of bangs in general, but on her, it's kind of cute."

"Blonde?" She asks.

"Brunette," I respond, rather quickly.

"That's *different*." She muses.

"Stop it," I growl, getting up from the bed and walking over to the kitchen, where my keys lay on the counter, and tucking them into my pockets.

"What? It's just interesting! You're usually mesmerized by blondes."

"Just because Carol was blonde doesn't mean that I only like blondes," I mumble into the phone.

"Say that to the line of blonde exes you have."

Okay, so maybe I did tend to lean towards them. But that didn't mean I was blind in recognizing a woman's beauty, and Sylvie was definitely beautiful.

Was she careless, overdramatic, and like a yapping Pomeranian?

Yes, yes, and yes.

But, nonetheless, she was still gorgeous.

"What else makes her beautiful?" Luisa asks.

I focus on my image of Sylvie last night, or at least the visual I had before my vision fogged from feeling my balls in my stomach.

"She's... curvy," I mumble into the phone.

"I'm sorry, what was that?" Luisa teases.

"I said she's a beautiful, voluptuous woman."

"Damn, you definitely took a good look at her, didn't you?" She asks.

My face heats up at her accusation, but I guess she wasn't wrong. But even if I hadn't seen her in a towel, she was a woman whose curves always stood out. And if she hadn't pissed me off in the first few seconds of meeting her, I would've been interested in her.

"It's not my fault, she was in a towel." I defend.

"Ew, Santi, now you're just a perv." Luisa scoffs.

"Okay, don't you have a job to go do?" I mutter as I walk out of the apartment and downstairs towards the entrance of the building.

"Okay, okay, I get it! You're not a perv; you just so happen to run into her almost naked. No worries, I believe you, friend."

I sigh and walk out into the fresh summer air. It was still morning, so the sun wouldn't start beaming with all its strength until around noon. This would be the best time for a run.

"Thank you," I murmur.

"I'll let you go because you're sadly correct and I do have to work, but we will be meeting up and speaking about this later."

I roll my eyes and let her know we'll meet later to talk and wish her luck on her day of work.

Usually, running seemed to clear my thoughts, mostly because of that running high I was chasing. But not today; my mind kept circling around that conversation with Luisa. That seemed to happen anytime Carolina was brought up. It had been six months since she left me at the altar. All the money and time that I worked hard and invested for us to have the wedding she wanted, and she left me there, waiting.

No contact after.

Just left me there without any clarity and looking like a fucking fool. I stalked her Instagram page here and there, and it was nothing out of the ordinary. Carolina continued her traveling and visiting family who lived outside of Spain.

From what I know, she hasn't been back. But every time I see a blonde, I do have to admit that my stomach drops and the knot in my chest begins to tighten at the thought of it being her.

These thoughts of Carolina must really get to me because I don't realize how fast I've been running until I get to the park much quicker than I usually do. I lower my pace and continue my jog, focusing on the upbeat music playing through my earphones. But a horrific scream breaks me away from concentration. And as much as I'd like to ignore it, I can't abandon someone in danger. I pick up my pace towards the sound of the screams and halt in place when I see her.

There was Sylvie, screaming bloody murder because a peacock was pecking at her.

"Get off of me!" She shouts at the colorful bird, who, for the most part, is always very calm and leaves people alone. But I guess the American found some way to upset him.

I walk over to the illegal cage fight and stand between the winning bird and the trembling American. It only takes the flick of my wrist and a "go away" in my native language to have the bird walk over to a fellow peacock friend.

I turn and look down at Sylvie, who's now fixing her outfit that must've gotten rearranged during her fight with the peacock.

"Jesus, why do they have these wild animals running around the park like that?" She grumbles.

"They're usually pretty docile creatures, I think you just have a way of pissing us Spaniards off," I murmur, walking around her and starting back on my jog.

"Wait!" A shout sounds behind me.

No.

"Santi, I can run too, you know." I hear beside me.

I turn and see the woman, jogging right next to me.

You've got to be kidding me.

I stop and look down at the bubbly American. I wasn't sure if she had put some sort of blush on this morning or if she was just flushed from her peacock attack. But regardless, it looked cute on her.

Santi, snap out of it.

This is your week off, and this American is ruining it for you.

"Do you run every morning?" She asks.

I lift a brow at her question, "Does it matter?"

Sylvie shrugs and looks around the park before looking back at me.

"Do you work?" She asks.

"Usually," I respond.

Why the hell was I responding to her?

"Oh, you got laid off?" She asks.

I bring my head back and furrow my brows at her assumption.

"What?" I huff, "No, I didn't get laid off." I mutter.

I turn and start walking away from her, wanting to continue my run. But a hand catches my wrist, holding me back from escaping this interaction.

I turn and look down at her French-manicured hand wrapped around my wrist.

"You're a very touchy person, you know that?" I mutter, shaking my wrist out of her hand. Sylvie complies and shrugs, her doe brown eyes looking up at me with a pleading look, and those plump lips, pulled out like a puppy's face.

"So, if you're not working, maybe you'd like to spend the day with me?" She asks, rather boldly.

This girl walks around like she's never been rejected a day in her life. And was I really about to be the first?

I guess I was.

"No." I turn and begin walking away, but Sylvie catches up right next to me.

"Please, please, please." She begs.

"Are you always this annoying?"

Sylvie stops walking and raises a brow at me, and I know this because I stop too for some odd reason and look right at her.

"You're not a ray of sunshine either, honey." She bites back, her lips pursed, and eyebrows furrowed. And seeing her annoyed like this was kind of… hot.

"Then why are you begging me to accompany you today?"

"Google maps and I aren't the best of friends." She admits.

"Ah, so you don't want to hang out with me. You just want me to be your tour guide." I cross my arms over my chest and look at her, baffled by her admittance.

"Listen, I've been trying to find this glass palace for an hour now, and I don't know where I'm going. And now I'm being attacked by peacocks, and I would just like it if you'd be nice for one second!" She shouts, obviously aggravated by the turn out of her day.

"Was I not nice to you when I allowed you to stay in my home for the remainder of the week?" I ask.

Sylvie bites her lip, probably stopping herself from saying something that would have me walking back home and changing the locks.

"Please?" She finally asks.

I stay silent, not wanting to give in to this woman I barely knew.

"Come on, I thought the French were the grumpy ones, not you guys." She jabs, a smile spreading across her face.

"The French are grumpy about tourists, and I'm beginning to see why," I mutter.

I'm sure Sylvie would rather shoot a menacing glare at me than a smile. But instead, she gives me the puppy face again and mutters a "por favor."

The only time I was ever a tour guide was when I was at my job, and I was guiding people around paintings that I studied and loved. And I didn't take this week off just to become a tour guide for this annoying American woman.

I was already allowing her to stay in my apartment, which was more than kind of me. And it's not like she was the best human in the world. She kicked me in the balls for crying out loud. And this whole puppy face thing was not going to work; I wouldn't fall for her tricks.

"Follow me," I mumble.

Sylvie hops up and down cheerfully and wraps her arms around me.

"Thank you, thank you, thank you! I promise I'll be the best person you've ever guided around the park." She states cheerfully.

"You're the only person I've ever had to guide around the park."

"Well, the ones that will come after me won't cease to compare." She promises.

"Sylvie, if I'm ever stuck in this same position again, my best friend and roommate will surely be dead," I grumble.

"Hm, but not me, right? You won't kill me?" She asks, looking me up and down as if to see if I could be capable of doing something like that.

"In this park? No." I joke, sarcastically.

"You know, actually, the map seems–"

"Let's go, Sylvie. As annoying as you are, Americana, you're definitely not someone I'd want to murder." I state, walking in the direction of the glass palace.

And Sylvie follows right behind.

CHAPTER TWELVE
Santi

"IS this park like your version of Central Park?" Sylvie asks, following right behind me.

"I guess."

"So, what's the history behind this park?" She asks.

"Absolutely not." I shake my head and continue moving further, trying my best to get this over with. All I needed to do was get her to the glass palace and around this park, and then I'd be free to go back to my daily routine.

"Absolutely not, what?" She asks.

"I agreed to take you to the glass palace, Sylvie, not to play tour guide and give you the historical rundown of the place." I had lived in Madrid for years and knew the layout of the park like the back of my hand. It's also very simple when there's a trail leading you in the direction. I don't know how the GPS could steer her wrong. But then again, this was the woman who didn't realize she had rented out a room rather than an apartment for her stay in Madrid.

"Hey Siri, what's the history behind–"

"It belonged to the Spanish monarchy."

I sigh and slow my pace to let Sylvie walk right next to me so I can explain the history behind the park.

"Belonged?" She asks.

"Yeah, at first it was part of the palace here, and it was mainly used for special events, or I guess as a vacation home of sorts. But then they opened some parts of the park to the public, then we had the Napoleonic wars, which damaged the park, and a few years later, after some other political turmoil, the royal gardens became public property.

"Huh, and what about the glass palace?" She asks.

"That came after, once the park was public property and when the Philippines was a colony of Spain," I explain, grabbing her arm to keep her from tripping, which she had done twice already on our walk. I was honestly beginning to think the GPS had nothing to do with our tour. Maybe she was just scared to break her neck all alone out here.

"Why is colonization important to this?" She asks.

"Well, the Philippines has beautiful flora, which the Spaniards were very interested in."

"You guys were interested in more than just flora and fauna. You know, have you guys ever even–"

"Sylvie, I am aware of my ancestors' wrongdoings, but the reason the glass palace came to be is because the flora of the Philippines was so beautiful that they shipped some plants and flowers over to Madrid, where they were kept in this glass greenhouse for everyone to see." I wave my hand forward and show the enormous greenhouse we are standing in front of.

Sylvie stares silently and gawks at the beautiful glass structure.

"Wow, this is beautiful, and much bigger than I thought." Sylvie makes her way around the perimeter of the structure, taking pictures like most of the tourists are doing.

"This was a good idea," Sylvie whispers to herself.

And though I know I'm not meant to hear it, I still step closer to her and ask, "What do you mean?"

Sylvie looks over at me and smiles, but I don't return it. It's not something I do often anyway.

"This trip didn't really start the way I wanted, and I thought maybe it was all just a mistake."

There's a slight pause before she clears her throat and speaks again.

"I'm kind of going through a breakup," Sylvie says.

"You? A breakup?" I ask. I stand corrected. I guess Americana has been rejected.

"Well, a couple of breakups, and one of those breakups is with my old self, you know?" She tries to explain.

"No. Wait. Is this like a polyamorous thing?" I ask, confused by her breakup.

"No, it's more like–"

"¿Les gustaría que les tome una foto?"* A lady near us asks in Spanish.

"No—" I begin to deny the lady, but Sylvie cuts me off completely and gives her phone to the lady.

"Sí, por favor." She says.

"What are you doing?" I ask her as she grabs hold of my bicep and brings me closer to the crystal palace to take a picture.

"I'm taking a picture so we can tell our kids in the future how safe life used to be back then, when we could stay at strangers' houses and not get killed," Sylvie states, fluffing her hair up for the picture.

"Our kids?" I ask, heat rushing to my cheeks.

"Yes, my kids with hopefully some nice Irish man and you with your kids with someone who can deal with your attitude." She explains, rubbing her lips together after having applied Chapstick.

"I don't have an attitude," I mutter, looking forward to the lady holding the camera.

"No? Then smile and look cute for the picture, honey." I roll my eyes, but catch myself mid-eye roll, not wanting to prove Sylvie right.

---

* "Would you like me to take a picture of you?"

"Can you not stand so stiff? My kids will think you're a weirdo in the picture." She grumbles.

"How would you like me to stand, Americana?"

"Put your arm around me or something." She says, finally facing the camera.

I bring my arm around Sylvie's waist and pull her closer to me, as I would with a girlfriend, and she instinctively leans into me.

We both smile up at the camera.

Or at least I try.

Though the minute we receive the phone back and look at the pictures, it does look more like a grimace.

"Why is your face like that?" Sylvie asks, furrowing her brows at the picture.

"It's the face I was born with," I say, bringing my hands up to my face to touch it subconsciously.

"No, your face is definitely not like this on the regular. I think you might've been tortured when you smiled as a kid, so now you instinctively make this face when you try to smile." She pauses for a bit and stares at the picture.

"It's almost disturbing to look at." She says.

"Well then, stop looking at it," I mutter, reaching over and shutting off the phone. Sylvie only laughs and points towards the line that's waiting to get inside.

"Would you mind waiting so I can take a look inside?" She asks, I shrug and lead us towards the line to go in. It's not like it takes too long anyway.

"Thank you," Sylvie says, looking up at me with those puppy dog eyes.

"It's fine, it's not like I had much planned for my day today," I murmur.

"Hm, what was it that you said you did for work anyway?" She asks, gluing her eyes back to her phone and chuckling at something she must have received.

"I didn't," I mumble.

"It's okay to not feel comfortable stating that you're a sex worker to random people. But don't worry, I'm all for empowering sex workers." Sylvie whispers, holding her fist up in solidarity.

My face pales at her absurd assumption.

Not that being a sex worker was absurd.

It isn't.

But I'm not one.

And I'm not even sure how the hell she came to think that I was one.

"I'm not a sex worker," I whisper back to her, not wanting to bring any attention to us.

"This totally makes sense." She states as if she's had a break-through.

"What makes sense?"

Sylvie leans in closer and looks around to make sure that nobody's listening to us.

"It makes sense why you were naked last night, you know—when we met."

It must suddenly be getting even hotter because I begin to feel my face heat up, and when I try to utter a response back to her, all that comes out of my mouth is incomprehensible gibberish.

"It's totally okay, Santi. I'm super okay with it. I'll promote you on my Instagram if you want. Here, what's your page?" She asks, turning her phone back on.

"No, stop it. Where did you even get an idea like this? I'm a tour guide at a museum for crying out loud. I'm an art history major, and I spend my workdays speaking about art pieces within the Prado museum." I explain, not even noticing that my hand is around her wrist, stopping her from trying to get on her social media.

Sylvie's eyes give her away before her smug face does.

"You were fucking with me?" I growl.

Sylvie shrugs and lets out a giggle.

"You're not big on sharing, so I had to come up with something that would make you want to share what you do for a living." She chirps.

"Sylvie–"

"Oh, look, it's our turn! Come!"

Before I can make my way out of this situation, she grabs my arm and pulls me inside with her.

After this was done, I'd give her instructions on how to get out of the park, and then I'd get back to my run and the rest of my day.

I wasn't anyone's tour guide, especially not to this nosey Americana.

CHAPTER THIRTEEN
Sylvie

SOMETHING very important to know about me is that I am a very persistent woman. My father used to say that there wasn't a single thing that I couldn't get in this world because I was just so determined to get what I wanted.

"Please?" I beg.

"No," Santi states firmly, like the last ten times I asked, but this time picking up the pace of his walk as if a bit of speed walking would deter me from my objective.

"Please?"

"No."

"Please?"

"No."

"Please?"

"Fine," Santi growls, turning back around to head towards the entrance of the rowboats.

"Yay!" I cheer excitedly, like a child who's just been told they're skipping school and going to Disney World.

And that is a childhood memory I don't have, and I will never forgive my parents for not making it happen.

"You're annoying, you know that?" Santi grumbles, paying the guy a total of twenty-eight euros. I take my wallet out to pay him back, but he pushes my hand down in disgust.

"Put your wallet back and don't embarrass me like that again."

I tuck the wallet back into my purse and put my hands up in surrender as Santi takes the tickets from the man in the booth and shakes his head in disapproval at my gesture of paying him back.

Santi leads us to a booth near the gates where they hand us life vests. Santi buckles himself quickly as I struggle with my own life vest. And even though he doesn't seem to be a man who likes to give out a helping hand, he adjusts the vest over my chest. And I can't help the chills that slide down my body as his knuckles accidentally graze my breasts.

Jesus Christ, Sylvie.

Get yourself together, girl.

The man's got a permanent crease between his brows from all the frowning he does for crying out loud.

"Come on." He says, leading me over to the boardwalk where two men are assisting people on and off the boat.

"Those boats don't look too sturdy as they go in and out," I mutter as I look over to a woman who's practically shaking as she tries to get onto the boat.

"It's a small boat on a body of water, what about that screams sturdy to you?" Santi scoffs, moving up in the line.

"Hey, I have a genuine question for you," I say.

"Hm?" He asks, showing the least bit of interest in what I have to say.

"Does someone spit or piss in your coffee every morning?"

"Excuse me?" He asks, finally turning to look back at me.

"Does someone spit or piss in your coffee in the mornings?" I repeat.

Santi furrows his brows, probably trying to process whether what he interpreted is what I actually said.

"Neither?" He says, though it comes out as more of a question.

"You sure, because you're awfully grumpy for a man who hasn't had his morning coffee pissed or spat on."

"Can we stop talking about ruining my morning coffee, please?"

I shrug and walk forward, the man holding the boat gestures for me to get on, and I hesitate for a moment, afraid of how unsteady it is. To my surprise, Santi walks onto the boat before me and puts out his hand to help me.

"Is this like a nice gesture you do to get me to trust you before you kill me?" I ask, taking his hand and stepping onto the boat.

"For a woman who's scared of being murdered, it's quite odd that you're still staying at my house." He mumbles and immediately grabs the oars of the boat and begins leading us out to the lake.

"Touche."

I look around and take in the park's surroundings. It was even more beautiful than the pictures online showed. But then again, the whole city had been. There were a bunch of other people rowing their own boats. On one side of the lake, people were admiring the monuments along the promenade. And on the other side of the lake, where we had made our way around, people stopped to look at the street performers.

"It must be so wonderful to live here," I murmur, inclining my head back to have the sunlight touch my face.

This is what I came here for.

I needed to feel this.

The sound of the lake, the birds, and the people's joy all around me.

The warmth of the sun caressing my face.

And the soothing movements of the boat as Santi moves us around the lake.

"Thank you," I mumble, not yet opening my eyes.

I wanted to enjoy this peaceful moment as much as I could.

"Thank me by remaining quiet. I think you look even more beautiful when you're like this." He mumbles.

I could easily ignore what he says and just enjoy this moment. But I'm a cancer, so that won't be happening.

I open my eyes and look back over to him, arching my brow in question. I even caught his stare lingering on me before he finally met my eyes and looked away.

"What?" He murmurs, his grip on the oars tightening as he continues to row.

"You said I look beautiful." I tease.

"Yes, I said you look beautiful when you're quiet." He rebuttals.

"No, you didn't." I chuckle, not being able to help the heat rising to my cheeks.

"Yes, I did." He argues, rowing the boat faster.

"No, you didn't," I say, with a shake to my head. "You said I looked beautiful — *actually*, you said I looked even more beautiful when I'm relaxing and taking in the beauty of my surroundings."

Santi's resting bitch face remains intact, and not even a sliver of heated cheeks shows. I raise a brow, challenging him to respond. It takes a few seconds before Santi shrugs and continues his rowing, which I hadn't even realized he stopped.

"I'm not blind, and you're not stupid." He mutters.

"What does my intelligence have to do with this?"

"You know you're a beautiful woman, and so you have to know that any straight man who looks at you can see how stunning you are." He explains, adjusting the ores on the boat.

Now it's my turn to blush and look away.

"I just happened to actually realize that beauty after I saw how you could be quiet for more than two seconds."

I stretch over and slap his leg playfully and scowl at his comment.

"I'm kidding, I'm kidding." He repeats, laughing at his own comeback at me.

"That was just mean," I mumble, crossing my arms over my chest.

I swear for a second I see his eyes linger down to my breasts for a moment, but he's quick to lift them back up at me.

"Not as mean as invading somebody's home and forcing them to give you a tour around the city." He says.

"Honestly, it's not my fault your roomie didn't tell you about his side hustle. It's also not like I had a gun to your head and forced you to let me live with you for the week and be my tour guide."

Santi only shrugs and picks the ores back up to move us around the lake again.

"I'm a bit confused." He finally murmurs.

"About the side hustle or the gun analogy?"

"Neither." He practically whispers.

"You might want to reconsider the volume at which you speak because I can barely hear you," I mutter.

"Why are you here?" Santi asks.

"Because the park is on my itinerary?" I state, but it comes out more like a question.

"No, not here. I'm asking why you are here in Madrid." He restates.

"Oh," I shrug and shake my head at him. "I already told you why."

"It was a bit confusing about breaking up from a polyamorous relationship. And then also with yourself. I may understand that one."

I want to preface that polyamorous relationships are real relationships and that love is love. But for some reason I break out into a laugh because I had no clue how Santi could've thought that I was in a polyamorous relationship from what I said before.

"What is it?" He asks.

"I'm not poly, I can barely handle monogamy. I doubt I'd be any good at handling more than one relationship." I explain.

"But you said you went through multiple break-ups." He explains.

"Ah, yeah." I shift myself on the seat of the boat, trying my best to unstick my sweaty thighs from the wooden surface. I had worn shorts knowing they would keep me cool from the summer's heat, but I hadn't thought a run would be part of today's itinerary, so the chub rub from it was bound to be brutal later on.

And trust me when I say chub rub is a big girl's enemy.

I look back over at Santi, who's still staring at me, waiting for a response. But I'm not even sure what to say or how to state it.

"It's complicated… um, you see, I'm more of a serial dater." I finally say.

"A serial dater?" He asks.

"You know, I date a lot and, I guess, love a lot — but not really?"

Santi stares at me like I'm completely insane.

"It's hard to explain." I finally mutter, giving up and feeling judged in the process.

"Maybe it's just that I don't understand because I'm the opposite." He says.

I lift a brow and nod for him to go on.

"I've always been in a committed relationship." He begins.

"My last relationship lasted eight years." My eyes practically bulge out of my eyes, and Santi seems to notice because the man laughs.

"Wait, eight years? That's almost a decade." I say.

"Almost, but not quite." He mutters to himself, letting out a light grunt as he pushes the oar.

"Wait, so how old are you?"

"Twenty- eight."

"I've beaten you by two years," I smirk.

"You're thirty?" He asks, the shock plastered on his face.

"Do I not look it?" I ask, and I'll admit his shocked face kind of gives me an ego boost.

"No, you just don't act like it." He jabs, and my smile instantly falls off my face, and I do the first thing that comes to mind and flip him off.

But despite the middle finger directed at him, Santi doesn't seem to be bothered and instead laughs.

Huh, I've made this grumpy man laugh twice already. And now, I'm sure that I want to make it into a game and see how many times I can make this man laugh or smile.

"So, you're here because you date too much?" He asks.

"I'm here to find something more enjoyable in life than finding ineligible bachelors," I explain.

"You know, Americana, I think I'm on the same boat." He acknowledges.

"You're only twenty-eight, and you're a man. I'm sure you'll find your soulmate."

And for that, I was jealous. Men never had that biological clock ticking. And I never really thought that whole biological clock thing was real. But the minute I turned twenty-five, I heard it tick for the first time. And I saw all of my friends running to get married and having kids, and suddenly I was thirty and my younger sister had beat me to the marriage and children portion of life. And I started realizing that maybe this just wasn't my path in life.

"And you're only thirty." He rebuttals.

I chuckle and give him a shrug.

"It's already considered too old," I murmur.

"How can you be old when your life is just starting?" Santi asks, lifting a brow to challenge my statement.

Honestly, I had never thought about it that way. In a way, thirty was exactly when life started. No more teenage rage, or the confused stage of life that comes with your twenties.

The thirties were the entrance to adulthood.

But that didn't fix my unresolvable issue of finding a partner for life.

The ringing of a phone brings me out of my daze, and Santi pulls the phone out of his pocket and answers it.

"No deberías estar trabajando?"[*] He says, and laughs at whatever response the other person gives him on the phone.

"Esta noche?"[†] He asks, looking around in deep thought.

"Vale, nos vemos allí."[‡]

Santi hangs up the call and rows around a bit more before we finally decide to call it a day at the park. I knew I hadn't seen it all, but I was starving and tired from all the walking and the peacock attack.

Santi rows us over to the boardwalk, and the man pulls us in. I

---

[*] "Shouldn't you be working?"
[†] "Tonight?"
[‡] Okay, we'll see each other there.

think it's scarier getting off the boat than it was getting in, but Santi helps me off and makes it easier.

He walks beside me this time, and at a regular pace I can keep up with. I'm pretty sure we're headed home after we exit the park, but just in case, I've saved the address in Google Maps so it can lead me back.

Santi suddenly comes to a halt and takes a minute to stare at something in the distance, but looks away instantly.

"Is everything okay?" I ask.

Santi looks back over at me, and that stoic face is there once again.

"Yeah."

There's a pregnant pause before he looks at me again and asks me if I'm hungry.

My growling stomach replies before I can, and Santi nods his head to the right for me to follow him.

But I can't help but look back as we walk away and try to figure out what had captivated his gaze for that long.

CHAPTER FOURTEEN
Sylvie

SANTI WAS MORE charming than he seemed. Behind all that grumpy exterior and nasty attitude, I knew he was a teddy bear. The man was a gentleman. He had defended me from my attacker earlier at the park, and I know most people will tell me that fighting off a bird is not much of a defense. But those people had never gotten into a physical altercation with a peacock.

Besides, it wasn't just about him saving me from that bird fight. He had walked me to the glass palace rather than continuing on his run. He also agreed to take me for a ride on the boats, which he paid for and rowed himself.

And even after a day of doing things he didn't want to partake in, he still took me out to lunch and had me try tortilla for the first time.

Now, I just lie here in bed, exhausted from this afternoon. Santi had left to go hang out with some friends. To my surprise, he actually invited me to come along. But I'm sure he only did that to be polite.

Regardless of his reasoning, I was still jet-lagged from yesterday. And tomorrow I expect to get a bit more done. The minute I got into the apartment, I took a shower and set myself down in front of the coffee table in the living room. As children, both Marlene and I would spend our weekends scrapbooking with our grandmother. It was something I enjoyed, even leading into my teen years.

But like most things we like doing, we find something that tears us away from it completely. My 'something' was school, and later on, it became dating and work.

I guess once you become an adult, you don't have time to enjoy the things you once loved. Until you get to retirement, that is, and enjoy your hobbies once again like my grandmother did.

But I wasn't going to wait for retirement.

That's just too far ahead.

I wanted to enjoy life again, and I want to enjoy the things that once made me happy.

That's why I had brought a bullet journal with me, along with some book-scrapping supplies. I wanted to make a bullet journal based solely on my travels.

My phone buzzes repeatedly, and I know it's Marlene nudging the messages for me to respond.

I sigh and pick the phone up to answer her. I hadn't been ignoring her, but just forgot to respond.

MARLENE

Wow, he's cute… but also constipated, I think.

You haven't fucked, have you?

SYLVIE

He's not constipated. That's just his face. But yes, he is a handsome man.

MARLENE

You've ignored my previous question, Sylvie.

SYLVIE

Of course not! I haven't even hit the 24-hour mark of having met him.

MARLENE

Says the girl who moves in with someone after a
week of knowing them.

SYLVIE

That was old Sylvie.

New Sylvie is only looking for fun in scrapbooking
and traveling.

MARLENE

How adventurous.

SYLVIE

Fuck off.

I roll my eyes and begin my scrapbooking, not paying mind to
anything that Marlene says. I know she's only messing with me. It's
our love language. But I also didn't want to repeat the same old
patterns.

Not that Santi would be interested in getting with me anyway. I
could barely get him to hang out with me today. And I think he only
invited me out to eat towards the end because it was the gentle-
manly thing to do.

Even his invitation to go out tonight seemed to be done out of
pity.

Regardless of his feelings, it didn't matter. I was here to live in
the moment and enjoy my time away, and today was a great start.

Day 2

CHAPTER FIFTEEN
Sylvie

IT'S CURRENTLY PAST MIDNIGHT, and I think I'm going to be kidnapped and murdered.

Or maybe they'll just skip the kidnapping part and just kill me.

Fuck me, I should've just gone to a hotel for the remainder of the week.

The ruckus outside my bedroom just increases, and I'm sure there are a few broken things outside. If I make it out of here tonight, Santi better not blame me for all the damage.

I creep out of bed, trying my best to make as little noise as possible, and make my way towards the locked door.

I felt that after the day spent with Santi today, there was no reason to build my fortress. That and I was tired of moving around the furniture. They were just too heavy, and it was annoying to move them around in the middle of the night when I needed to use the bathroom really badly.

I crouch down against the door and take a peep under it where there's enough space between the floor and the door for me to see feet passing by.

"Joder, como pesas, tio."[*] I hear a female voice murmur from the hallway.

Tio?

That means uncle, right?

Is this a family of robbers or murderers?

"Joder como la extraño, Luisa."[†]I hear a man respond.

Wait, is that Santi?

Yeah, of course it is, Sylvie.

It's probably Santi coming home from a drunken night out. And the girl is obviously his… niece?

Is he old enough to have a niece who's going out for drinks with him?

Whatever, it doesn't even matter because this just means that I'm not dying and that I can go back to sleep.

I pick myself up from the floor and walk back over to my bed. I stayed there for a moment just listening to Santi's niece clean whatever was broken and then leave.

I try my best to fall back asleep, but something doesn't feel right, especially when I hear shuffling outside my door and the knob of my door moving.

"Javi?" A groan comes from the other side of the door.

Just ignore it, Sylvie. He's drunk.

"Javi, can we talk? It hurts."

At this moment, I should be quiet and pretend like I'm asleep, and hopefully, he will just go away. But instead I lower my tone in voice to sound as manly as I can and respond.

"What hurts?"

There's silence, and I'm sure that he's come out of his drunken haze and realized that I am definitely not Javi.

"My heart." He responds, and I guess the man really is super drunk.

---

[*] "Fuck, you're heavy, man."
[†] "Fuck, I miss her, Luisa."

I sigh and remove the covers from my body and walk back to the door, this time unlocking and opening it.

But Santi isn't there.

"You're not Javi." I hear him say, the sound of his voice coming from the floor. Where he happens to be sitting right next to my room.

"No, I'm not." I sigh, not sure of what to say to him.

"Who are you?" He asks.

"His girlfriend?" I state, though it sounds more like a question.

Santi scoffs in disbelief and shakes his head at me.

"As if."

"What's that supposed to mean?" I ask, crossing my arms over my chest.

"Javi, could never get a girl like you." He murmurs.

"A girl like me? What does that mean?"

"It means, you're too beautiful to be with a man like Javi."

"Oh," I utter, not sure as to what to say to that.

"Come on, let's get you off the floor and into bed." I bend over and help him up as best I can as Santi tries to stabilize himself.

"Why are we speaking English?" He asks, and I realize his accent is even thicker when he is slurring his words.

"Because I'm American." I manage to choke out as I lift his arm around my neck and lead him to his bedroom.

"La Americana." He murmurs.

"That's me," I grunt, entering his room and helping to lay him down on the bed.

"Americana?"

"Yes?" I respond, pulling a blanket over him.

"My heart still hurts." He murmurs.

"It'll heal in time," I assure.

"How?"

That was a good question, one that I didn't really have the answer to, being that I was never as in love as he was to be feeling such pain.

"I'm sure that some day you'll find someone who'll calm the

storm in your mind and glue back the shattered pieces of your heart."

I wasn't sure where that reply came from, but it must've been enough of a response because Santi only stares at me with those hazel eyes of his before they flutter close.

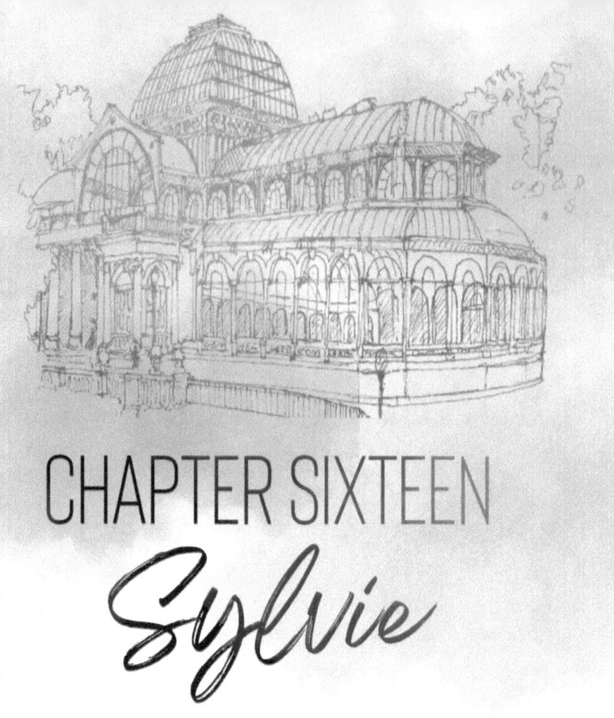

CHAPTER SIXTEEN
Sylvie

THIS MORNING I woke up and made my way out of the apartment as quickly and quietly as possible. I knew that Santi was still sleeping because I could hear his light snores coming from his room.

After I tucked him into bed last night, I had heard him murmur someone's name a couple of times as I was cleaning up the damage he had done in the living room. But I didn't stick around much after cleaning it all up.

MARLENE

Are you sure it's safe for you to be staying there?

SYLVIE

Yes, Marlene. He wasn't hostile, and I'm sure the items he broke in his own home were an accident.

MARLENE

Yes, and him trying to enter your bedroom was normal; there's no need to be afraid at all of a stranger trying to walk into your room while you're sleeping.

SYLVIE

You're going all mama bear mode on me.

Reminder: Sylvie is your OLDER sister and knows what she's doing.

MARELENE

Reminder: Marlene loves Sylvie and would love for her to come back home in one piece.

SYLVIE

I'm fine, I promise. I will speak to him about the incident afterward.

Reminder: I love you, too.

I had texted Marlene about what happened last night as I was getting ready this morning. I hadn't expected her to freak out about it. It wasn't that big of a deal anyway. I know this is only my second day of meeting Santi, but he just wasn't like that.

Santi was too organized and too much of a stickler to be a serial killer.

Plus, last night he was obviously reminiscing on a heartbreak and looking for his best friend to talk to him about it.

I don't even think that he would recall anything from last night.

I make my way towards the cafe where I had met Emilio yesterday.

Not because I was hoping to see him again, even though I wouldn't mind that either. But rather because the words free always sounded nice to my ears.

And it was a quiet place to work on a project that Aaron was too much of a dumbass to lead on his own.

I wasn't sure how he got his managerial position to begin with, but I was sure it involved a lot of ass kissing. Which is something that they couldn't pay me to do.

"¿Señorita Sylvie?"* The waiter asks, approaching me as soon as I enter.

"Yeah, I mean sí," I answer.

The waiter chuckles and waves a hand for me to follow him to a corner of the cafe. It's quiet and dim and relaxing. The perfect place to code, actually.

I look through the menu and give him my order of an omelette and coffee.

I set up my computer and put on a stopwatch for a maximum of two hours. That's as much time as I was giving Aaron on my day off. And he better be appreciative.

My phone buzzes on the table as I open up my programming platform. I try not to answer it to devote the two hours solely to my work. But the continuous buzz makes me curious.

EMILIO

No churros today?

And how dare you show up to the cafe when I'm in a meeting I can't get out of?

I look around the cafe to see if anyone's staring at me directly. So now the waiters were also spies? At least it would look great on their resume when applying to work for the CIA.

SYLVIE

I wasn't aware you liked to stalk your customers.

EMILIO

I can't help wanting to know if the beautiful American woman came back.

SYLVIE

I believe you said the words, "free." That brings every person running back.

---

* "Misses Sylvie?"

Emilio

How about a date? Where does that bring you?

To an indecisive state of mind. I'll get back to you on that.

But until then, thank you for the breakfast.

I roll my eyes and place my phone back down, this time focusing on my work.

A date?

Yeah, right.

No one dates a tourist.

They fuck them, but they don't commit. And I wasn't looking for commitment or a summer hook-up. I was just taking this time to look for myself again and find a happy place in my life that doesn't involve a person's head in between my legs.

Regardless, I still had so much I wanted to see in Madrid, and the men weren't on that list.

Puerta del Sol was beautiful and crowded, which became somewhat of a challenge when I kept looking at the floor, trying my best to find a plaque called kilometer zero that, according to google was something I shouldn't miss out on seeing.

It's considered the starting point of the roads in Spain.

Or something like that, all I knew was that I wanted a picture of it. And I wasn't sure where on the floor I would find it.

I pass through the herds of people and try to step out of their way, but a broad shoulder slams into me, sending my phone sliding across the floor.

Crap.

I walk over to the phone, but a hand reaches for it before I can, bringing it up toward me.

"You don't seem to be the luckiest of people." The British voice chuckles, and my eyes move away from my phone and up to the blonde woman from the airport.

"Oh, hey," I murmur, a bit embarrassed about having to meet her like this again.

I take the phone out of her hand and tuck it into my pocket.

"Thanks, I guess Madrid isn't too fond of me," I mumble awkwardly.

The blonde woman lets out a chuckle and shrugs.

"Trust me, you just haven't caught me on a bad day yet. Because I have had my share of bad days in this city, trust me." She says.

"My name is Carol, by the way." She says, extending her hand in a greeting.

I smile and give her my hand to shake.

"Sylvie."

"Are you traveling alone?" She asks.

"Why does everyone keep asking me that? Do I look like I'd travel alone?" I scoff.

Carol looks at me and then around the area as if looking for someone that I could be with.

"Okay, yes, I'm traveling alone. But if a man asks you otherwise, you say I came with a group of people that would miss me if I were to disappear."

Carol giggles and shakes her head.

"Well, I wasn't asking you so that I could hire a hit man; I was asking you to see if you wanted a buddy to tag along with. I'm not doing much anyway." She shrugs.

"Oh!" I'm a bit thrown off by her suggestion.

I had to beg Santi to lead me out of a park I was lost in, and this girl is offering to join me, even though I'm sure she's seen everything already, despite her British roots.

Alright, calm your bisexual beating heart down.

She's just offering to join you on an excursion, not asking for you to join her in bed.

"I wouldn't want to intervene on your—"

"You're not, I'm offering because I want to. It's not like I have much planned for today. I was supposed to meet with my brother after he was done with work, but his meetings got extended, so I have nothing else to do until he's out."

I pretend to ponder the thought for a bit before staring back at Carol. "Fine, I guess you can be my tour guide. Besides, the one I had yesterday was a grump."

Carol chuckles and nudges her head for me to follow.

"Did you meet him at the airport too?"

I laugh and shake my head.

"Worse, in my apartment."

CHAPTER SEVENTEEN
Sylvie

"IF YOU THINK this place is pretty now, you should be here during the sunset. And if you think it's packed, come back during New Year's." Carol explains as I continue to take pictures of the Puerta del Sol. She had taken me around the city before heading back. Stating that the crowd would ease up around lunchtime, so I would be able to take my pictures.

And she was absolutely correct.

I told her about my living arrangement, and she even offered for me to come and stay with her if I felt uncomfortable around my gentleman roommate. But I let her know that he wasn't too bad, just overly grumpy and antisocial.

"So, why Madrid?" She asks as I look back at the pictures I've taken.

I shrug and think back to the decision.

"It was something that happened in the moment. It was the first country that came to mind, so it's the one I stuck with. Besides, I plan to travel throughout Europe, so it didn't really matter where I began."

Carol nods, taking in my explanation but not saying much. But that's how it seemed the whole time we were talking. It reminded me of a journalist who asked the questions that were needed and often pondered on if the response meant more than it actually did or if there was a way to manipulate it to mean more than it did.

I wasn't even entirely sure why I thought that. Carol hadn't done anything to me, and she seemed to be a sweetheart the entire time. I was just being irrational.

Regardless, she was just trying to buy some time until her brothers' schedule freed up. It's not like she was trying to make any friends.

Speaking of which, didn't she have any around here?

"If you think the exteriors of these buildings are pretty, you should take a look inside some of them." She chirps, almost as if she expected me to ask her why she was adamant on tagging along with me to tourist attractions.

"Any place you have in mind?" I ask.

"Come, we can head over to the royal palace." Carol grabs my hands and pulls me in her direction.

"So, don't take this the wrong way, but why is it that you're so keen on spending the day showing a tourist around?"

Carol shrugs and gives me a tight-lipped smile.

"I don't have many friends here." She says, clearing her throat before continuing.

"I grew up with my mom in London and only came to Spain in the summers to spend time with my dad and my brother." Carol inclines herself over to the right, until our shoulders are touching, before whispering in my ear.

"I was the evidence of my father's affair."

A gasp leaves my lips before I can help myself, and Carol lets out a giggle.

"Really?" I ask.

Carol nods and shrugs.

"Yeah, but Papi and Lourdes are still very much together. Meanwhile, mum married my step-dad Victor, when I was around eight."

"And you have half-siblings?" I ask, curious about her family dynamic now.

"Yeah, one half-brother on my dad's side. He's taken over Papi's businesses, so we haven't had much time to spend with one another."

Carol gives me a forced smile, and I can't help but feel bad for her. Maybe I was a bad judge of character. All that Carol seemed to want was to spend time with someone. And as much as she knew this city by the back of her hand, the city didn't know her.

"Where's this real estate property you were speaking of? And how many rooms are we talking?" I ask.

Carol chuckles and grabs my hand to pull me towards the direction of the palace.

"Jesus, they have a room for every color of the rainbow," I whisper, taking a picture of the purple room we're standing in.

"I think at some point they ran out of ideas and just started throwing whatever they wanted at these walls and stuck with it," Carol says.

"I hope the royal family has some better taste now." I murmur.

"I'm sure they've gotten with the times," Carol murmurs, passing through the large group of tourists who are following the guide around.

"You'd be surprised, some people struggle to get with the times."

"Tell me about it. I had an ex who wouldn't even download social media." She scoffs.

"Hm, what's wrong with not having social media?" I ask, not seeing anything wrong with not wanting to be sucked into a virtual world of detox beverages and blepharoplasties.

"Nothing, except that's what I do for a living, and it would be nice to have someone who supports what I do and posts a picture of us now and then." She murmurs, seeming to be deep in thought on the whole situation.

"Well, coming from someone who's had many significant others post her on their socials… it doesn't define a relationship. If it did, I'd have been married by now."

Carol looks at me and sighs.

"That's one of the reasons why I came back, you know?" She asks.

"Not really, I just met you," I mumble, but if anything that I heard from her phone call at the airport was correct, then the bun in her oven was bringing her back to the man who put it in there to begin with.

"Well, I loved him, I mean, I still do love him. But, I think we're just too different."

"Hm, I don't know, some of my best relationships were with people who were different."

"And what happened to those relationships?"

"Oh, we broke up because of our differences."

Right as the words escape my lips, Carol gives me a knowing look. I roll my eyes and give her a light shove.

"Oh, shut up, even the people I shared similarities with ended with a breakup."

"I know, but in my case. It wasn't just the differences. He was just so caught up in his work and living in Madrid forever, and not willing to start our lives somewhere else rather than in a country that doesn't really feel like home to me."

"Ah, so you wanted him to quit his job, move back to a predominantly English-speaking country so that you could feel like you were at home?" I ask, trying to make sure I gathered all the details.

"Precisely."

"Well, sometimes life is about sacrifice. I mean, did you consider that maybe he doesn't speak English as strongly, and it would be harder for him to move to a country whose primary language is not Spanish? Or that maybe he loves the job that he has here and it'd be hard for him to find something similar back in England?"

"That's the thing, though, Sylvie. He can speak English, and he could easily change jobs."

"What is it that you do again?" I ask.

"I'm an influencer, and I also do freelance marketing and social media management."

"So you work from home?" I ask.

"Yes."

"And he works in person?"

"Yes."

"So, you're able to move anywhere you would like, and it wouldn't disrupt your life majorly?"

Carol sighs and rolls her eyes in defeat.

"You're just like my brother, he thinks I'm being selfish and inconsiderate."

Well, that's one way to put it.

"I think that you're not seeing it through your ex's perspective." I try to rationalize.

"But, this doesn't feel like home." She says, opening her hands to gesture around her.

"Of course it doesn't, it's a royal palace that's open to the public. It's not even home to the royals anymore."

Carol gives me a death stare, and I roll my eyes at her.

"A city isn't supposed to feel like home, Carol." I sigh.

"It's not?"

"No, but a person is," I say.

"Hm, I guess you're right." She murmurs.

"Of course I am. I'm thirty, that's the age everyone gets granted wisdom."

"I thought that was what happens at twenty-five."

"No, that's when your frontal lobe snaps into place, and then after that you spend the next five years going over all your mistakes and horrible situations that you put yourself through just because your brain wasn't fully developed," I mumble.

"That explains all the overthinking and the headaches that have been happening since I blew out those candles last month." She groans, stepping outside of the palace with me right behind.

"I'm pretty sure those are just migraines."

"Shut up." She giggles, this time shoving me for a change.

The ringing in her pocket pulls her out of our conversation and into a new one with someone I assume is her brother on the line. I don't capture what she's saying exactly because she moves from English to Spanish, but I don't pay much attention to their conversation regardless.

Instead, I walk over to the center of the courtyard and take pictures of the palace.

"My brother said he'll meet us here shortly. I hope you don't mind, I'd like to introduce you guys." Carol chirps.

"I don't mind, the more people I meet, the merrier."

"Speaking of people you meet, let me get your number. Just in case we don't see each other around the city, maybe we can meet again when your travels take you to London."

I give Carol my information and even share my Instagram with her, which is nothing compared to the thousands of followers she's built up.

"Jesus, I didn't know you had this much of an influence."

"Yeah, it's nothing too crazy, but I'm really trying to build a career out of this."

"Sylvie?" A rough voice calls from behind me.

Both Carol and I turn to look at the man who's announced my name, and right before us stands Emilio.

"You two know each other?" Carol asks, cheerfully throwing her hands around Emilio in a hug.

"I met him in one of the cafes he owns," I answer.

"Oh, so you're the beautiful woman he told the entire staff to give everything for free to. That demand has made its way all around the employees and to my family's ears."

My face heats up immediately from embarrassment.

"Oh, I hope I didn't get you into any trouble."

"Oh, please, trouble? It's his business. We're all just nosey and extremely curious who would make my brother break his rule of no free items to friends, let alone a stranger." Carol teases and nudges her brother's arm.

Emilio rolls his eyes, and his own face flushes to a light pink.

"Shut up, Carol." He grumbles.

"It seems we have similar tastes. Sylvie seems to be a magnet for us. She reels us in without even knowing it." Carol teases sending me a wink.

"You'll be paying for lunch if you keep this up." He threatens.

"No, I won't, because Sylvie is coming with us and you wouldn't want to make a bad impression." She argues.

"Oh, I wouldn't want to intrude."

The last thing I wanted to look like was a mooch. Apparently, the whole family and their staff seemed to know I was getting a freebie. Never mind them finding out I was joining in on their family luncheons.

"Nonsense, you're coming. It'll make lunch with this one bearable." He says, nudging his head towards Carol.

"Oh shut up and let's go, us girls are famished." Carol barks out the order and grabs my arm before I can think of making up an excuse.

And Emilio follows right behind.

CHAPTER EIGHTEEN
Sylvie

"IS THIS CONSIDERED A DATE?" Emilio asks, after the intense staring contest we've been playing throughout dinner.

We hadn't brought anything up until now. Carol had kept us occupied with her work talk. But I could feel Emilio's stare on me the whole time when I wasn't making eye contact.

"Do you usually have a chaperone on your dates?" I tease, taking a sip of my wine.

"I do, if that's the only way I can get them on the date." He reasons.

"Get a lot of rejections?" I ask.

"You're the first."

I suck my teeth and roll my eyes at his cheesy response.

"But I have to say it makes me want you even more."

"I'm sure it does, but I'm on a no-boy rule during my travels."

It's not that Emilio wasn't attractive; he was extremely attractive. And though something casual isn't necessarily a bad thing, it only leads to feelings in some way or another.

"Lucky for you, I'm a grown man." He replies.

I smile and shake my head at his cheeky response.

"Am I really that lucky?" I tease, sending him a wink before looking towards the restroom where Carol has just stepped out of.

"Fine, then let's go out as friends." He murmurs.

"As friends?" I ask.

"Yeah, come out with me tomorrow night to one of my rooftops. It's going to be fun." He guarantees.

"What's going to be fun?" Carol asks, sitting back down next to me.

"Oh, your brother was just saying that you and I should join him at his rooftop clubs tomorrow," I announce cheerfully.

Out of the corner of my eye, I see Emilio's smile fall right off his face.

"Funny because he banned me from even showing up." Carol chirps, her face now completely joyous at ruining her brother's party.

"That's because you always do more harm than good at these parties." Emilio bites back.

"Hm, that's upsetting. I really would've gone if you were going to be there, Carol." I sigh and look over at Emilio with sorrowful eyes that I know will get him to say yes.

That and the possibility of being able to see me in a black lace dress that I had bought just for a nice occasion. Something told me that the black dress would hold more memories of Europe than I would remember.

"Fine, Carol, you're invited." Emilio bites back.

"Hm, I'm not sure if I really want to go."

"I don't think you're sure of many things." He mutters.

And though the two siblings seem to have a relationship based on bickering, I can tell that his comeback had hurt more than any others had.

"Well, I know that I'm sure of many things, but some people are just too persistent," I state.

Emilio's eyes slide back to me, and his lips turn up into a smirk.

"Sometimes we aren't even sure of things until we've experienced them."

"Oh, trust me, I've experienced them enough to know that you wouldn't be the miracle that changes my sureness of things."

Carol spits the water that she had been drinking, causing others to look and stare, but Emilio's eyes stay on me, and he struggles to keep a straight face himself.

"Carol will be there." He states.

"Will I?" She asks.

"Yes… You will." He establishes.

"Hm, so I guess I'll ponder on the idea of showing up. I have time to think about it, don't I?" I ask.

"Of course." He replies.

"But I thought you said that the guest list had to be submitted no later than tonight." Carol teases, knowing her brother is breaking another one of his rules just to impress me.

"Carol, I'm sure the Zara across the street is having a sale," Emilio says through gritted teeth.

"There is no Zara across the street." She remarks.

Emilio pulls out his wallet and hands her a shiny black card.

"How about now?" He asks.

Carol swipes the card out of his hands and stands up from her chair.

"Well, Sylvie, I'm sure we'll see each other very soon. Like at that party." She says, giving me a side hug and walking out.

"Do I get one of those cards if I leave, too?"

Emilio chuckles and leans back in his chair.

"No, but I guarantee you'll get one with your name if you stay."

I shrug and take a sip of the remainder of the wine left in the glass.

"What a shame it is that I don't have a visa."

Emilio rolls his eyes and shakes his head at my stubbornness.

"Come tomorrow night."

"I'll think about it." I sigh.

"I'll make it worth it." He promises, inclining himself forward to get as close as he can with the table in the way.

"That's exactly what I'm afraid of," I admit, and that comment is enough to bring a smile right back on his face.

CHAPTER NINETEEN
Santi

MY MEMORIES from last night are quite foggy, and I'm not sure exactly what happened, but what I do remember is seeing Sylvie hovering over me in bed, and she looked ethereal.

I know nothing has happened, I'm sure of it, because I woke up fully clothed in the same thing I went out in last night. And I reek of alcohol. I knew going out with Luisa and a few friends would not go well.

Especially after the glimpse I had of that woman, who I was sure was Carolina.

But what would she be doing back here?

She had family here, but it's not like she was ever that close to them.

Regardless of whether it was her or not, I was currently caught up on the idea of where on Earth Sylvie was. She had been out from the moment I had woken up. It would be getting dark in a few, and she was still nowhere to be seen. I had even gone on a run through a different tourist attraction, hoping I'd run into her.

I wasn't even sure why I cared so damn much.

I guess I was just worried.

I wasn't sure what I could've said or done last night. And I'm surprised she hasn't come home by now, at least. The girl obviously didn't seem to be fond of the stranger danger thing. I mean, she decided to stay here and live with me.

What sane person did that?

Two days with this girl and she already had me worried.

I should've given her my number just in case she needed something.

The front door creeks open, and I shoot up from the couch and walk right over to the entrance.

"Where the hell have you been?" I mutter, staring at Sylvie, who's just walked in with chocolate on her face from having enjoyed the chocolate-covered churros from one of the cafes.

"I'm sorry?" She asks mid-chew, letting the door close behind her and walking right past me.

I lock the door and follow her to the kitchen, where she drops her things on the counter.

"Churro?" She offers, extending her hand out to me.

"No, I don't want a churro," I grumble, walking over to the sink, where I rip off a sheet of paper towel and wet it under the faucet.

"Why are you extra crabby today?" She asks, taking another bite of the churro.

I rinse the napkin and walk over to her and wipe the chocolate that's smeared on her face. I'm not sure why I cleaned it off myself rather than just giving her the napkin, but that was the least of my worries.

"Thank you?" She says, though it comes out more like a question.

"Where have you been?" I ask again.

"Well, unlike you, I don't live in Madrid, Santi. So, I was following my itinerary for my vacation." She mutters.

"Besides, what do you care? We both agreed that we would do our own separate thing and that we wouldn't bother one another."

"Yeah, well, where was that yesterday when you forced me to parade around the park with you?" I argue.

"Oh, you're so right, dearest Santi." Sylvie mocks me by gasping and bringing her hand up to cover her mouth.

"I completely forgot that I held a gun to your head!" She shouts.

"All I'm saying is that while you're living here, you should at least let me know what's going on and what you're up to." I rub my temples, trying my best to calm down the headache that's starting to develop.

"I wasn't aware that my Airbnb came with a father-like figure. Does the apartment come with an ankle monitor as well?" She fumes.

Sylvie is upset, she's upset, and she looks hot when she's flustered and contemplating my murder.

Maybe I was taking this out of proportion, I mean, she's nobody. She's just someone who passes through your life, and you never really see again, unless you become mutuals on social media.

Which I don't have… officially.

"I would just like to make sure that you're alive."

"Well, sadly, I'm here listening to you, so I must be very much alive or in hell." She grumbles, shoving past me and walking into her room, slamming the door right behind her.

I sigh and rub my hands through my face.

I'm sure Javi would say there's a better way of stating that you're worried about someone without making them feel bad for doing nothing wrong. But, if I were like Javi, I'd be an emotionally intelligent man who would still be with his ex and most likely even married.

I grab the churro from the bag and take a bite as I rethink my outburst. But it's quickly snatched away along with the bag on the counter by an upset Sylvie.

"Dickheads don't get to eat my churros." She grumbles, marching back to her room.

And brats who don't let their roommate know where they are deserve a spanking, but you don't see me marching to the bedroom and bending you over.

Though the idea is extremely enticing.

"Just apologize to her before I get a bad rating." Javier sighs on the other end of the phone.

I roll my eyes and dump the pasta into the strainer.

"What does it matter? You're not going to be renting out this apartment anymore." I mutter, making sure we had got that clear.

As annoying as it was, I got lucky to have Sylvie here as my roommate rather than a random weirdo.

"Yeah, yeah, yeah, I got it. But you really did cross a line."

I roll my eyes and continue cooking while Javi continues to go on about what I did wrong. And as annoying as it was to hear him say it, I know that it's true. I should've never talked to her the way I did.

"It's fine for you to be worried, dude. But, it's never what you say, rather the way that you say it that upsets people." Javi explains.

This time, I sigh into the receiver and take some time for myself before admitting that he's right.

"What do I do now?" I ask.

Speaking about my feelings was always hard for me, and apologizing was even worse. I was sure that was one of the reasons why Carolina ended up leaving me.

"Just try telling her what you actually meant to say before. And then apologize for not stating it the way that you should have."

I was sure apologizing wouldn't be enough.

I had usually gone to Javi when I needed to apologize to my ex, but that's because most of the time I wasn't sure why we were arguing to begin with. And even after I apologized, she still remained angry for days on end until she decided to let go of the issue.

"Why do you care anyway?" Javier asks.

"Because I obviously hurt her feelings."

"No, I mean, why do you care about what she was doing. She's just supposed to be renting out a room. Despite you morphing into her tour guide yesterday, it doesn't matter. She's supposed to be doing her thing, and you're supposed to be doing yours. And soon enough she'll be gone, and you will have the apartment all to yourself again." Javi explains.

And I wasn't sure why I cared so much. Maybe it was just because, in reality, Sylvie wasn't a bad person. She seemed to be sweet, and she was definitely funny when she wasn't being annoying. But most importantly, she was naive, and that scared the fuck out of me. I didn't want her naivety to land in the wrong hands. People would use her to get something out of it for themselves, and Sylvie didn't deserve that.

"She's a good person." I finally answer, causing Javi to retort with a snort.

"I'm a good person, and you never go out of your way to cook something and apologize to me."

"Yeah, well, that's because most of the time you're in the wrong," I mutter, while scooping the pasta carbonara I made onto a plate for Sylvie.

"Yeah, I'm sure that's why."

"Goodbye, Javi," I say, through gritted teeth.

"Bye, lover boy." He retorts, before hanging up the phone.

Loverboy?

I'm not a lover boy. I'm just apologizing because I feel bad. No feelings besides guilt are tied to this apology. Especially not any romantic ones.

I pick the plate up and make my way toward Sylvie's room, and give it a knock. There's no response, and I'm unsure of whether I should walk in or not. But I take the chance and turn the knob, poking my head inside.

Sylvie's on the bed, her hair tied in a messy bun at the top of her head. Headphones on her ears with music loud enough for our neighbors to hear. She's in one of her oversized t-shirts again and her pajama shorts. And scattered throughout the bed are a notebook, scissors, tape, and pieces of stickers and paper.

I call out for her again, but as one would assume with the music blaring in her eardrums, she can't hear me. I take a step closer, and it's not until my shadow greets the bed's comforter that she jumps up, finally aware of my presence.

"Jesus Christ, don't you knock?!" She shouts, her right hand on her chest, and the other one pulling off the headphones.

"I did knock and call out your name. But, I think you were too busy breaking down your eardrums." I was sure I'd get a comeback from her, but instead, she just stares at me with a blank expression.

"This is for you," I say, pushing forward the plate of food.

Sylvie raises a brow and looks at the plate in my hand. She waits a few seconds before taking it from my hand and looking at the food.

"It's carbonara, I hope you like it," I say, unsure of what I could do to make this interaction any less awkward.

"I'm sure I will." She murmurs, going back to her craft project.

I wait for her to look back up at me or at least acknowledge my presence, but she keeps herself busy picking out the best stickers for her notebook page.

"So, what are you doing?" I finally ask.

Sylvie pauses the action and looks back up at me, rolling her eyes. "What do you want, Santi?" She finally asks, setting down the bag of stickers in her hand and looking at me.

"I wanted to apologize." I sigh.

"For?" She asks, lifting a brow and changing her posture to show she's listening.

"I'm sorry for getting upset with you the way that I did."

"And?" Sylvie asks.

I sigh and run my hand through my hair, trying my best to gather my thoughts on how I want to say this to her.

"Sylvie, I shouldn't have gotten as angry as I did. And I shouldn't have talked to you the way that I did. I was just upset and worried about where you had been. I know we're just temporary roommates, but for the time being, I would really appreciate it if you could update me that you're safe throughout the day." I say the words exactly like I had discussed with Javi on the phone.

Sylvie stares at me for a few seconds before nodding her head, reaching for the plate I had given her, and taking a bite of the food.

"The food is delicious, thank you." She says mid-chew.

"That's it?" I ask, completely thrown off by her reaction.

"Um… It's scrumptious?" She says, taking another bite.

"No, Sylvie. Not about the food, I mean, about the apology. I apologize, and you have nothing else to say?" I ask, completely annoyed at her nonchalantness.

"What do you want me to say?" She asks, setting her plate back down on the nightstand.

"I don't know, that it's okay, that I'm a dick, and that yes, you will communicate that you're safe." I list off all the suggestions, and as I say these things to a stranger, I do realize that I might be insane. But I think Sylvie just may be even more insane for sticking around.

"Fine, you're forgiven, it's not like it was a big deal." She says, shrugging it off.

"Not a big deal? You practically chopped my hand off for eating a churro." I scoff.

"Someone's being dramatic." Sylvie sings, grabbing the bag of stickers again to look through them.

"I'm being dramatic? You're the one who isn't taking the apology."

"I thought I just did." She remarks, looking back up at me with a raised eyebrow.

"Fine, Sylvie, what is it that you want?" I ask, knowing she must want something out of me to receive some sort of forgiveness from her. And obviously, dinner wasn't enough to patch up the wound of our argument.

"Nothing." She says, looking back down at her notebook.

"Fine, do you want dinner for the remainder of your stay? Free translation at any moment?" I list out the options, but Sylvie doesn't move an inch toward my suggestions.

"Fine, I'll be your tour guide tomorrow." I sigh and take a seat on the bed.

"But, I need to do my morning run. After that, I'm all yours."

Sylvie hums as she ponders the agreement before grasping me in a hug.

"Okay, all is forgiven. But I still expect dinner every night." She murmurs near my ear.

"Okay, that's enough with the hugging." I groan, tapping on her arm.

Sylvie sighs and lets go immediately.

"God, you're just as much of a grump as my sister when it comes to physical touch." She whines.

"Should've added that to your agreement." I snicker, getting up from the bed.

"I'm sure you'll piss me off soon enough to make that agreement happen."

I roll my eyes and wave her off as I walk out of her bedroom.

"Wait!"

I turn around and meet her eyes from across the room, those chocolatey hues looking straight at me with such an immense amount of emotion in them.

"I need your number." She says, though it barely comes out as a whisper.

"There's a sticky note underneath the plate. My number is on it. I was sure that if my apology didn't work, the minute you spotted the sticky note, you'd come to your senses."

Sylvie scoffs and rips the sticky note from under the plate.

"I'm sure you did, which is why you ended up agreeing to being a free tour guide and a personal chef every night." She challenges,

"What can I say? I felt guilty." I admit.

"It's okay, Santi. I've forgiven people for worse." She mutters, going back to eating her food.

I'm not quite sure what to say to that, so instead I wave to her good night and close the door. And even though Sylvie didn't seem to care much about her comment, something in me boiled in anger at the thought of anyone taking advantage of Sylvie and her allowing it to happen.

Regardless of her forgiveness, I'd make tomorrow the best day of her whole trip, and nothing could get in the way of that happening.

Day 3

CHAPTER TWENTY
Santi

HER FACE HOVERS over me in the dark, and I'm not sure it's actually Sylvie until the night's breeze pushes back the curtain, allowing the moonlight to peek through and reveal her figure.

"Sylvie?" I manage to croak, struggling to focus my vision on her.

"What are you doing here?" I ask, lifting my upper body to face her.

"I couldn't sleep." She murmurs, and her voice sounds so sultry and sweet. It pulls me in like a siren calling out to a sailor at sea.

"What's wrong?" I'm not sure what possesses me to even reach up and push her hair behind her ear, but I do it. And the way she leans her cheek onto my palm warms me.

I allow my eyes to look down at her body. She must've switched out of her clothes because she's not wearing her normal nightwear. She's in a sexy tank top that does very little to cover any of her cleavage.

The skin of her stomach peeks through the small section between where her top ends and her shorts meet. God damn those shorts, they seemed to be holding on to the curves of her hips for dear life.

I'm sure if she turned around right now, those shorts would barely be covering half of her ass. And as much of a gentleman as I want to be and try not to look, I also want to bend her over my lap and give her the spanking I've been craving to give her since she appeared in my apartment.

"Santi." She whispers.

"Yes?" I ask, my eyes now on hers, taking in every emotion that she spills through them.

"I need you." She whimpers, causing the heat in my body to lead straight down to my cock.

Fuck me.

I bring my hand behind her neck and pull her down to me. My lips are colliding with hers, fighting for dominance. I let my head fall to the pillow and glide my hands down her full curves, stopping only the minute they meet her ass. I grip them tightly, making a breathy moan escape her beautiful, plump lips.

I grip her thighs and pull each one on either side of her legs so that she's straddling me. Our lips never separating from each other. I slip my tongue into her mouth and grab her throat to bring her closer to me.

Fuck, I needed her close to me, I needed to be inside of her, grasping onto her hips as I pushed myself deeper and deeper into her.

Sylvie pulls away from my lips and sits up, straddling my torso.

Fuck, she looks unreal.

Her breasts rise with each breath, and my cock hardens even more at the thought of being between them.

I grab her hips and flip us over, my cock pressed firmly against her mound.

And as my eyes meet hers in this position, I can feel my heart beating in my ears and my stomach fluttering with nerves.

What the fuck is happening?

"I'm sure that some day you'll find someone who'll calm the storm in your mind and glue back the shattered pieces of your heart," Sylvie whispers, her lips forming into a sincere smile, and her hand caressing my face.

"What?" I ask, pulling away, confused.

"It's healing already." She whispers, her hands now on my chest, pushing me off of her.

A gasp escapes my lips as I push myself off the bed, the morning's sun shining through the curtain.

My skin is covered in sweat, and my bed is free from Sylvie's scent.

She wasn't here.

It was all just a dream.

I groan and push the comforters off of me.

I needed a cold shower and a run to start my day. Especially after that fucking dream.

I stand up and stretch, but don't realize that my bedroom door has been swung open until Sylvie lets out a yelp.

I look over and follow her eyes down to my groin, which is currently creating a tent in my underwear.

"Get out!" I shout, grabbing my bed sheets and trying my best to cover the hard-on caused by Sylvie infiltrating my dream.

Sylvie slams the door and shouts an apology from the other side of the door. I'm sure she's gone after a moment of silence, so I grab some joggers and pull them up before heading outside my bedroom.

Only to find Sylvie in the kitchen with breakfast on the counter.

"At least you're a shower and grower." She jokes, giving me a shrug.

I groan and move towards the bathroom to calm my erection down.

This was just the start of the day, and it was already proving to be difficult.

CHAPTER TWENTY-ONE
Santi

I TAKE a bite of my toast and stare at Sylvie, who sits across from me taking a sip of her coffee.

"Don't you know how to knock?" I mutter, taking another bite of my toast.

"I did knock, but you couldn't hear me over your groaning." She mutters.

I can feel my face heating up immediately at her words.

"Were you having a nightmare?" She asks, adjusting herself on her seat so that she's sitting criss cross on the seat. And I can't help but stare at the slightest movement of her breast under the t-shirt she wears to bed.

"Yeah, something like that." I sigh, rubbing my hands across my face. At this moment I would moan in mortification, but my morning had been embarrassing enough without having to show Sylvie how much she's done to my fucking mind in the span of two days.

"So, what are the plans for today?" She murmurs, taking a bit of the scrambled eggs she had made for us this morning. I was surprised to have even seen her here, let alone making us breakfast. The first two days she stayed here she had gone out for breakfast. At least I hoped she'd had something to eat before walking around all day.

"The plans are that I will go out for a run and then when I come back we can do whatever your heart desires." I say, opening my phone to look at any messages I'd gotten while I was deep in that dream of mine.

"A run around the park sounds nice." She muses.

"Does it?" I ask, only paying half attention because the name that shows up on my screen makes my heart freeze its beating immediately.

The name Carolina is bright and white on my phone screen. It's also at the top of my text messages.

CAROLINA

Hey, I know we haven't spoken in a while. But I had some time to think and I'd really like to talk to you. I'm back in Madrid for a couple of weeks. Let me know if we can talk. I have some things I have to get off my chest.

And I know this is sudden and unfair. But, I really need to speak to you.

Please, just think it through.

"Yay, I'll go get dressed."

CHAPTER TWENTY-TWO
Sylvie

"I'M SWEATING in places I've never sweat before," I admit, huffing for air as we make our way through the park.

Santi lets out a snort as he slows down his pace for me. I'm sure it bothers him to have to adjust his speed for me, but he doesn't show it.

I had run track in high school and always loved running, but work seemed to get in the way of that enjoyment as well. Thanks to Santi, I realized how much I've actually missed it.

"Watch out!" Santi shouts, but before I can stop, I trip over a peacock and fall right on my face.

"Fuck, are you okay?" Santi asks, helping me up from the floor.

"Depends," I groan. "Am I allowed to hunt those fuckers?" I ask, throwing a glare at the bird.

"No." Santi chuckles.

The bird seems to taunt me by spreading out its feathers.

"I bet you it's the same one from last time," I growl, aiming daggers at the bird with my stare.

"I doubt it's the same one, but I will agree that you don't seem to be this breed of bird's favorite human." Santi squats down and wipes off the dirt from my knees, and I can't help but blush at his act of kindness.

"Are you in any pain?" Santi asks.

"Yes, but not physically," I mutter, rubbing the pain that developed in my chest from the embarrassment.

Santi grabs my wrist and flips my hands so that my palms are facing his direction. He wipes any excess dirt off of them before letting them drop back to my sides. I wonder if he realizes how much of a mother hen he is, but by the way he nudges his head for me to continue walking with him, it doesn't seem like he does.

"I'm sure you'll heal up quickly."

Santi doesn't pick up the pace; instead, he walks by my side as we make our way out of the park.

"Are you upset?" I ask, worried that I've ruined his run.

"Yes, very, I've never had any issues with these birds until now. I think I'm going to have to stop being seen with you if I want to make sure I stay on their good side." I roll my eyes at Santi's sarcastic reply and give him a shove with my side.

"No, I'm not upset. I enjoyed our run today." He murmurs so low I barely catch what he said.

"Then how come you're cutting the run short?" I ask, "I can still run. It's going to take a lot more sweat and more than a peacock getting in my way to stop me from running.

Santi rolls his eyes and chuckles and I have to admit any time I get something close to a laugh or smile out of him I feel a sense of accomplishment.

"I'm cutting it short this time because I want to have time to show you around the places you want to see."

I grab hold of Santi's arm and bring him closer to me, enough for me to lay my head on him in a loving gesture. I can feel Santi's body stiffen, but I'm sure that's because just like Marlene, physical touch freaks him out.

"Thank you, Santi. That means a lot." I murmur, letting go of his arm.

"It's not that big of a deal." He shrugs.

"Sure, it is, I'm aware that you could be doing anything else with your free time."

"Like getting drunk?" He mumbles, obviously referencing the other night. And along with the reference is a darker undertone to his voice. I don't push it or say anything else. The last thing I want to do is bring up any bad memories from that night.

"Where are we going, anyway?" He asks.

I bite my lip and look up to face him with my best attempt at puppy dog eyes that I can do.

"No." He groans.

"Please," I beg.

"Absolutely not, Sylvie."

"Please!"

"No, I'm not changing my mind on this, so pick another place." He says, his tone aggressive and clear.

"Fine." I sigh, dropping my shoulders and walking a couple of steps ahead of him so he can see the change in my demeanor.

Santi is silent, and I make sure not to say a thing. A few moments pass until we are finally back on our street, and Santi sighs behind me.

"Fuck me."

"I can't believe you have me at work on my day off," Santi growls, pulling up next to me as we enter past security, free of charge.

The grouchy man is back, but I don't mind one bit because I got a free entrance to the museum and a free tour guide who knows everything up on these walls.

"You seem pleased about this situation."

I walk beside Santi and turn my head to look up at him, giving him a devious smile. "You mean, I shouldn't be pleased that I coerced you into doing your job for free on your day off?" I feign a shocked expression and smile up at the brooding man that he is.

"It's okay, it'll be quick anyway. I don't have the attention span or interest to go through all these paintings. It's not like they interest me." I shrug, as I rummage through my purse and pull out a paper where I had listed all the works that I would like to see.

"That's despicable. Let me see that list." Santi rips away the list from my hand and peers down at it.

"All you have written down is Goya."

"No, I also wrote down Picasso."

Santi flips the page to take a look at any further writing before looking back at me.

"Sylvie, there's nothing else on here."

I shrug and take the paper from his hand and pretend to acknowledge it.

"That's odd, must've been in the other paper," I murmur, taking out the map that was given to me at the front to see where I can find those paintings.

"Give me that," Santi mutters, ripping the brochure from my hands and tossing it in a nearby trash can.

"Was this your plan all along?" He mutters, walking ahead for me to follow.

"What do you mean?" I ask, doing my best to play dumb, but I love it when he catches onto my antics.

"You're purposely annoying me to get what you want."

"First of all, that's insulting. I am not annoying, and I don't even try to annoy you. You just get annoyed by everything."

I was lying.

I knew he would hate to come to work on his day off.

But I also knew he loved what he did and was very good at it.

The copious amounts of art history books that were placed all around his apartment told me so.

"You will stay quiet during the remainder of this tour and listen to me as we go through every, and I do mean *every* work of art in this museum."

"Oh no, this is complete torture, I hope you don't go into depth with the explaining." I fake a groan and follow Santi as he takes me to the first painting of the museum.

"You brought this upon yourself, Sylvie." He tisks.

"I sure did, now start working, big boy." I encourage, slapping his ass, making Santi jump and look around to see if anyone spotted us.

"Don't do that." He mutters through his teeth.

"Fine, I'll keep it inside the bedroom." I sigh as an elderly couple passes by us, giggling.

"Sylvie."

"Santi."

"Don't start."

"Then please begin." I gesture towards the paintings down the hall, and Santi begins talking about the first piece we are coming up to, and I follow right beside him.

CHAPTER TWENTY-THREE

Sylvie

"WHAT ARE WE LOOKING AT?" I ask, as we take longer than usual to stare down at this portrait of a man.

"What do you think we're looking at?" He asks, his eyes not moving away from the painting.

Santi was ensuring that this tour was both boring and informative. I was sure he didn't usually share this much information on his tours when he was working. But nonetheless, my snarky comebacks and comedic timing made this tour less of a punishment on his end.

"A picture of a king, or nobleman of some sort." I finally answered.

"Drawn by who?"

"I don't know, some man that I have no recollection of learning about?"

Santi's lips curve up into a grin, and he finally takes his eyes off the painting to look at me. "A woman," He muses, "a woman you have no recollection of learning about, painted this painting of King Philip II."

"And she did a mighty good job, I knew that this portrait was better than the others we've seen."

"I'm sure you did." Santi murmurs, a small smile appearing on his lips.

One thing I've learned about Santi is that smiling is a rarity for him, and I have made it my unofficial job to see how many times I can break him out of his hard exterior and make him smile at me.

"So, what's her story?" I ask, curious as to how I've gone through twenty years of education and never once was I taught about a woman Renaissance painter.

"Her name is Sofonisba Anguissola. She was an Italian Renaissance painter. She came from a noble family that valued education, even for their daughters. And this is a large reason as to why art classes should be funded and remain a part of the curriculum in schools." Santi continues to educate me on the painting, and for some reason, all I can focus on is the glimmer in his eyes as he speaks about the history behind a simple portrait that I wouldn't have thought to look twice at.

"She later on served as the court painter for Spain's King Philip II and became his wife, Queen Elisabeth of Valois's lady-in-waiting."

"Why isn't she taught in schools?" I ask, wondering why something so simple as putting down a name in textbooks is so hard for people to do.

Santi sighs and gives me a shrug before grabbing my wrist and bringing me over to one of her other paintings of Queen Elisabeth of Valois, holding a portrait of her husband. Santi stands behind me, but it doesn't feel like hovering, even though I can feel him so close, our bodies pulling closer and closer together as the seconds pass.

"Don't the paintings look so much more beautiful now that you know her?" He whispers.

"Don't they speak to you differently?" He asks, his hot breath on the back of my neck, sending shivers down my spine.

I give him a small nod, my eyes remaining on the painting before me, taking in every detail and inch of the painting.

"This, Sylvie, is what I love about my job. I love knowing about the artist, their struggles, their life, because they make the paintings tell us something completely different than what we see."

This was much more intimate than it should be, and I should walk away and act as if there's nothing tense between us right now. But there seems to be a magnetic pull keeping us in our same positions. I clear my throat and look over my shoulder, where Santi stands hovering over me. His eyes aren't on the painting, but rather on me.

The air around us seems to thicken, and the small murmurs of the crowd hush into silence. And I know Santi must be feeling something similar by the way his tongue peeks out to swipe his lips, providing moisture for something that's to come. Something that shouldn't happen, but the way that we pull closer and closer together tells me it's going to happen anyway.

"Ah, you're introducing her to Sofonisba Anguissola." A woman's voice snaps us out of our haze. I take a few steps forward and squint my eyes to look a little closer at the painting, trying my best to pretend that I wasn't about to kiss this man I barely know.

This man with whom I'm currently living and spending my days with.

Oh, fuck, what am I doing?

"Luisa, perfect timing," Santi mumbles from behind me.

"Was it?" She asks, her voice chirpy and obviously enjoying this awkward moment.

Wait– had he said the name Luisa?

I turn my body around to face the conversing pair.

"This is your niece?" I ask, taking in both of them together. They seemed to be the same age to me. How much older could Santi's sister be? Better question yet, how old were his parents?

"My what?" Santi asks, the creases in between his brow becoming more prominent.

"Your niece?" I ask again, looking between a confused Santi and a laughing Luisa.

"Luisa, this is not funny." He murmurs, giving her a shove.

"Why would you think we are related?" He asks.

"Well, she called you, tío, that night you came into the apartment," I clear my throat and take a step closer before whispering the next word, "intoxicated."

Luisa controls her laughter and gives Santi a pat on the back.

"Entiendo ahora por qué me habías dicho que es una mujer magnífica, tío." *

"See? She said it again. I know I can barely keep up with a conversation, let alone understand someone speaking the language to me. But, I did pay attention to the family tree section in my high school's Spanish class." I mutter, feeling a bit embarrassed because obviously I'm being left out on the actual meaning of the word.

"You are funny, Santi was right." Luisa grins, looking up at Santi, who's scowling down at her.

"Oh," I manage to speak, flipping my hair and giving Santi a bright smile as he rolls his eyes at me. "You didn't tell me that you think I'm funny, actually, you have said quite the opposite."

"I didn't say you were funny, I said you were entertaining at best." He snaps.

"Well, if I seem to be some sort of entertainment for you, then I would appreciate a tip."

"You're living in my home, that's more than enough for a tip." He remarks.

"A home I've rented out for the week, and you don't seem to mind when you're opening the bathroom door to take a peek," I mutter, exaggerating the truth just because he's pissed me off.

Santi's cheeks flush, and Luisa keeps her eyes on us, moving them back and forth like some sort of tennis match.

"I did not–" Santi tries to clear up his name, but I quickly turn my head to Luisa and give her an ultimatum.

"Luisa, who do you think is telling the truth? Me, a helpless tourist or your grumpy six-foot-tall uncle who grunts at a yes or no question?" I ask, bringing my hand on Santi's chest to push him away so that I can stand in front of her.

"We are not related, tío can be seen as the equivalent to bro or dude," Santi remarks from behind me.

------

* "Now I understand why you told me she's a wonderful woman, man."

"Keep grunting, caveman. We women, are planning a retribution."

Luisa's smile brightens as I focus my attention on her, as Santi continues to mutter something behind me.

"What was your name again?" Luisa asks, bringing her hand up between us.

"Sylvie," I respond, taking her hand in mine and giving it a firm shake.

"Well, Sylvie, it's best that I tell you that my *uncle* wasn't always like this, but over the years, the man has become even more senile." Luisa teases.

"Okay, that's enough. Putting you two together is like adding another circle of punishment in Dante's Inferno." Santi grabs my shoulders and pulls me back towards his chest.

I spin around and face Santi and bite my lip as a thought I know I shouldn't say lingers in my mind; ultimately escaping my lips without a fight.

"Don't go all historic and philosophical on me now, Santi. You know what that does to me." I wink, referencing our almost kiss before.

Santi's eyes darken, and Adam's apple bobs before he clears his throat.

"Luisa, I'll call you later. We have plans to see Picasso and Goya."

"Goya? How romantic! I'll see you later, my lovely senile uncle, and you too, his future trophy wife." I take a second to stop and model for her, as she pretends to take a picture, but Santi quickly pulls me away from her.

"You cause too much trouble." He mutters.

"Yeah, I do, but somehow you still think I'm magnificent."

Santi's face pales at the reference to what Luisa had mentioned to him before.

"I guess high school Spanish stuck with me more than I thought." I shrug, moving along down the hall.

CHAPTER TWENTY-FOUR
Santi

SYLVIE ME QUITA de quicio.* And the only reason I don't leave her here to look at paintings on her own is because I made her a promise that I would stay. And I also get this rise of guilt that forms in my chest at the thought of abandoning her just because I'm annoyed.

I'm not even annoyed that she got along well with Luisa or that she is, without a doubt, a pain in my ass. But instead, I'm annoyed that I almost kissed her, right in the place where I work, in front of Luisa.

And I don't even want to think about all the messages and teasing I'll be receiving from her later today. Granted, I had no idea she was even working today.

I had stopped to show her some of my favorite paintings along the way, but didn't get into too much detail about them or their history. Which was extremely difficult not to do. I have already

---

* Sylvie drives me crazy

purposefully condensed my knowledge on the paintings because there has to be enough detail to give information to the tours, but fast enough that it doesn't waste any time.

"Are you upset with me?" Sylvie asks, walking beside me, as we head towards the entrance of the black paintings.

I let out a low grunt and walk into the dimly lit room.

"There's my favorite caveman." She coos, as if I'm some sort of baby.

"Stop that."

"Then answer my question." She demands.

"No."

"No, you're not mad, or no to denying my demand?"

"Sylvie, I am not upset. Now look at the paintings that you wanted to see."

Sylvie pouts her fuckable lips at me and slides her hand down my arm.

Wait.

Did I just say fuckable lips?

"You don't have to get so grumpy. I can still kiss you if you play nice for the rest of the tour." I feel the tips of my ears heat up instantly, and if my ears are red, then that means my whole face looks like a tomato.

Sadly, I don't blush; I fucking flush over beautiful American women.

Or just one very annoying one.

"You're looking at the black paintings," I explain, trying to move away from this topic. The last thing I needed was to complicate anything between us. I was still mending a heartbreak, and Sylvie was mending her life according to her. At most, the only thing that could come out of this interaction was an Instagram follow from my nonexistent account.

But even as I begin to explain the dark background behind these paintings, there's a small yearning that I'm unable to tuck away. A yearning I won't give into but will allow it to linger for as long as it stays because it's the best feeling I've had since my heartbreak.

We move on to the next painting, and Sylvie gets distracted by her phone, which automatically makes me send her a look of disapproval, and it sends my brain into a fantasy of what I could do to punish her.

Punish her?

She's my temporary roommate for Christ's sake.

"I didn't know your phone was more interesting than Goya; we could've just stayed home if that were the case."

Sylvie looks up at me and smirks, "Nothing is ever more important than whatever you have to tell me, honey."

Was she flirting with me?

Or was she just enjoying the sudden change in the color of my skin?

"I'm confirming plans for us, for later tonight." She muses, taking a step closer.

"Tonight?"

"We've been invited to a rooftop event in the city." She smiles at me like a Cheshire cat. And I don't want to tell her that I don't usually enjoy party events. But I swallow my discontent down to not ruin that smile of hers.

"By who?" I ask, wondering who the hell had invited her out tonight if she wasn't even close to anyone here.

"Some guy I met a couple of times throughout the city." She mentions nonchalantly, sending out a reply and tucking away her phone.

"Don't you Americans rave about stranger danger? Why the hell are you trusting random men throughout an estranged city?" I know the crease between my brows has made its presence and so has the headache that tends to rile up at the sides of my head when I'm met with stupidity.

"Relax, I was always in public places, and I made them think that I had friends here that would send out a search team if I were to disappear." She waves me off with a flick of her wrist and walks over to the next Goya painting, and I follow right behind her.

"I'm serious, Sylvie."

Sylvie scoffs and rolls her eyes.

"What will happen when you actually don't know anyone in the city you're in? What if you have no other accidental roommate? Which you should make sure you don't fucking have because that in itself is another god damn problem. There are freaks out there, Sylvie." I can't believe I was lecturing this grown woman on the safety of traveling.

"Jesus, Santi, I'm thirty years-old. I think I know how to travel and keep myself safe." She mutters.

"No, you don't."

I honestly didn't believe that Sylvie was actually thirty. I look Sylvie up and down and take her in completely. There's absolutely no way that this is a thirty-year-old woman who has no sense of responsibility when it comes to keeping herself safe.

"Are you sure you're thirty?" I ask.

Sylvie lifts a brow and crosses her arms over her chest, probably offended that I'm emphasizing her age.

"Yes, I am. Are *you* sure you're twenty-eight?" She asks, with a little spunk in her tone.

"I'm twenty- eight, but age isn't an issue here. Your lack of understanding of the dangers in the world at your age is what's concerning." I say, not wanting her to think that I was grilling her about her age.

Sylvie raises a brow and takes me in for a second. I'm not sure what she's thinking. Maybe she's just taking in my words and trying to process how crazy it actually is that she doesn't see the danger of the situations she puts herself in.

"I've actually never been with anyone younger than me, and somehow that makes me want you more." Her lips tilt upward into a smirk, and she sends me a wink as I groan into my hands.

"Sylvie."

"Yes, yes, yes, I know. I made sure that all of the other places I'm staying at are people-free. And I will make sure to stay mute on any further travels to ensure that I won't get abducted or murdered in a faraway European country."

"I'm serious," I mutter.

"As am I," Sylvie assures, nodding her head and then pouting her lips at me.

Those damn fucking lips.

"But that still doesn't mean we can't take advantage of the socializing I did while I was out in the city." Sylvie looks up at me with pleading eyes, wanting me to join her later tonight.

"I don't know." I sigh, unsure if I'm feeling up to going out.

"Please." She asks, taking a step closer.

If she were to take one more step, her breasts would be pressed right up against my abdomen, and I don't think I'd have another option but to agree. And I'm sure Sylvie herself is aware of that when she closes the distance between us and allows her breasts to press up against me.

"Por favor, Santi." She asks again, looking up at me with those puppy eyes.

Fuck me.

"Fine."

CHAPTER TWENTY-FIVE
Sylvie

I WAS KIND OF LOOKING FORWARD to going out tonight. And I think a small part of Santi was, too. I had texted Marlene and told her about our almost kiss. She hadn't responded right away, but ultimately sent a text stating not to get attached. I know I don't need Marlene's approval to have sex, but I didn't want to disappoint her. I've never held any secrets from my sister, so that was out of the picture as well.

Besides, I wasn't sure I even wanted to have sex with Santi. I didn't even know he was attracted to me until today. I mean, he's such a cold fish; he's never shown any interest in me. This was all just because he was still dealing with his breakup, and now that I've broken into his personal space with my insistence, he was starting to let his guard down.

And I guess now he was ready for a rebound. But I have been too many people's rebound. And Santi wasn't anyone special. He was just some grouchy man that I happened to be rooming with for a temporary amount of time, and then I would be on my way out to

Paris, and he would be here on to the next. Maybe even with someone like Carol.

There we go, I could introduce them tonight.

And then if I really want to get freaky with someone, I can jump Emilio's bones and then never see him again. Because we are here for a short time, not a long one.

"Hey, Sylvie, what are you wearing–" Santi walks into the room and is at a loss for words as he stares down my body. I was wearing a dress that shaped me perfectly, and that had a sheer layer of lace showing off some skin that left someone, like Santi, obviously wanting to see more.

"You just happen to have that in your suitcase?" He asks, his eyes still staring down at my body rather than my dress.

"Of course," I shrug. "You never know when your travels lead you to a nightclub or rooftop events."

"How convenient." He mutters slowly before clearing his throat and turning around.

"Just give me a moment, I'll be ready shortly." He says, walking straight out of my room, but even as discreet as he tries to be, I still notice the way he adjusts himself as he walks toward his room.

Maybe it is attraction.

"Do you know this place?" I ask him as the bouncer lets us into a hall that leads us to the elevator.

"I've been here before it got sold. Now it's been bought and revamped." He replies while adjusting his linen shirt that he looked so goddamn good in.

"How did you even get into a situation where you're invited to an exclusive opening like this one?" He asks, pressing the elevator door to go up.

"I was at a cafe on my first day here and sat next to a man who happened to be the owner. We kind of found ourselves running into each other again in the city, and he kept on insisting that I come." I explain, giving him the shortest version of the story.

"So what you're saying is that this man thinks you're very attractive and wants to get into bed with you?" Santi mutters.

I lift a brow as I look back up at him, kind of offended that he thinks that Emilio is only interested in me for one thing.

He's probably right.

But still, I'd like to think that my wit got us here today.

"What he wants and what he gets are very different things, Santi." I end up saying as the elevator doors open for us to exit. I take a step out and feel Santi's eyes on me. And for some reason, his stare feels cold, causing shivers to erupt down my spine.

He takes a step closer and lowers his head to my ear.

"And how does someone get you, Americana?" He whispers into my ear, and I'm tempted to turn around and kiss him. But instead, I swallow and look up at him with sheer confidence and a grin.

"I think you're very close, baby," I remark, and kiss him on the corner of his mouth.

Santi stands there frozen for a second before allowing a smirk to rise on his face.

"Now, come, I need tequila in my system right now." I shrug off the sexual tension as if nothing happened between us and move towards the bar, knowing Santi is right behind.

The rooftop looks beautiful, and there are high-top tables around the edges for people to sit and enjoy the city view. It's a quarter till midnight, so the place is starting to fill up. In the center, crowds of people have started to dance and move to the DJ's choice of songs.

Santi orders us a round of tequila shots that we down instantly, and then he orders a beer for himself and a rum and Coke for me.

"You're treating me nicely this evening, aren't you?" I tease, taking a sip of my drink.

Santi scoffs and takes a sip of his beer, "I always treat you nice." He says, placing the bottle back on the bar.

"No, you don't, you're always so rude and passive," I argue.

"It's because you're annoying." He mutters, his eyes finding mine as he says the words.

My lips move up to a sly grin, and I inch a little closer to him.

"Annoying, but yet you still tried to kiss me."

Santi smiles once again and brings his face down so that our noses touch.

"I said you're annoying, I never said you weren't sexy. And I think we both know that a man would have to be blind or completely and ignorantly stupid to not want to be with you." His hot breath touches my lips, and I can't help but wonder if this moment is the result of the alcohol in our system or simply just insatiable yearning.

"Let's dance," I whisper into his lips before pulling away, downing my drink, and hoping he follows me into the crowd.

I sway my hips along with the music and wait for Santi to come and pull up beside me. Instead, he wraps his hands around my waist and pulls me close to him.

"Why are you tempting me, Sylvie?" He groans in my ear, his body pressed up against my own. I can feel him hardening against me.

I try to separate and turn around, but Santi grips my hips tightly, stopping me from going anywhere.

"This is a stupid and dangerous game," I murmur.

"It is." He admits.

"A kiss was just a kiss. But this wouldn't just be a kiss; we would want more. And more leads to complications that we can't get into."

"You think I'm attractive." He mutters in my ear.

"I'm a serial dater, I think a lot of people are attractive," I say, hoping the idea of me being with other people might deter him from me.

"So you say." He says, his voice barely decipherable with the music blasting. "But still, something tells me you don't usually fight off men the way you're fighting me off."

"Santi, it seems that with you Spaniards, I'm like pollen to a bee. And I didn't come here to complicate my life with sex." This time, Santi allows me to step away and turn to look at him.

"You're hurting my ego." He says, a smirk playing on his lips, letting me know he's not serious.

"You'll live," I mutter.

"Sylvie."

"Yes?" I ask, my eyes set on him, my breath shallow as I continue to stare.

"You're looking at my lips."

"I am."

A moment of silence passes between us as we just stare at each other, and before I know it, Santi's lips are on mine. My hands instantly slither up his arms and around his neck, pulling him closer to me. His hands grip my ass and bring me as close as I can possibly be to him. This kiss is passionate and full of lust, but most of all, it's full of yearning. It's like a fire has been lit within us, one that won't diminish until we get more of one another. Our tangled tongues and firm grips on each other's bodies aren't enough, and that's what I was most afraid of.

Because this kiss is different.

This kiss is unlike anything I've felt before.

"Santi?" The female voice pulls us away from our lustful haze, and I'm not sure if I even heard his name be called until I hear my own name leave her lips.

"Sylvie?"

My head turns, and standing there are Carol and Emilio. Carol looking every bit shocked, and Emilio looking annoyed.

I clear my throat and open my mouth to say something, but Santi beats me to it. His voice is calm, but almost pained as he utters the question:

"Carolina?"

CHAPTER TWENTY-SIX
Sylvie

"SHOULD we go there and stop them?" I ask Emilio who's now perched up against one of the rooftop's glass walls with a Negroni in hand.

Emilio shakes his head as he continues to peer at the bickering ex-couple. Santi's fuming, and Carol– or Carolina looks hurt and upset.

"They need to get this over with." He says, taking another sip of his drink.

I don't say anything else and instead sit there on the stool awkwardly as I stare out at them. I don't think I've ever seen Santi this angry, not even when I pushed all of his buttons.

"So, you invited a friend to come along with you so that I could watch you make out with him on my rooftop?" He asks, turning his neck to look at me. I adjust myself in my seat to look at him.

"Those weren't my intentions," I say, taking a sip of the water that I had asked Emilio to order me. I didn't think another alcoholic beverage would help me in this case.

"Then what were your intentions?" Emilio asks.

I could be honest and tell him that, for a moment, I was thinking of entertaining him for a bit. But I didn't really like his attitude.

"Well, I was hoping I'd meet up with your sister here and that maybe I'd just convince her that women are superior to men in bed. And then we'd leave you alone at this party while we entertain ourselves in other ways." I spit the words out like venom and grab my cup of water, drinking it all before setting the cup down on the table harshly, wishing that I had chosen something stronger instead.

"Really? You didn't seem to show any romantic interest in Carol." He remarks.

"I didn't show much romantic interest in you either, but somehow we are still here."

"Then why are you here, Sylvie?" He asks, but he doesn't sound annoyed or aggravated, but rather curious and possibly amused.

"I don't know. To have fun?" I say, though it comes out more as a question because it was never supposed to be something so serious. We were just supposed to have fun tonight. And now I have an upset stomach, and an upset Santi barely holding it together as he continues to argue with Carol.

"Are you having fun?" Emilio asks, breaking my gaze away from them again.

"My temporary roommate is arguing with his ex in a corner of a rooftop bar, and I'm here with said ex's brother, who is butthurt by me kissing someone he knows," I mumble.

"I'm not upset." He remarks.

"Sure, that's why you're sitting there pouting."

Emilio straightens himself on the stool and turns to face me across the table.

"I'm pouting because I'm jealous, not because I'm hurt, and honestly, I'm not sure what about the guy makes you and my sister fawn over him."

I furrow my brows and scoff. I was not fawning over Santi; in fact, Santi was fawning over me. He's the one who showed his cards and the one insisting on that damn kiss. And I just followed the pull of the magnet right into his arms and my lips onto his.

"What's not to like about him?"

I was curious as to why Emilio hated Santi. From what I know, Carol broke up with Santi. It's not like Santi broke her heart. And he hadn't done anything wrong because Carol made that clear when she spoke to me about her ex. Though at the time I had no idea that it was Santi that she was talking about.

"He's boring and a cold fish."

That was rich coming from a man whose whole personality is being good-looking and rich.

"Maybe he's just not around the right people that could make him smile and show them his persona."

"What, so you're saying that my sister had to change herself for him to be a little bit more human around her?" He asks, his voice snarky and rude.

"What I'm saying is that sometimes certain people don't mesh together, no matter how much you try. If you aren't compatible, then you shouldn't force it." I mutter the words, trying my best not to lash out at him. I didn't like the way he was trying to twist my words. I had nothing against Carol.

"I don't know, I think that Santi and Carol, for the most part, were pretty compatible. They had a lot of things in common."

"Having things in common doesn't mean you're compatible. Sometimes opposites attract. What you need to find is someone who balances you out. Maybe Santi was boring for her, but maybe she was boring for him. A storm needs its calm. If everything were always just storming or calm weather, then it would be too monotonous."

Emilio hums and takes a sip of his Negroni once again and peers off at his sister and Santi, who now seem to be coming down from their argument.

"And you think you and he are compatible?" He finally asks.

The answer to that question didn't even matter. Santi and I were just having fun; he was trying to get over Carol, and I was trying to let loose. That was it.

I mean, I've only known the guy for three days.

"I don't think he's boring." Is all I manage to say, and Emilio lets out a chuckle.

That response gave him all the information that he needed. Carol seems to burst into tears, and Santi pulls her close to his chest, while mine aches a bit.

"I see Carol has brought out her crocodile tears," Emilio smirks into the rim of his cup and then peers back at me.

"I thought you were against, Santi." I muse.

"I'm not against anyone. I just state the obvious: Santi is boring and just likes sticking to the same things in life. And my sister can be selfish and inconsiderate. There's not much to work with in that type of relationship. And though she may be upset about her breakup with Santi, running back and begging him to give the relationship another chance isn't going to change the fact that there's no chemistry." Emilio finally sets the empty cup down onto the table and looks up past my shoulder.

I turn around, and Santi is there hovering over me.

"We're leaving." Is all he says.

And I follow him because I can tell by the look on his face that now isn't the moment for any jokes or to giving him trouble.

Santi and I walk home in silence, not a word uttered between us. He doesn't look angry or upset at me for not having put two and two together. But right now, I don't think I'm anywhere near his thoughts. I think the only thing he wants to do right now is figure out his relationship with Carol.

Santi opens the door to the apartment and takes a step inside, removing his shoes. I follow the same movements and stand in the entrance of the apartment, unsure of what is next.

Santi stands there for a few moments, possibly contemplating everything that's happened tonight. Finally, he looks up at me and gives me one of those awkward smiles of his again.

"Night." He practically croaks before walking into his bedroom, shutting the door behind him, leaving me in the dark.

"Goodnight, Santi."

Day 4

CHAPTER TWENTY-SEVEN
Sylvie

"I THINK HE MIGHT BE DEAD," I murmur into the phone's receiver. It was past eleven in the morning, and I hadn't done anything but cook breakfast and pace around the living room contemplating whether I should barge into Santi's room or not.

"I'm sure he hasn't died." Marlene groans into the phone, obviously still groggy from being awoken by my call. "Here's an idea: how about you knock on his door and see if he's awake." Marlene sighs into the phone. I can hear Yousef murmuring something, but can't quite pick up what he's saying.

"I made breakfast this morning, and he hasn't even woken up, and you know everyone wakes up to the smell of bacon," I whisper into the receiver, not wanting Santi to overhear me.

"Haram," Yousef mutters, this time making sure his tone is loud enough for me to actually hear him.

"Being that I've seen him down a bunch of Iberian ham and chorizo, tells me he doesn't follow your Islamic beliefs, Yousef."

"I want bacon now." Marlene groans into the receiver.

"No, you don't, you want to sleep. So hang up on your codependent sister and tell her you'll call her at a reasonable hour." Yousef states it matter-of-factly, and Marlene hums in agreement.

"My dear sister, I fear you're coming between me and my sleep."

"No, I think the problem is that I'm coming between you and your husband," I say.

"That too!" Yousef shouts enough for his voice to reach the receiver.

"I'll talk to you in the morning, Sylvie," Marlene whispers before hanging up the line. Leaving me alone with a possible corpse a couple of feet away.

Marlene was right, I just had to open the damn door. I know personal space was something we had agreed on when I moved in here, but he hadn't come out of his room all day, and it was beginning to become worrisome.

The walk home had been silent; no questions were asked, and not even glances were shared between us. And we sure as hell didn't talk about that kiss.

That goddamn kiss, that had me tingling from my head down to my toes.

I hadn't even shared that little piece of information with Marlene yet. I didn't want to hear what I already knew.

That I shouldn't have kissed the guy I'm rooming with, that it makes things more complicated. And she would also add the little reminder that I'm leaving in three days, and nothing would come out of this hookup.

But that was perfect, wasn't it?

That gave me the boundaries that I needed in order to stop myself from jumping into a relationship with anyone.

Look at you, Sylvie, so horny that you'll find any excuse to jump your roommate's bones.

Fuck, he might be dead.

Concentrate, Sylvie.

I give the door a light knock and wait for a response, but I'm met with silence instead. Which wasn't surprising because I'm already picturing a corpse under the damn covers.

I open the door slightly and peek my head in to look at the lump that lies under the covers. I open the door enough for me to step through and quietly walk over to his bed.

My goal wasn't to disturb him but rather check up on him. It just didn't feel right to leave him here all alone without at least checking in.

While I would be galavanting through the city, he'd be here sulking over a woman who left him at the altar.

"Santi," I whisper his name in hopes of receiving a quick response. But Santi is silent, and I assume asleep, because one thing is for sure: this man is very still.

The only thing that gave me hope was the color on his cheeks that I see as I peer closer to him.

Okay, Sylvie, you don't need to wake him up. You just need to check his breathing. I put my finger under his nose and check for any sign of life.

My eyes are so focused on my finger under his nose that I don't realize that Santi is looking straight at me.

"What are you doing?" I pull back in a screech and bring my hand towards my chest.

"I don't– I was just– I thought you were fucking dead." I finally mutter, catching my breath from the scare.

"Why would you think I'm dead?" He asks, lifting one of his arms over his head, and I can't help looking at the way his biceps flex in the process.

"I thought you were dead because it's twelve and you're silent." The words come out from my brain and out through my mouth, but it seems I'm too distracted to actually state a precise sentence because even I know that didn't make any fucking sense.

"So you thought I was dead because it's noon and I was silent because I was sleeping?" He asks, raising his brows at the absurdity of that sentence.

"Ugh, you know what I'm trying to say, Santi," I mutter, taking a seat on the bed beside him so that I now face the wall rather than at a shirtless Santi.

"I thought you were upset about yesterday," I mutter.

"About what, exactly?" He asks.

"Don't act like you didn't have an argument with your ex-fiancée after she saw us tonguing each other," I growl, crossing my arms over my chest.

Santi sighs, and from the corner of my eye, I can see him turn his face away from me to look up at the ceiling.

"Well, I am upset about having to see Carol." He admits, and for some reason, that sends a pang of jealousy to my heart.

"I mean, no one is ever happy to see their ex, especially not when the last time you saw them was the day before the wedding. The wedding in which she left me like an idiot waiting at that damn altar."

I look over at Santi, and I can see real pain in his eyes.

"Was she mad that we were kissing?" I ask.

"I think she was mad that I had moved on enough to be kissing a pretty girl at her brother's club. Which I didn't know was his, to be fair. You never mentioned Emilio's name, and I didn't know that he had bought the rooftop from the previous owners." Santi promises, and I believe him because, for some reason, it would hurt more than it would with anyone else to find out that Santi had only been using me to make Carolina jealous.

"What about the baby?" I ask, knowing that it's none of my business, but that I certainly would like to know what's going to happen now that she's pregnant.

"The what?" Santi asks, pushing himself out of bed.

"The baby?" I ask.

"What baby?" He mutters, his green eyes peering down at me as if I were the one withholding the child from him.

"The one in her uterus?" I ask.

"Not my baby." He mutters, either pissed that I've accused him of being the father or that his ex is pregnant with another man's child.

"I don't know, I overheard her talking on the phone once, and she said she wasn't going to tell him that she was pregnant. And I just assumed that you were him." I try my best to connect the dots, but something is definitely missing.

"She's not pregnant, at least not with my child," Santi mutters, lying back down on the bed. I peer over, this time feeling bold enough to extend my arm to his other side and hover over him.

"How can you be so sure? I know what I heard." I mutter.

Santi's gaze shifts from my eyes down to my breasts and back up to my eyes. And I have to say, it feels good to know that last night wasn't just the alcohol in his system that made him want to kiss me. There was a real attraction between us.

"Well, the last time I would have been able to conceive a child with her was six months ago." He says, bringing his fingers up to curl one of the strands of my hair that's hovering over his face. "And correct me if I'm wrong, but I'm sure she'd be showing by now if she were carrying my offspring."

"Six months?" Is the only thing that tumbles out of my mouth.

"Six months." He confirms with a nod.

"Without sex?" I ask.

Why the fuck did I ask that?

Santi smirks and gives me a shrug.

"No one has piqued my interest." Santi murmurs, removing his finger from my hair and trailing it down my chest to the crevice of my breasts. His eyes on mine, not breaking contact for a second.

I clear my throat and nod before pulling away.

"Well, congratulations are in order then, as Maury would say, you are *not* the father," I say, trying my best to make my way off the bed without tumbling off it.

"This calls for a celebration. There's no reason for you to be moping in bed all day, upset that you've spotted your ex in public." I walk backwards as Santi lifts himself to look at me.

"I'm not moping." He mutters, there he is back to old grouchy Santi again.

"Then why didn't you go out for your morning run?" I ask.

"It's raining."

"It's barely drizzling," I argue.

"She asked me for another chance." He admits, stopping me in my tracks.

"And?" I ask, not even realizing that I've started to hold my breath.

"I thought about saying yes." He answers sincerely.

I swallowed a knot that I hadn't realized had been building up in my throat.

"You thought about it, but you said no," I ask, to make sure I'm understanding.

I know I shouldn't feel jealous. Santi and I had only shared brief moments of tension and a kiss. And it wasn't like we would ever talk again after I left for my next destination. We would just be strangers we'd met along the way in life. The type of strangers that we'd learn something from, and think about every so often when the lesson they taught us repeats itself in life.

"I thought about it when I remembered all of the years spent together and the good times we had." He admits, but I really wish he would stop telling me everything.

"I was with her for so long, I proposed to her. I invited my family and friends to a wedding that didn't fucking happen, Sylvie." He mutters, getting up from the bed and dragging his hand across his buzzcut that had begun to grow out a bit.

Santi walks over to his dresser and pulls out a white shirt, covering his tattooed skin with it. I have to admit I'm quite disappointed that I didn't get the chance to look at all the tattoos he has placed around his torso. And now I was wondering if any of them symbolized *her*.

"I didn't hear from her until last night. That was the only ounce of clarity I got, and it took her six fucking months." Santi utters the words through his teeth and pulls out gray sweats from the dresser, tugging them on.

"That really fucking sucks, Santi."

Santi looks at me and then walks right over to where I am and stands close enough for our bodies to touch.

"Do you know why I'm off from work this week, Sylvie?" He asks, as if it were the easiest question in the world.

I shrug and give him a shy smile.

"Summer vacation?" I ask.

Santi scoffs and shakes his head, looking away almost as if he's gathering his thoughts before looking back down on me.

"This was supposed to be the week of our honeymoon."

The words seem to echo in the room, and I'm not sure what exactly to respond to that revelation, and Santi seems to realize that as he walks away, leaving me there to take in his words.

CHAPTER TWENTY-EIGHT
Sylvie

"THIS IS STUPID," Santi mutters, putting the corner pieces of the puzzle in a pile.

"It's not stupid; it improves our cognitive skills," I explain, passing any corner pieces over to him while running back to the stove to flip the tortilla.

He had insisted on cooking us lunch, but I was keen on learning how to do it myself. I wasn't the best cook, but how bad could someone fuck up an egg, potato, and onion recipe? Besides, he had been here the whole time giving me the instructions. It wasn't until we were actually cooking the tortilla that I asked him if he had a puzzle. He muttered something about Carol loving to do puzzles and about her leaving behind one she had gifted him during their relationship, in hopes he would pick up the hobby as well.

Once the puzzle was complete, we would end up with the Birth of Venus, which would be nice to frame. But I wasn't sure that Santi wanted something gifted to him by his ex to be hung up on any of his apartment walls.

I press the plate onto the pan and grip the pan's handle. I try my best to flip it over, but struggle with the weight of the pan.

"Wait, I think I might need help," I say, my voice in a panic, afraid of dropping the tortilla. Santi comes up behind me and puts his hand over mine, helping me flip the tortilla onto the plate, then slides the uncooked side back onto the pan to finish cooking.

"That's the hardest part. Now, all you have to do is wait for it to finish cooking, and you can officially file for Spanish citizenship." Santi teases, his hot breath on the crevice of my neck.

"That easy, huh?" I ask, peering over my shoulder to look at him, but he doesn't respond. Instead, he just looks at me, the delicious smell of the tortilla making my stomach growl, or maybe that was just my body giving me an excuse to pull away.

"Wow, I'm really hungry. I can't wait to eat this." I move around Santi and walk back to the puzzle pieces spread out on the table.

"What's going on?" Santi asks, coming to stand right next to me as I continue to pull side pieces into the pile.

"Nothing is wrong." Except that there's a lot of fucking tension between us, and just yesterday your tongue was in my mouth, and your ex crashed our moment in hopes of getting back together with you, and you actually thought about saying yes. And it shouldn't even fucking matter, because Madrid is just a place I'm visiting, along with a list of other European countries I will be visiting until I return home to where I have an apartment and a job waiting for me.

"The way you're ignoring me and pushing through those pieces says otherwise," Santi mutters.

"I'm not ignoring you. I'm literally taking time out of my day to stay here with you while you mope about your ex." I bite the inside of my cheeks to stop myself from saying anything else.

Santi scoffs and turns back around to finish the tortilla, and honestly, I'm not sure if I like this reaction better than the moody one I was expecting.

"I'm not moping." He finally mutters as he brings over the cooked tortilla and the chorizos we had cooked before making the tortilla.

I take the plates from his hands and put one by where each of us is sitting. I don't respond; instead, I take the cutlery and begin cutting the tortilla.

"You're the one who asked me what happened last night, and I was honest and told you." I nod and pull a piece onto his plate, then another onto mine.

"I didn't really need to share any information with you to begin with. It's not like you're anything to me."

And there it was. That was the Santi I was used to, brutally honest and grumpy. And as truthful as his words were, I can't help but admit that there was a pang in my chest from how easy it was for him to say them. As if he had hit me with a dagger straight to the heart.

"You're right, which is why I don't understand why you care that I want some personal space," I mutter, trying my best not to show that his words had actually stung.

"Fuck, Sylvie, we kissed, and it was a fucking good kiss." Santi groans, taking a seat right beside me.

"I'm aware."

"And now you don't even want me near you." He adds.

"I just think that it's best not to complicate things anymore than we already have." He was just looking for a rebound, and anyone could be his rebound. He just needed one night in the city, and he'd be home and in bed with his conquest of the night.

And I know I could be a rebound, too, but it felt different with Santi. Whatever happened with us would never be more than just sex, but I also knew that I didn't want to lower myself to just being a rebound.

"Is this because of Carol?" He asks.

"It's not just about that."

"Then make me understand." He pleads, finally taking a seat next to me and taking a bite out of his tortilla.

"The truth is that you don't have to understand. You just respect that I don't want to pursue whatever it was that we were even starting." I rebuttal, taking another bite of my food. And I already feel so fucking bad for stating it like he's done something wrong. Especially because Santi does deserve an answer after last night.

Santi reaches over the table and settles his hand on my own, rubbing his thumb in comfort, and I look up from my meal to finally meet his eyes.

"You're right. I'm sorry, I don't want to ruin anything or make you uncomfortable. You can be annoying, but you're a good person, Americana. And I appreciate you coming home with me last night." He says, cutting the chorizo in half and placing it on my plate, then his.

"You don't have to thank me for that. Of course, I would go with you." I say, taking a bite of the Chorizo.

The minute the meat's juices burst into my mouth, I moan at the goodness. This was the perfect combination, and though it was so simple, it was so delicious.

"You know, you can at least make it a little easier on me." Santi murmurs, looking right at me.

"Sorry." I blush and go back to concentrating on the puzzle.

"Don't you have an itinerary to follow today?" Santi asks as he begins combining the puzzle pieces together, building the edge of the puzzle.

"It's raining." I shrug.

"It's drizzling." He rebutted, using the same excuse I had before.

"Yeah, but I'd rather enjoy my day here with you."

Santi doesn't say anything at first; he just hums in response and continues on with his puzzle. We remain silent for a few minutes before Santi finally breaks the silence.

"I was enraged when I saw her yesterday." He admits.

I don't answer right away; instead, I stay silent and let him find his next words.

"You were right this morning." He sighs, lying back in his chair, his eyes stuck on the puzzle piece he kept on moving from finger to finger.

"I was moping." His eyes reach mine again, and I only give him a subtle nod for him to continue.

"I was fucking pissed that she had come back to Madrid during the time she knew that we had scheduled our honeymoon. And fuck I was even more pissed that she felt the need to bring you up like you were just a rebound." Santi growls, his eyes now focused on the raindrops hitting the window. And I knew he must've been recalling last night's interaction with her.

"I don't care what she has to say about me." I scoff, "But just out of curiosity, what did she say?" I ask, obviously fucking caring about what she said about me after we had spent our time together. I had even flirted with her fucking brother to get her into his rooftop.

"It doesn't matter, what she said was stated out of jealousy." He reasons.

"So she called me fat?" I chuckle and shake my head.

"I didn't say that." He mutters.

"You don't have to, it's the first insult in the mean girls hand-book, when the girl they're mad at is an actual nice and sexy woman." I shrug my shoulders and take another bite of food.

I was a fucking millennial. I knew a thing or two about mean high school girls, and the blonde skinny bitch was always the leader.

"I'm glad you know that," Santi says, giving me a sincere smile.

"But seriously, what did she say?" I ask.

"Nothing about your weight." He mutters.

"If you don't tell me, I'll just continue to think about it."

"She said some other words that aren't respectable to call a woman." He sighs.

"Oh, a whore?" I ask.

"Yes."

"Because I kissed you?" I ask, raising a brow.

"No– well, yes– but something else."

"Spit it out, Santi." I bark, getting annoyed at the guessing game with him.

"Did you sleep with Emilio?" He finally asks.

"Is that what she said? That I slept with her brother?" I ask, crossing my arms over my chest. I was sure that if I spotted Carolina in public again, I'd punch her straight in the fucking face.

"Did you?" He asks, and for a moment, I see the brief look that passes his face. He wasn't just asking out of curiosity or to get the story straight. He was asking because Santi was fucking jealous.

"You think I would've kissed you if I had fucked him?"

"You flirted with him." He shrugs.

"Flirting is harmless. I once flirted with a sixty-year-old man from an auto body shop to get a discount on my oil change."

Santi furrows his brows at that, and I only shrug.

"It was college, money was tight, and instead of a discount, I got it for free."

"So you don't like him?" Santi asks.

"Not as much as I like free things." I tease, continuing to build on the puzzle.

But Santi doesn't seem to find it amusing because he just continues to stare at me.

"No, Santi, I didn't like him like that."

I should have left the conversation at that, but something about Carolina trying to steer Santi away from me with a lie bothered me.

"Did you believe her?" I finally ask.

Santi takes a moment to reply. I'm not sure if he's contemplating answering honestly or if he's just recollecting the memories of last night.

"No, but I did picture you two together the moment she said it, and it pissed me off." He admits.

"Why?"

"He's an ass."

"Funny, he said something similar about you." Santi rolls his eyes and looks down at his plate of food.

"The food is delicious, by the way, thank you." He murmurs.

"Thanks, don't expect much cooking from me though. I'm usually very terrible at it and am lucky to have had you next to me to flip the tortilla."

"You mean you won't be my personal chef for the remainder of your vacation?" He teases.

"Listen, buddy, today is just a break-up ritual. After this, we go back to normal." I say, furrowing my brows to look as serious as I can.

"A break-up ritual?"

"Yeah, you know the things you do to make yourself feel better after a break-up," I explain, though I had already assumed he knew exactly what I was doing when I asked him what his comfort meal was and then proceeded to cook it for him. But Santi continues to stare at me with a blank expression on his face.

"Like, eat your favorite food, pick an activity that distracts your mind from the break-up, watch your favorite rom-com movie, and eat a bucket of ice cream." I gesture to the scattered puzzle pieces and plates of food around us to help him get the gist.

"But, I'm not going through a break-up." He states.

"Santi, your ex-girlfriend shows up on the week that was supposed to be your honeymoon and asks you to give her another chance after having left you at an altar with millions of guests watching you."

"It was not millions of people." He disputes.

"There was more than one, and that's enough to feel humiliated and hurt," I murmur.

I didn't need Santi to admit that he felt his heart shatter into a million pieces the minute he saw Carol last night because I saw it myself. And last time I checked, the only time a man proposes to a woman that's not pregnant is because they're very much in love with her.

And Carol fucked that up.

"Sylvie?"

"Hm?"

"What's your favorite Rom-Com?"

I lift my eyes up from the puzzle and let my brown eyes find his blue ones, and allow for my excited grin to take shape on my face.

CHAPTER TWENTY-NINE
Santi

I'VE LEARNED a few things today.

1. Carol was not the woman that I thought she was.

2. She did me a favor by leaving me at the altar.

3. Sylvie is the most caring person I've ever met.

4. She's a very beautiful woman, but looks even more beautiful crying over a Rom-Com she states she's watched a billion times, but rewatches it like it's the first time.

5. She's a big believer in someday finding the one.

6. I suddenly have the urge to be that one.

And I don't know why that last thought is taking up occupancy in my brain when it shouldn't. My heart is just confused with all the kindness being thrown at me today. That and it's painfully obvious how attracted I am to her, and I almost had her until Carol and Emilio interrupted us last night.

I obviously respect her boundaries; if she didn't want to pursue anything, I could live with it. But thinking about Sylvie leaving after this week hurt a little more than it should.

Fuck, we should've just stuck to the rules we had established in the beginning.

I should've done my thing, and she would've done hers. There was no reason for me to be walking around the streets of Madrid with her, taking her to my damn job, where she met one of my closest friends. And I shouldn't have even been at that rooftop with her last night.

And I shouldn't be sitting here, allowing her to nurse a heart that's not even broken. Because the truth is, when I saw Carol again, for once, I didn't feel pain or loss. Instead, I felt fucking frustrated that the woman had decided to show up the moment I found something that made my heart beat again. And I'm not really sure why my heart decided to beat for someone who won't ever be in my life again, but damn it, I can't control it.

Maybe this is one of those things where you have to get it out of your system. But then, when I look at Sylvie in the face, I quickly realize that she's not someone that you get out of your system.

And even I, someone who's usually always annoyed with the world, can understand that.

"He shouldn't have let her leave Ireland." I finally say, wrapping my arm around a sobbing Sylvie.

"That's what I always say."

She sniffles and wipes away the remainder of her tears.

"But Marlene always says that would ruin the whole point of the movie."

Marlene was right, but it wouldn't have killed Declan to have admitted his feelings to Anna.

"What's it like to fall in love with someone?" Sylvie's voice barely comes out as a whisper, and I don't even think she realizes that she's spoken the words until I answer.

"Haven't you been in love before?"

"Pfft, I don't think it was ever really love more than it was an infatuation or better yet a hunger for wanting that sort of fated love."

"You speak of it as if you've seen it."

Sylvie adjusts her body to face me, our noses now only a millimeter away from touching.

"My parents are annoyingly romantic, and Marlene and Yousef fit. I mean, they are complete opposites, but they balance out somehow. Sometimes I'm a tad bit jealous that she's found her love before I have."

My hand finds Sylvie's thigh, and I give it a squeeze of assurance.

"You'll find them, Sylvie."

Love is a very strange thing, and I was sure that I knew what it was because I had been ready to marry Carol. But now that time has passed and healed, I was more hurt by the embarrassment of being left at the altar than by the actual break-up. Fuck, I was pissed that she had done things the way she did. I wanted to argue and fight, but she never responded. And I was left without answers.

Even yesterday's reunion didn't give me the answers I deserved.

"I'm thirty, and I feel as if the clock is ticking." She admits.

I look up at her and see actual sorrow in her eyes. And something about seeing Sylvie be anything but bubbly gutted me.

"We all feel the clock ticking," I tell her, trying to show her that she's not alone in this thought.

"Not all of us are women who want to be married and have children." Sylvie scoffs, as if what I had said was ridiculous.

"You can still have kids," I argue.

"Yes, if I settle for the next person that comes around."

Settle?

"You're not settling for anyone, Sylvie. You are a woman that deserves the Universe handed to her, and I think that the real reason men end up leaving you is because they realize that they'd fail to give you just that."

Sylvie raises a brow and stares at me with a look that says, *be so for real.*

"Men leave because I'm overbearing."

"Sylvie, you are not overbearing; if anything, you're altruistic. And with dating altruistic people, sometimes we people who suck with emotions and genuine human interaction feel that we aren't enough."

Some men liked the idea of having a woman who knows exactly what she wants. And Sylvie was that kind of woman. And not only did she know what she wanted, but she got it.

"Is that what you found attractive about me?" Sylvie's bubbly personality comes back with a wiggle of her brows as she asks me the question.

"Yes." I lie.

The truth is that the minute I saw Sylvie in that bathroom with the towel held tightly against her body, I knew she was the sexiest woman I had ever laid my eyes on.

Those bark brown eyes, the plump pink lips, the perfect divide between her breasts when tightly squeezed under the towel, and those god damn hips that peeked out from said towel.

Sylvie was sexy.

But then I got to know her annoying, bubbly, overdramatic, and over-caring persona, and I realized Sylvie was heart-stoppingly beautiful.

"Why are you looking at me like that?" Sylvie whispers, her nose only millimeters away from my own as we look at each other.

"Like what?"

Sylvie opens her mouth to speak, but closes it once more, her gaze shifting from my eyes down to my lips. Almost as if she's either contemplating what words to say or rather to show.

"Like..." She starts but doesn't finish, and instead relieves herself of a shaky breath.

Like what, Sylvie?

Like you're the most beautiful woman in the world?

Like you're making me break down the hard rock exterior that I spent months building after Carol broke me?

Like, I'm completely taken aback by the human that you are?

Like, I'm all of a sudden feeling my heart beat for you?

"I don't know, you're just looking at me differently. If you keep it up, I'm going to begin thinking you want to be my friend." She teases, turning her head away to face the film again.

Jesus, Santi, what the fuck are you doing?

This won't ever go anywhere. She came here to avoid any interaction with men. And more importantly, she already said no, so I'm going to respect that. The quicker that settles into my head, the easier it'll be to get rid of this newly developed crush.

My eyes shift towards the window, where a few remaining rain droplets begin to slide down the window's glass. Though Sylvie had stated that she skipped her itinerary plans because of the rain, I knew that hadn't been what really stopped her. She had stayed for me, to make sure I was okay after what happened yesterday.

She had adjusted her itinerary to accommodate my needs. And I wasn't deserving of that, not when I had been rude to her during her stay here. That would be another thing we'd have to talk about before she leaves. She can't be nice to men who are complete assholes to her.

I wait for the film to finish before telling Sylvie to go get changed.

"Where are we going?" She asks.

"We haven't had the last thing on that breakup list of yours," I say, lifting myself up from the couch to walk into my bedroom.

"Ice cream?" She chirps, following me into my room, but stopping by the frame of the door.

"Yes, and I owe you a little history lesson for your friendship today."

Sylvie lets out a cheerful yelp and runs into her bedroom to get changed. I check my phone to see how much time we have left until sunset. It wouldn't take too long, and the fact that it stopped raining meant that there would be a line.

But the way the sun lowered on the horizon of the park would be worth it.

And the way her eyes would brighten along with her smile made this even more important.

CHAPTER THIRTY
Sylvie

"I THOUGHT you were taking me to get ice cream." I pout, as Santi leads me on a random stroll, rather than taking me to an ice cream parlor like he had promised at home.

"Stop complaining, you make it difficult to do nice things for you." He mutters, but there's no frown to indicate his annoyance.

"I would just like to know where we are headed." I reason.

But as I think about the statement I've made, I realize that I do, in fact, want ice cream, regardless of whether he intends to take me there.

"You know, actually, I want to make sure that you'll do as you had promised and get me ice cream because now I'm craving it."

Santi chuckles and shakes his head as we begin to approach some steps that lead to a park.

"Te lo prometo: tendrás tu helado, Americana."

"That better have been a promise." I threaten.

"It was."

As we make it up the steps, my eyes widen in shock at the monumental stonework that lies in the middle of the park.

"What is this?" I ask, walking closer to what seemed to be a temple.

"It's the Temple of Debod." He states as if it's something everyone knows.

"Oh, right, I know all about the Temple of Debod, that looks like it should be in Egypt or Sudan and is somehow in the center of Spain."

Santi's lips turn upwards into a grin, and I can't help but notice how good it makes me feel to get that reaction from him. "Well, you're right. It was at the time located in the ancient kingdom of Nubia, also known as Kush. Which took up the South of Egypt and the North of Sudan. So you're on track with history." Santi says, grabbing my hand and pulling me to the line of people that are heading into the temple in groups.

"So, how exactly did it get from South Egypt to the center of Spain?"

"As you know, a lot of temples and ancient burials are being ruined by floods and the overall rise in water levels. In this case, a dam had been built near the historical architecture. So, when temples like the one here were going to be threatened by possible submersion, Egypt decided it would be best to move the historical monuments." Santi explains the story as if he's heard it plenty of times before.

As he speaks, I can't help but picture him in his clean-cut sheets of a bed, nothing like the rumpled mess of blankets I left behind every morning. He'd be reading his book, the kind others would jokingly call a textbook, which I know would annoy him, not enough to stop reading the books out in public, but enough to have him growl a fuck you and return to his reading. But he still prefers to read in the comfort of his bed, with no one around but him and the story of history.

"Anyway, Spain ended up helping save these monuments, and as a gift, Egypt had the Temple of Debod dismantled and shipped over to us. And now it lies here for anyone who'd like to come see it."

I take a look around the park, where a group of people are practicing their evening yoga class. There are some children running around and a few people on their bikes. All of them are completely normalized to having an ancient temple in the middle of the park.

"What's inside?" I ask.

"You'll see, but mainly it's hieroglyphics, and they do have panels on the interior that tell you a bit about the history of the temple."

"Who needs to read them when I have you as my tour guide?"

Santi rolls his eyes and pulls me forward to follow the line.

"Usually there's a much longer line, but since it rained earlier today, it seems that not a lot of people came to see it."

"Why did you bring me here?" I ask, curious as to why he decided to pull us away from our hangout with the promise of ice cream, only to bring me here.

"Because in a few moments, when the sun begins to set, and it shines along the horizon of the park, you'll want to take a picture to add to those notebooks you like to fill with paper, and trash." I slap Santi on the arm, and another grin appears on his face

That's two already.

"It's not paper and trash. It's the little things that I want to remember about my trip."

"I saw you tape a candy bar wrapper to the corner of a page, Sylvie."

"They were huesitos, and they were so damn good. I had to put them in my scrapbook of memories." I defend, making a mental note to stock up on some of those when heading over to Paris. I wasn't sure if they could be found outside of Spain.

"I can't blame you, they're delicious." He admits, looking out past the temple as the sun slowly begins to set. The security lets us know that we are next, but Santi states something about letting the others pass and pulls us to the side.

"What's happening?" I ask.

"I don't want to be inside the temple when the sun sets. I want you to see how beautiful it looks." Santi stands behind me, his body close but not close enough to touch. But damn, do I wish we were.

It was better this way. Nothing promising would come out of this, and I had to keep reminding myself just that.

The sun begins to meet the horizon, and its orange hues expand across the park, complementing the greenery and illuminating the temple that stands right before it. It was breathtaking.

"It's so beautiful, Santi," I murmur, taking in the beauty of nature.

"It's exactly what I imagined." He murmurs right next to me, and I turn my head to look at him, already facing me.

"I'm sure you must've had some idea, you've probably been here a bunch of times."

Santi lets out a chuckle and nods his head over to the temple's entrance.

"Come, let's go see the interior before they close it for visitation."

I follow Santi inside the temple, where the walls are filled with hieroglyphics. The interior is quite tight and small, but nonetheless very interesting.

"The temple was dedicated to the gods Amon and Isis, and years after it was even used by the Romans," Santi whispers behind me as I take in the written walls.

"The Romans? Weren't they Christian?"

"This was at a time when the Romans were part of a polytheistic religion, influenced by what we know as Greek mythology. Hence, the names of the gods, such as Zeus, also being known as Jupiter, Hera being Juno, Poseidon being Neptune, Hades being Pluto, and so on." Santi explains as he points a finger at the stairs illuminated by the lights leading up to the second floor.

We make our way up the stairs while Santi continues to explain the history.

"So, to the Romans, all polytheistic religions were the same. It didn't matter who you prayed for because it would all lead back to the same god that was represented."

"And then after came Christianity?" I ask.

"Well, first it was Judaism, followed by Christianity, and lastly Islam."

"Do you like the History Channel, Santi?" I ask, smugly walking up the stairs.

"Love it." He says, reaching the top with me.

"Hm, I think they should give you your own show, and I should obviously be there for comedic relief." I tease.

"Hm, I'm sure it'd be for comedic relief and not at all for the *free* travel." He says the words like a taunt.

"Don't use that word around me, Santi. You know it turns me on." I nudge his shoulder as he says it, and a hint of red rises up his neck and towards his cheek.

God, I liked making him blush just as much as I liked making him smile.

"What are these?" I ask, walking over to the glass display cases.

"It's supposed to be a model of what the temple would've looked like in its original state."

"Who would've known that my first look into an ancient Egyptian temple would be in Madrid?"

"Who would've known that I'd be playing tour guide to an American tourist who happened to find herself living in my apartment?" Santi says, mimicking my tone.

"Okay, you win," I say, letting out a dramatic sigh and following Santi down the same flight of stairs we came from in order to make our way out.

Santi makes it down to the bottom, waiting for me. But as I get closer, I feel my heart drop to my stomach when I miss a step and fall forward. I close my eyes, ready to break the fall, but a pair of hands grab ahold of me, one on my torso and the other firm on my ass.

My eyes shoot open, and Santi stares down at me with his casual smugness.

"You know, it's been a while since your last klutzy moment. I was beginning to worry you were coming down with a sickness, or worse, that you were captured and replaced by aliens." His hands remain firm in their position as he stands me upright, but he makes no effort to pull them away. On the contrary, I feel the slight movement of his thumb on my ass, and I'm sure he doesn't even realize that he's doing it.

"If you keep making these types of jokes, I'm going to think the same thing myself," I say, clearing my throat and stepping out of his embrace. Santi is quick to realize that he's closer than he should be and takes a step back, shoving his hands into his pockets.

"Thank you," I say.

"You don't need to thank me for that."

I shrug and nod my head for him to continue in front of me so that he can lead us.

"Do you want to take a picture outside?" He asks.

"Will you be in it?" I ask, giving him one of those pleading looks I know he can't say no to.

"Ugh, sure, where do you want to take the picture?" He asks, pulling out his phone and opening the camera settings.

"We can do it further down the gateways," I suggest, where there's already a group of people standing at the very end of the aisle.

Santi and I walk over to the group and ask one of them to take a picture of us, which they kindly agree to. Santi stands near me, obviously unsure of what exactly to do in these circumstances.

"If you can cop a feel while inside an ancient temple, you can surely put your arm around my waist to take a picture." Santi narrows his eyes and shoots me a glare, obviously annoyed that I brought the ass touching up.

"I did not cop a feel, I stopped you from landing on your face."

"Whatever you say." I shrug and grab his arm to bring it around my waist. I then step into his frame and lean into him.

The woman in front of us takes a couple of pictures, then hands the phone to Santi. He takes the phone from her grasp and mutters a thank you before scrolling through the photos.

I inch a bit closer and peer over at the phone to look at them with him.

"Oh, they're so cute. Send them to me." I pull out my phone and open WhatsApp, immediately waiting for the photos to arrive.

"Are you still hungry for that ice cream?" He asks, as we step away from the temple and onto the darkening park.

"Always, maybe we can get some ice cream and then go back home to complete that puzzle. You think we can finish it before I leave?" I ask.

"Possibly, if we get home every day from whatever tourist attraction we've been to and force our tired brains to concentrate and put odd shapes together."

"What do you mean by when *we* come home?"

Santi shrugs and lets out a longing sigh.

"It's not like I have anything planned for the remainder of the week. Might as well use all my knowledge to teach you about the city I live in."

"Aw, you want to hang out with me." I tease and stick my tongue out.

"I'm having more fun than I would've sticking to my regular routine and stalking my ex on Instagram."

"I thought you didn't have Instagram."

I was sure that Carol had mentioned it before.

"How do you know that?" Santi furrows his brows.

I'm sure at this exact moment, he's trying to recall our past conversations to see if we've ever spoken about his use of social media. And I'm unsure if it's even relevant for me to bring up Carol after the day we just had. But it's not like lying would take me out of this.

"Well, Carol may have mentioned something about her ex not having any social media," I admit.

"Ah," Santi takes in a deep breath and lets out a sigh as we walk by one another.

"What else did she say?" He asks.

"Does it matter?"

"It doesn't, but I'd still like to know, just like you wanted to know what she had said about you."

The words come out like a taunt, and I roll my eyes. I know he's mimicking my own words from yesterday. And I see his point. I understand why he'd want to know everything his ex said about him. But I also realize that knowing the other side of the story makes me see that Carol wasn't always in the right, and after what she told Santi yesterday, I knew she wasn't trustworthy or as nice as I thought she was.

"She just said that you were opposites and that it was best that you broke up."

"So, the exact opposite of what she was trying to do yesterday." Santi looks more confused now than he did at the beginning of the conversation.

"God, Santi, she only said that yesterday because I told her that she should see things from your perspective and that maybe if she was still thinking about you, then she should reach out to apologize and try to make it work. But that was before I knew that you were the man she was talking about and way before I knew she was two-faced." I don't know why it feels wrong to share this. There is nothing wrong with the conversation I had with Carol.

I had thought she was just a woman in need of guidance in life; hell, I was a woman who needed guidance, and I was in my thirties. But admitting this to Santi feels like a betrayal.

"Relax, Sylvie, I'm not upset that you talked to Carol. I was aware that you guys had conversed prior to now, and I was sure that you obviously hit it off, or you wouldn't have been at her brother's rooftop. I'm just shocked that Carol had admitted any of her doubts with you." Santi stops by a bench, takes a seat, and I sit right next to him, letting him take the moment he needs to speak.

"It almost feels like a slap in the face." He sighs and brings his palms across his face, rubbing them aggressively against his skin, and then lets them fall onto his lap dramatically.

"I tried my best to open up to her in our relationship. And that was the biggest reason I proposed in the first place. I know that I'm not the easiest person to love. Fuck, I know I'm a grump with a frown constantly sewn to my face. But I can't change who I am, and with Carol, it didn't seem like she minded that or made a fuss about it. She knew I wasn't a fan of social media; she knew I preferred to keep to myself. And I knew we were complete opposites, but I was sure it didn't bother her. I mean, I respected her work, and she respected mine. I knew she probably wanted to post about us occasionally, but she never seemed to make a big fuss about me not wanting to be in the public eye, especially given the number of followers she had. I like my simple life, and I thought that Carol didn't mind sharing that simple life with me, that is, until our wedding day, of course."

I'm not sure how to respond. I had admitted to Carol that she was being selfish and should have been open about her feelings with Santi. But Santi had done the same in some ways. And I kind of understand where Carol was coming from now. I didn't want to defend the girl, but I now knew what she meant when she said that she felt somewhat shoved into a corner.

"Would an Instagram picture kill you?" I ask.

Santi chuckles and shakes his head.

"No, but she never made a big deal out of it, so I never insisted either." Santi sighs and lies back on the bench.

"Communication goes both ways."

"I proposed to her, Sylvie. I think I communicated what I wanted from our relationship."

"But you didn't communicate why you didn't want to be a part of this bigger world she was a part of."

"It's social media."

"It's her job." I defend.

"And what about my job? She expected me to move away from a place that I love, from a place that I worked, to follow her to her second home in London. Did she tell you that?" He asks, but I don't miss the heat in his tone.

"Hey, I'm on your side. She wasn't too nice to me last night, so I don't have a reason to defend her. But you're also here telling me how upset you are, and I don't know, Santi. What are we doing here? Why are you even telling me this?"

"I don't know, because I'm going through some sort of fucking crisis, or because you brought up what she said. Maybe it's because she never said a fucking thing after leaving. And damn it, Sylvie, you're easy to fucking talk to, and I haven't even spoken to Javi about this, my best friend." The admittance hangs in the air, and my throat tightens at the revelation.

"I'm sure Carolina must have felt some type of reassurance around you to admit her feelings and her faults, too."

It's obvious that Santi isn't looking for advice but rather for a way to express his emotions. He doesn't want me to sit here and fix what's been broken; he wants me to listen and validate him.

"I'm sorry, I always feel the need to figure things out. But sometimes situations like these don't need a resolution, but rather support. And I'm here, Santi, to support. I don't know what went on between you and Carol. You can both tell me what went wrong in your eyes, but the truth is, it wouldn't matter because I wasn't there. But one thing I have some words of wisdom on is that relationships are always complicated, and trust me, I've been in a couple of them. But fights with the person you're meant to be with should never be enough to allow you to let them go. I've let them all go, and sure, I'd try to tell them to stay, but I never *actually* tried. I kind of knew what the outcome would always be, and I was okay with it."

Santi nods as I speak, letting me know he's appreciating every word, and I'm grateful for that because I hate talking about how much I sucked at my last relationships, but mostly because I hate to admit I wasn't the best partner either.

"So, what I'm trying to get at is that if you really wanted to be with Carol. You wouldn't have let her leave Ireland." Santi's lips curl up at the reference to the movie we watched earlier today. It takes him a moment before he finally gets up off the bench and extends his hand out to me.

"Ice cream?" I ask, actually excited for the change of subject and mood.

"And puzzle." I take his hand and let him lead me out of the park and towards the busy street of Madrid again. I wasn't sure how I felt about holding hands, but my body tightened its hold on his fingers before I could even think about letting go.

I guess this was the least amount of contact I could allow myself. And if Santi offered his hand, it's because I think contact is what would help him right now.

"You deserve someone like that, too, you know." He mumbles the words so low that I almost don't catch what he says.

"Deserve what?"

"You, Sylvie, deserve someone who won't let you leave Ireland."

I give him a tight-lipped smile and tighten my grip on his hand nervously, because as he said those words, a thought slithered its way through a crack in my subconscious. And it made my chest tighten just to think how much I wished he'd said that he didn't want me to leave Madrid.

Day 5

CHAPTER THIRTY-ONE
Santi

"WHATEVER YOU DO, don't answer her back," Luisa mutters, stopping at the crosswalk for a car to pass us by. I was sure that her kindness wasn't truly based on wanting the car to go first, but rather that she just wanted to take her time before heading into work.

"I'm not going to respond to her, I have nothing to say."

Carol messaged me an apology last night and said she wanted to talk. But I didn't pay her any mind. I couldn't, when just a room away, there was Sylvie, who had taken a day out of her trip to distract me from my thoughts and problems.

"Interesting." Luisa sings.

"What's interesting?"

"Santi, how are things with you and the Americana you left sleeping on your bed last night?" she asks.

I tighten my jaw and roll my eyes at her little assumption between Sylvie and me.

"Being that she's asleep in Javi's bed and not my own, I'd say that things are the same as they were." The words left my lips as if they were true.

I mean, sure, there was some truth to it. Sylvie was still bothersome, like with that damn puzzle of hers that she was too tired to continue to try and put together last night, but ended up shoving to the corner of my kitchen table for us to complete later on. And I was not as angry as I had once been with the world, but still brooding over the bubbly morning bird I was stuck with for seven days.

And somehow along the way, I began to wonder if I was still brooding over the fact that I had to share a space with her, or rather that she'll be gone soon enough, leaving me in the apartment all alone.

"You guys did it on Javi's bed? That's kind of gross. I'm going to tell him that the next time I see him." Luisa makes a fake gag sound, and I shove her lightly.

"I'm serious, Luisa, there's nothing there."

Actually, there was so much there between us. In just a few days, Sylvie managed to cling to my brain, and now the only thing my mind does is think of her every single second that she isn't with me. Fuck she was even in my dreams every night now.

"I think what you mean is that both of you are too scared to try to pursue anything."

"She deserves more than just a one-time thing, and I also know that if she gets with anyone, her ultimate goal is to end up with them." Sylvie had made it clear that she was trying to focus on herself and not jump into any sort of relationship.

"I agree, but I think that you like her more than you let on. And I also think that this is the most I've ever seen you have some color and emotion in your life again. God, you were just a walking gloomy figure before."

"Are you saying that I was a ghost?" I ask.

"You might as well have been dead with the way you were walking around like nothing in life was worth it."

I don't respond to Luisa, mostly because I know she was somewhat correct. But also because I wasn't sure I was ready to admit that to her.

"I just think that she brought some color back into your life, and I think a person like that is worth keeping around. Whether it's romantic or not."

I give Luisa a nod to let her know I'm listening, but I don't mutter a single word because I don't really know what to say. Luisa is right to some degree. Sylvie has that thing about her that makes a gray-and-white world turn technicolor. So, yeah, she probably did bring some color back into my life, but there's no good reason as to why we would develop anything between us, especially when it wouldn't lead anywhere.

Even if we were just friends, there would still be a large body of water and a time difference that would stop us from talking. And it's not like I was any good at maintaining the friendships that I already had, given that they lived in the same city as me.

"I have more than enough friends, but she will definitely be a good part of my story when I tell my future children."

Luisa scoffs and begins to drag her feet as we get closer to the museum.

"Come back and make working bearable, please." Luisa sighs and brings her head against my chest and groans aloud. I'm sure the passerby's think she's going through a mental breakdown, but really, she was just clocking in to work with people she could barely stand.

"I only have a couple of days left, you'll make it," I assure.

"You don't understand. Diego has been trying to speak to me all week. And if I have to hear about his centipede collection again, I think I'll slam his head against one of the paintings." Luisa takes a step back and looks over at the entrance of the museum as if it's her impending doom.

"Where does he even get all of his centipedes from?" I ask.

"A lot of them are mainly online or from other arthropod hobbyists."

"Arthropod hobbyists?"

Luisa shrugs and waves my question off, as if she's unsure of it herself.

"I don't know, that's what Diego said. They're just people who like to collect creepy crawlers as pets. And listen, I get it, I have a pet gecko, which isn't seen as the most normal pet to have. But, all I'm saying is that they freak me out and I'd prefer not to have to talk about it."

Her discomfort around bugs was rational, but now I found it concerning that she had a pet gecko, which, as far as I knew, ate bugs.

"I get it, but now I'm wondering how you feed Leo."

Luisa gives me a cheerful smile and chuckles, "Clara takes one for the team, all for our little Leo."

"Of course she does, she makes sure that you're spoiled."

"Hey, I feed him his occasional hornworm from time to time."

I look at her in disbelief and know she definitely doesn't feed that gecko; she only has it because Clara wanted one.

"Why did you let her buy a gecko, if you knew you wouldn't like knowing that you would have to feed him live bugs?"

I'm not sure I would've agreed to bring anything into the apartment that involved maintenance. Not even for Carolina at the time or for Javi now.

"We share a home, and I want her to be happy in life. If Leo does that, then I can live with the occasional cricket escaping his enclosure as we try to feed him. They also don't freak me out as much as Diego's centipedes." Luisa utters the words with a grimace and shivers, most likely at the thoughts of Diego's centipedes.

"Don't act like you wouldn't buy a dog for that American girl who's in your apartment. You were practically drooling over her while she was looking at paintings in here." Luisa scoffs, looking down at her watch, probably trying to see how much time she still has to grill me about Sylvie before heading into work.

"I wouldn't because she isn't staying here permanently," I state matter-of-factly.

"Interesting response, so if she had said she would stay, you would have gotten her a dog." Luisa's eyes brighten as she says those words, and I know she wants me to admit that I have some sort of feelings for Sylvie, but there's no point in doing that.

"Luisa, let it go."

That's all I mutter before giving her a hug goodbye and heading back towards my apartment, where Sylvie will probably be up by now and ready to head out.

I hated being brusque with Luisa, especially when she only meant well. But she was pushing on boundaries that I wasn't okay with. For fuck's sake, it was Sylvie's fifth day here; after this, she had two more days to go, and then she'd be gone. There was no reason to think about a hypothetical world where we would ever be more than just people who happened to cross each other's paths in life. I learned a lot about myself and my relationship with Carol through Sylvie, and maybe that's why she was put in my path.

She wasn't meant to be anything more than a woman I happened to meet in life that taught me a lesson I would cherish, and maybe I was the same for her. I practically jog back home and take out my keys to unlock the building's door, but come to find it completely open. This wasn't anything to worry about; usually, the older women in the building leave the door open for whatever reasons. Sometimes it's just someone coming in and out with groceries.

I make my way up the stairs and towards my apartment door, where I hear murmuring and movement from the other side.

Maybe Sylvie was on the phone with her sister.

No, that couldn't be it because her sister would probably be sleeping by now.

Had Javi come back home?

The mental image of Javi walking into his room where Sylvie was spread out on his sheets in a deep sleep created a fury within me that tightened right in the center of my fucking chest.

I turn the knob, expecting it to be unlocked, but I was proven wrong when it doesn't budge.

I enter my key and unlock the door, ready to march over to Javi.

But the minute I open the door, I spot Sylvie in a pair of sweats and a tank top, her hair tied up in a ponytail, but she has enough hair where it still trails down her back. She giggles at something, and her cheeks seem rosy from all the laughing she's doing.

It's quite adorable; she types something on her phone, and it begins translating whatever she types into Spanish. And it's not until I hear the words "Santi had the cutest cheeks" in Spanish that I look over to her left and realize that Sylvie is talking to my mom.

CHAPTER THIRTY-TWO
Sylvie

MY PARENTS HAD ALWAYS SAID I was good at feigning sleep, and I would have to agree. As a child, it granted me a free pick-up ride from the car, straight into my bedroom. And as I got older, it was easy to pretend to be asleep early in the night to then sneak out through my bedroom window. Though that came to bite me in the ass when I struggled to get back up onto the second floor and reach my window.

And as an adult, it also helped me get out of uncomfortable conversations that I wasn't yet ready to have with my partners. And I know it's childish, but if I hadn't pretended I was asleep, I wouldn't have overheard Santi talking to Luisa on the phone and letting her know that he would walk her to work today. I also wouldn't have noticed the way that this man opened Javi's bedroom door and walked over to my bed to see if I was okay, only to then cover me with a blanket and bring my hair behind my ear before leaving.

Fuck.

Why would he do that?

He likes you, Sylvie, that's fucking why.

And damn it, I liked him. He was an actual good man under that hard exterior, and that pissed me off even more.

My phone buzzes, and I stretch out from the warmth of the blanket that I'm spread under to look at the email that's come through. A simple reminder that in three days, the cheap flight I had found from Madrid to Paris would be ready for me.

And you'd think that a girl who's dreamed of traveling Europe would be excited for her next adventure in the city of love. But instead, a ball of dread sinks deep into my stomach.

Maybe it's just the thought of having to fly in general that's making me feel this way.

Yes, Sylvie. Maybe the thought of having to fly for two hours to a neighboring country after having travelled across the fucking Atlantic Ocean is causing you to feel anxious.

Maybe this unease was caused by the feeling of time passing by so fast, and that soon I'll be back in my cubicle working through codes and thinking about what Lean Cuisine I want to remove from the freezer when I get home.

But, I had plenty to see before I would be stuck in the city overworking myself for a company that didn't see me as someone that they could promote for whatever reason.

Fuck, I knew what this ball of dread was about, and it had everything to do with the reason I was cuddled up against the knitted blanket that was spread on top of me.

I shouldn't have fucking kissed him, and as much as I want to blame it on the shots of tequila, they had no fault for my decision to press my lips against his that night.

And now, what did I expect from this?

And knowing Santi's feelings about whatever is between us didn't help my thoughts either. He wanted me just as much as I wanted him.

Why couldn't he continue being a total ass?

I place my phone back on the nightstand and finally pull the blanket off from on top of me. It was better if I just started my day alone rather than waiting for him to join me. He probably had other things to do anyway.

I walk out of my bedroom and wave a good morning to the woman in the kitchen before stepping into the bathroom.

Wait, woman in the kitchen?

I swing my body back and scream at the middle-aged woman who's made herself at home in Santi's home.

Oh my god, who is this?

She stares at me in disbelief and continues to clean the counter as if she's been here before.

Did Santi have a cleaning lady or something?

And if he did, why hadn't he mentioned that she would be here today?

"Hola, soy Sylvie."[*] I say.

The woman peers up at me and smiles. There was something similar about her, but I couldn't quite put my finger on it.

"Eres la novia de Javi?"[†] She asks, setting the damp rag on the kitchen counter and walking around it to meet me.

"Javi?" I ask.

Did she mean Santi?

"La habitación de la que acabas de salir es de Javi, a menos que se haya mudado y mi hijo simplemente haya decidido no decirme nada."[‡] As she says the words, I realize this is definitely not the cleaning lady, and she realizes that I do not belong here.

And there was obviously a language barrier here. Fuck, how did I tell her that I lived here temporarily? Or maybe I should just tell her that I am Santi's friend? She obviously knew Javi, so she had to know Santi as well.

I think about the translation of the words a couple of times in my head before finally spitting out: "Yo amiga de Santi."[§]

---

[*] "Hello, I'm Sylvie."
[†] "Are you Javi's girlfriend?"
[‡] "The room you just came out of belongs to Javi, unless he's moved out and my son just decided not to tell me."
[§] "Me friend of Santi."

Which I'm sure isn't exactly correct, but she can probably get the picture.

"Tú eres amiga de Santi? No, es que esto no tiene ningún sentido. ¿Cómo es que Santi nunca mencionó que se quedaba una amiga? Y de dónde eres?"* Now the woman looks more annoyed than concerned.

Okay, think Sylvie, think.

How can I communicate with her?

My mind goes back to the phone I left on the nightstand, and I raise my finger up at the woman who's continuing to speak to me in Spanish and tell her to give me a moment. I walk into Javi's room and grab my phone, opening it to the translation app.

"Hi, my name is Sylvie, I'm from America. I'm currently staying here for a couple of days because Javi rented his room out to me. But I didn't know that I would be sharing an apartment. So, now I'm here because Santi has allowed me to stay the remainder of my trip." I ramble out the words before the woman has time to call the police on me, and bring it closer to her as the words start appearing on the screen and Siri begins voicing them aloud.

I give her the phone, and she speaks something into it, and I listen as Siri translates the words aloud for me.

"Javier is an idiot." I laugh at her response and listen for the next translation.

"I'm Santi's mom. I don't usually stop by so abruptly, but I had a Doctor's appointment in the neighborhood and thought I'd stop by. He would know that if he answered the phone once in a while."

Santi's mom, this woman was Santi's mother.

This made so much sense now. Of course, she looked familiar; she looked like Santi. Or rather, Santi looked like her.

"Where is my son anyway?" She asks.

I grab the phone, speak into it, and let her know he should be back soon and that he stepped out to walk Luisa to work.

That was probably more than I should've said because that

---

* "Are you friends with Santi? No, this doesn't make any sense. How come Santi never mentioned that a friend was staying over? And where are you from?"

wasn't a detail I was supposed to know anyway, since I was too busy pretending to sleep.

"Do you want a coffee?" She asks, as if she were the one inviting me into her home.

"I feel like that's something I should be asking you." I chuckle and follow her into the kitchen. I reach for the coffee pot, and she slaps my hand and points over to the kitchen chair for me to sit.

No translation is needed for that. I understood my place very well.

I sit at the table and consider sending Santi a text to let him know his mom is here. But I'm sure that he will be back soon anyway, so I decide against it. Santi's mother gives me a brief smile, finishes up the coffee, brings it over to the table, and takes a seat across from me.

This was the most awkward meet-the-parents interaction that I've ever experienced, and I wasn't even dating the guy.

"What's your name again?" Santi's mom asks again.

"Sylvie and yours?" I ask.

"Lourdes."

No more than fifteen minutes have passed before I see a figure standing in the doorway as Lourdes continues to show off pictures of Santi as a baby.

"Mamá?" Santi shrugs off his thin jacket and hangs it up by the door. It must've been a little chilly this summer morning for him to have gone out with the zip-up.

And for him to have covered you with that blanket this morning.

I let Santi speak to his mom alone as she gets up to hug him. It's not like I could understand a single word they were saying. I focus my eyes back on the pictures of little Santi and a young Lourdes. Marlene and I had only a handful of baby pictures because mom and dad had lost some during their multiple moves across the states. And at one of our semi-permanent homes, the basement ended up flooding, taking away many of our childhood memories that were scattered across the floor rather than in protected boxes.

It's hard to decipher from my memories whether that was when we were living in Florida or Pennsylvania. My parents, unlike what I learned from Santi, had moved around a lot for my dad's job. But I also think my parents liked the nomadic lifestyle of picking up and moving on to a new adventure. And though it may seem like fun now, when you're growing up and trying to establish a friendship, it fucking sucks. Which is why Marlene was really the only friend I had. Also explains a lot as to why I have no boundaries.

From what I know about Lourdes, Santi has grown up his whole life outside of Madrid. His father passed away a few years back, with who he seemed to be pretty close to. He gets along with his mom but barely calls nowadays (his mother's words, not mine), and he's had the same best friend since he was a kid, Javi.

"Sylvie, why didn't you tell me my mom was here?" Santi asks, pulling me away from my thoughts.

"Oh, I didn't want to bother. Besides, I was having fun learning about every single detail of your childhood. How's that mole on your ass, by the way?" I try my best to keep a straight face as I ask the question, but let a giggle slip when I see a pink hue rise to his cheeks and his eyes darken in annoyance.

"I see my mom has kept you entertained with the stories of my childhood." He says through gritted teeth.

I smile and rise from my seat, excusing myself so I can head into my room and get ready for the day. I wasn't sure what I would do today, but that's because I was kind of going by Santi's itinerary.

I rummage through my clothes and pick out a nice outfit for the day. I set everything on the bed and grab a towel to head into the bathroom to shower when a knock makes me look up.

"Come in."

Santi steps into my bedroom, and he looks almost relieved to be in here rather than in the living room.

"Why didn't you tell me my mother was here?" He whispers, as if his mother would understand English.

"I don't know, I knew you would be right back." I shrug.

"You knew because you were awake." His lips rise into a grin, and he knows he's caught me.

"I see your mom was quick to tell you everything."

"My mother is Spanish. By the time she sets foot outside of this building, the whole country will know that I've allowed an American woman to room with me." Santi walks over to my bed and takes a seat on the mattress, right in front of me.

The sudden urge to walk right in between his legs is dangerous, but so fucking tempting.

No, Sylvie, behave.

"Is she upset that I'm here?" I ask, and Santi looks at me like I'm stupid.

I know he's a grown adult, but some cultures frown upon their kids living together with the opposite sex. I mean, my parents never really gave a crap about anything. But that didn't mean I wanted to disrespect other people's cultures.

"No, because I'm a twenty-eight-year-old man who pays his own bills and has his own life. Would your parents feel some type of way with you rooming with me?" He asks, almost as if trying to prove a point. But the truth is that Santi had never met Fred and Donna, who are unapologetically liberal, and instead of acting like parents, sometimes act like they're Marlene's and my best friends.

"My parents would probably assume we are sleeping together and just encourage me to make sure you're wearing a condom and that I have an IUD placed in."

Santi chuckles and shakes his head in disbelief at my words, but Donna and Fred tend to get that reaction from a lot of people, including their kids.

"Your parents seem fun."

"That's a nice way to say batshit crazy."

Santi leans back on his hands and rolls his eyes. He allows himself a moment to drag his eyes down my body, not that there's much to see, but it doesn't seem to stop him from tightening his grip on the sheets and shifting himself on the bed.

"So, your mom left?" I ask, refocusing his brain onto something else and refocusing mine as well.

"Yes, but she will be back. I hope you don't mind, but she asked to stay and make us something for lunch. I thought maybe you and I could step out for a bit and come back once she's done cooking."

"Wouldn't that be rude?" I ask, taking my bottom lip between my teeth and peeling at the dead skin. I didn't want to come out as being rude right after meeting his mother. Maybe she wanted to join us, or maybe she wanted us to partake in her cooking, too.

Santi stands up from the bed and walks over to me until he's standing as close as he can. His hand rises up to my face, and he cups my cheek. His thumb grazes my bottom lip, demanding that I release it from my teeth's grasp.

And I do.

He doesn't need to say a single thing.

His actions are demanding enough.

And his eyes.

Those *fucking* eyes.

They're staring right into my soul.

"You're making this hard on me, Sylvie." He doesn't have to tell me what *this* is. Because it's the very thing we have been trying our best to ignore since I got here.

"You're the one in my room." I defend, the heat of my breath touches his thumb, and he pauses a moment before sliding it away, dragging my lip down with his movement.

"You're the one in my home." He remarks, my lip still under his hold.

"Tell me to leave," I whisper.

"No." Is all he whispers in return as he lets go of my face and takes a step back. Suddenly, his whole demeanor shifts, and he's guarded again. Back to the Santi I met on the first day.

"Get dressed and then let me know when you're ready."

With that statement, Santi leaves my bedroom, leaving behind a heat I don't think a cold shower could diminish.

CHAPTER THIRTY-THREE

Sylvie

"I HOPE I didn't make a bad impression on your mom." I sigh, taking a sip of my Dunkin coffee. Santi just stares at me with utter curiosity, wondering why I chose Dunkin over any of the cafes around us.

In thought, he's not wrong. It would probably be best if I helped out smaller businesses, especially ones that have helped establish this city, but Santi just doesn't seem to understand the actual claws of fury that Dunkin has inserted into the folds of every American's brain.

I mean, for Christ's sake, America runs on Dunkin.

"Sylvie, she was showing you my naked baby pictures and went straight to the fish market to make us a paella. No sane woman would make a paella out of the blue for a person they don't like." I shrug and look away as we continue down the paved roads.

I try to hold back the grin that comes from knowing that his mom likes me. I'm not sure why that even matters because it's not like I'm anything permanent in Santi's life.

"So, Santi is short for Santiago?" I ask, bringing up the name that escaped his mother's lips here and there as she showed me various pictures of his childhood.

Santi smirks and gives me a nod, as if it were something I should've already known.

"And what about your name?" He asks.

"What about my name?" I mimic back.

Santi rolls his eyes and pushes me lightly with the weight of his body as we walk side by side.

"Is it short for anything?"

"Nah, my parents made it short and quick, quite different from my sister's name, Marlene. She still complains about the name to this day. She used to scream at my parents and swear that she would change it the minute she turned eighteen. The joke was on her because my parents wouldn't give a shit if she did."

Santi looks at me like I'm crazy, but most people do when I show them a glimpse of how my parents are.

"Are you close with your parents?" He asks, and it actually takes me a moment to think.

I mean, I don't talk to them as often as I should, and living states away makes that even harder. But they weren't your typical, everyday, strict parents. Marlene and I spent our childhood jumping from state to state. I think it's because of that reason that both Marlene and I chose to stay in the same city.

"Not as close as I am with Marlene, we barely text or call. I kind of just send them texts here and there." I shrug off the pity look that Santi gives me.

I know it isn't the norm to not have some sort of relationship with your parents. Usually, a relationship like the one I just described carries negative connotations. But we just aren't big on calling or texting often. And my parents would drop everything to come help both Marlene and me.

"What about you? Obviously, you're close to your mom. What about your dad?"

Santi gives me a slow nod and sighs.

"I was, but he passed away a few years ago."

I halt my step and look at him. I reach my hand out to grasp his arm.

"I'm sorry to hear that."

Santi shrugs and waves me off.

"It's been two years already, so I've had more than enough time to come to peace with everything. It was a car accident that killed him. A drunk driver ended up killing both himself and my father. Of course, it wasn't easy losing my dad, but I think it had to have been harder for my mom."

Santi's green eyes peer into my soul, and fuck, he looks so sincere and honest about this tragedy. He doesn't have to tell me his feelings or anything about his past, but he's choosing to share anyway.

"Did he get to meet Carol?"

The question slips out of my lips before I can even think it through. And Santi looks taken aback by the question. Because, of course, the last thing this guy wants after telling me a story about his dead father is to connect it with the woman who left him at the altar.

Why the hell would I even ask such a dumb question?

"He did." That's all Santi says, and I think he's waiting on a follow-up question, but I don't ask anything else. Instead, I sip on my coffee and begin walking with him again.

And for some reason, a painful pinch of a nerve strikes my chest, and it's not something I feel often, but something I'm very familiar with.

And one thing is for sure.

Jealousy has no business making itself known right now.

"Come, I want to bring you to one of my favorite places." Santi grabs my hand, which stops the green-eyed monster from making its way out.

Santi leads me to a storefront with a dark green-covered door and windowpane.

"This right here is my favorite bookstore in Madrid, it's where I buy most of my art history novels." Santi pushes against the door as he turns the knob and nudges his head to the side for me to enter before him.

I walk into the tiny store whose walls are packed with literature. And packed seems to be the right word to use. There doesn't seem to be much structure; rather, books are piled and pressed against one another to make as many fit on one shelf.

"Is this like a book trade of sorts?" I ask, reaching out and grabbing one of the books that looks like it's been here for a long time.

"It is, but it's got some of the best history books around, especially for art history. Which can be really hard to find, but Fermín is great at always finding me new books." Santi looks giddy as he talks about the books that Fermín, who I assume must be the owner, has gotten for him.

"Santi, eres tú?"* A thick raspy voice calls out from what seems to be a back room behind the counter of the register.

"Sí, Fermín, soy yo. Salte de tu cueva, que tienes invitados."†

A surprisingly short man comes out from the back room, years of hair loss noticeable at the top of his head. His round belly touches the wooden counter slightly as he makes his way around it to give Santi one of those manly hugs that come with a good, strong pat on the back, one that I've only ever experienced when choking on a hot dog as a child.

"Y quién me has traído?"‡ Fermín gestures to me with a smile and wide eyes as he looks back at Santi for an answer.

Santi smiles and nods his head towards me.

"Fermín, esta es Sylvie, una amiga de los Estados Unidos. Vino a pasar unos días aquí en Madrid y, por supuesto, no le pude dejar ir de la ciudad sin haber visitado la mejor librería de toda España."§

Fermín lets out a loud chuckle and slaps Santi on the arm. I wasn't so sure what Santi could have said to be so funny. Between

---

* "Santi, is that you?"
† "Yes, Fermín it's me, come out of your cave, you have visitors."
‡ "And who have you brought to me?"
§ "Fermín, this is Sylvie, she's a friend from the United States. She's visiting Madrid for a few days. And of course I couldn't let her leave the city without visiting the best bookstore in all of Spain."

the two of us, I was the comedic one. So I'm guessing it's an inside joke.

"Mucho gusto, Sylvie."[*] Fermín puts out his hand for me. I take it in mine and give him a firm shake.

"It's a pleasure." I give the man the old smile and nod when you have no clue what the fuck they're saying or when it's too awkward to say anything else.

Santi chuckles beside him, then grabs my hand, mumbling something to Fermín again, who only chuckles and says something about the word *'novia'*.

I swear I've heard that word before, but it would take a while for my brain cells to rummage through the files listed as high school Spanish.

"What did he just say?" I ask Santi as he brings me to the art history section.

"Nothing of importance." He shrugs, not letting go of my hand as he peers through the book's titles.

I look at Fermín, who's busy reading a book behind the counter, and take this moment to really look at him. The little hair he does have has a curl pattern that reminds me of the same curls Santi used to sport, from the pictures his mom showed me.

Why he chose to keep his hair in a buzz-cut was wondrous, but to each their own.

His sharp nose and pink-colored cheeks were similar to Santi's, too, in a way that made you almost think that they could be related.

"Santi."

"Yes?" He sighs, releasing my hand and finally picking out a book from the shelf.

"Who is Fermín?" I ask.

"The owner of the bookstore." He answers immediately, as if there's nothing else to it.

"Santi?" I ask again, this time with a tone that would make a child admit their secrets.

---

[*] "It's a pleasure, Sylvie."

"What is it, Sylvie?" He sings back, continuing to peruse through the book in his hand.

"Who is Fermín to *you*?"

Santi snaps the book closed and stares down at me with a heated gaze.

Looks like the grouch is back.

"Why are you so nosy and insistent on getting the answers you want?" He grunts, shoving the book back into its place on the shelf.

I shrug and lean on the bookshelf, my eyes not moving from him for one second.

"Why am I suddenly meeting the family, Santi?" I ask, nudging my head towards Fermín, who I know is definitely listening to our conversation. And even though he can't understand English, he can definitely understand tone and body language.

"You're not." He mutters.

"So your mom just showing up—"

"Was just a coincidence, I promise." Santi runs a hand through his hair, which is slowly growing in, and I can't help but wonder how often he shaves it down, along with his five o'clock shadow that's beginning to show.

"I brought you here because I actually enjoy it. I'm always here to have some time alone. I usually stop in before or after work, but lately I've been exploring the city with you, so I haven't stopped by as often as I used to. Which is why my mom came by, because Fermín mentioned I hadn't been by in a while." Santi admits the words in a whisper, as if Fermín could understand us.

"They just get worried sometimes. I lost my dad, and then I lost my girlfriend. And they just—"

Santi seems to pause on the thought, maybe unsure of which word to use, and instinctually, I grab his hand and say the words for him.

"They're just afraid you'll lose yourself, I get that."

Santi nods slowly and takes a moment to compose himself before clearing his throat.

"He's my uncle." He admits, giving a nod towards Fermín.

"He's my dad's brother, he's kind of the only person I have left that reminds me of him." Santi looks over at his uncle, and I'm sure he's thinking about how similar the man is to his actual father. And how he misses him.

Truthfully, I've come to realize I've never lived a life as raw and tender as Santi. He was a grouch, but that's because he's felt more than I ever have. I can't say that I've felt the heartbreak of a loss of a parent, and I don't think I've ever felt the pain he did when he lost Carol. No wonder he can barely stand me when I'm out here preaching about rainbows and unicorns.

I reach my hand out and gently take his chin and pull his head to face me.

"I'm sure he thinks the same when he looks at you, Santi." I lovingly caressed his cheek, then nudged my head back toward the books. I just wanted to enjoy the quiet of the store, the smell of the books, his comforting presence, and the undeniable feeling of falling for someone I could never have.

CHAPTER THIRTY-FOUR
Sylvie

THE HALLWAY to Santi's apartment smells marvelous, and I could practically do a backflip the minute I realize it's coming from his apartment.

"That smells delicious." I moan, my mouth salivating immediately.

"Better than the tortilla we made?" Santi asks, unlocking the door.

I raise a brow at him and roll my eyes.

"As delicious as that tortilla was, nothing can compare to whatever I'm smelling right now. So, please open the door quickly so I can take a seat and eat that deliciousness."

Santi turns the doorknob and opens it for me to enter.

"Llegasteis a tiempo; ya la paella está lista para servir." *Santi's mom says as she grabs the plates from the cabinet. I make my way over to her, grab the plates, and ask Santi to tell her to take a seat.

---

* "You guys made it on time, the paella is ready to serve."

The least we could do was set the table after she went out to buy all the ingredients and came back to make the paella.

"Santi, tell her it smells delicious and that I cannot wait to try it." Santi looks over at his mom, who's seated at the table, and translates the words to her.

"She says she hopes you like it; it was Dad's favorite of all her meals, but I think it's just because that's the only thing she can actually cook well by the grace of God. But don't tell her I said that." Santi whispers the last things as he hovers over me to help me with the cups.

I shove him to the side with my hip to get him to stop his teasing.

But he only bites his lips to hold his laugh, and his mother looks like she's reprimanding him. I'm not sure what she is saying, but her body tells me she has a hunch that her son just teased her about something.

Santi rolls his eyes and grins as he heads back to the table.

"My mom wants to know if you've ever had it before." He asks, taking a seat beside me and lifting the lid on the pan that holds a colorful dish filled with yellow rice grains, round green peas, and a multitude of seafood. The scent of the warm dish wafts up to my nose, and my mouth begins to water immediately.

"God, this smells amazing." I moan, trying my best to stop myself from salivating.

Santi translates my compliment, and Santi's mother grins as she serves my plate first.

"Funny enough, I've actually never eaten seafood. Just canned tuna and a salmon fillet, I tried at a restaurant before. But it gave me food poisoning, so I've never eaten it again." I admit.

Santi pauses as he lifts his plate up to his mother and looks at me with bewildered eyes.

"What?" He asks.

"What?" I parrot.

"You've only eaten canned tuna and one single salmon fillet?" He asks, as if it's absurd.

But I had met many people who had never eaten anything but chicken and beef.

I shrug and twirl my hair around my finger, waiting for Santi's mom to finish serving herself before taking a bite.

"I was a picky eater as a kid; I barely ate any meat in general until I was ten."

Santi shakes his head in disbelief as if I've just told him something unbelievable, but ultimately shrugs and takes a bite of his meal.

"Buen provecho." * He says, and his mother and I mimic it back.

I bring the rice to my mouth and immediately lean back in my chair to savor the flavors.

"Wow." I take another bite, this time trying the shrimp.

"This is delicious, I could eat this every day of my life," I say to Santi's mother. By now, Santi knows his job as a tour guide has been promoted to my personal translator.

"She's glad you like it, she says she is more than happy to share the recipe."

"I'd love that." I smile and keep digging into my plate.

"My father taught my mother how to cook paella, actually, he taught her the few things she knows how to cook. He was a really good cook." Santi says, and I can tell by the way his eyes light up as he looks at the dish that he's recalling some of his favorite memories with him.

"It's nice to know where you get your cooking skills from," I say, gently giving his arm a squeeze.

Santi and his mom go on to have their own conversation, and I clear my throat as it begins to tingle. There must be some spice I'm not used to, so I just drink some water to rush the discomfort down.

I take another bite, ignoring the itchiness on my throat that's now leading into the inside of my ears. I clear my throat this time and bring my hair up in a bun, suddenly feeling hot.

I take another sip of water, and it's not until Santi's mother peers over at me and gasps that I know something is wrong.

____

* "Enjoy your meal."

Santi turns to face me, and his eyes practically bulge out of his head.

"Sylvie, are you okay?" He asks, bringing my face into his hands and observing my skin.

"I-I don't know, I'm kind of hot, and my throat and ears are itchy." My heart rate begins to pick up, and I'm not sure if it's because of my body's current reaction or if it's because I'm nervous about just how close and worried Santi is.

Santi's mom begins to speak quickly to Santi, but I'm sure that even if she slowed down, I still wouldn't understand her.

"It's an allergic reaction, Sylvie. I think you're allergic to shell-fish." He mutters, taking out his phone immediately and searching up what to do, I assume.

"I'm sure I am fine. I think I have some Benadryl in my bag." I try to get up, but Santi pushes me back into my seat.

"We are going to the hospital." Santi orders.

"Santi, I'm not sure—"

Santi ignores my protest and mutters something to his mom while grabbing hold of my arm.

"Come, we are leaving. I don't know how long this will last. And I don't want it to get any worse. Your face is already swelling up as we speak."

Santi drags me out of the door, with no time to even utter an apology and goodbye to his mother. He practically drags me down the stairs, and I have to slap his hand just for him to let go.

Santi stops and turns around to stare up at me.

"Are you okay? Are you losing your breath? Should I call an ambulance? Is your tongue or throat tingling? Mierda, deberia—"

"Santi, chill, I'm fine for now. You're just dragging me down these stairs, and it's hard to catch up when there's already so much happening. I'm sure a Benadryl could help me just fine." I try to reason and calm him down, and Santi only stares at me with that stoic expression of his.

"We are going to the hospital, the Uber is right outside, let's go."

Santi grabs my hand again and, this time, pulls me gently down the remaining flight of stairs and out the door, where a black Volkswagen sedan is waiting to take us to the hospital.

Santi opens the door for me to slide in and confirms the address with the driver as he settles down in the seat beside me. His hand is now on top of mine, the other one running his fingers through my hair, trying his best to relax me.

Truthfully, I should probably be more afraid of dealing with an allergic reaction. But as long as I can still breathe, that's all that matters and all that I should focus on, even though I can definitely feel my face swelling up by the moment.

"Tell your mom I'm sorry," I say, turning my head to face Santi, whose eyes have been on me the entire time.

"What are you sorry for?" He asks.

I shrug and clear my throat to try to alleviate the itchiness as much as I can.

"I don't know, for ruining lunch."

"Sylvie, you didn't ruin a single thing. How were you supposed to know your body would react like this to seafood when you've never tried it? I'm just glad you're okay and hope that the minute we get to the hospital, they can take you quickly."

"I'm sure we will be fine," I assure him, bringing my hand over to his and giving it a squeeze. I was hoping to get to the hospital soon because I was too scared to tell him that my tongue was starting to tingle, and I was scared that soon I wouldn't be able to breathe.

CHAPTER THIRTY-FIVE
Santi

"ARE YOU A FUCKING IMBECILE?" I shout at the front desk receptionist of the damn hospital emergency room.

"Sir, there is no reason to act out in this way." The woman replies, putting her hand up as if that would stop me from wanting to get them to do their job.

"This is a damn emergency; she is having an allergic reaction and can barely even speak, right now."

"I am aware and am just trying to get all her information in order, sir. Please have a seat. They will be bringing her in shortly." The receptionist sighs, goes back to typing at her computer, then turns to one of the girls behind her and has them check us in quickly.

Thank God that Sylvie was smart enough to get international health insurance while she was traveling, because I was sure that if she had nothing, they'd allow her to fucking die waiting for them.

"Santi." Sylvie croaks from her seat in the waiting room, and I quickly rush over to her to see what she needs.

"What's going on? Are you alright?" I ask, fucking nervous with just the thought of her going into anaphylactic shock.

"Calm down, I am fine. I'm sure they'll take us in soon. We just got here."

How the hell is she so calm when she can barely speak?

"I'm just uncomfortable, not dying."

I sigh and sit beside her. Sylvie lays her head on my shoulder, and I'm sure it's not to make herself comfortable but rather to make sure that I don't get up a third time to harass the front desk.

It takes about five minutes for someone to call out Sylvie's name, and we are taken to a room for proper assistance.

"What brings you two in today?" The male nurse asks, typing away at his computer.

I gesture to Sylvie's condition as if it isn't obvious.

"She's having an allergic reaction, obviously."

What the hell is wrong with these people?

Did I bring Sylvie to an incompetent hospital?

The nurse types my response into his computer and looks over at Sylvie.

"And who are you to her?" He asks, raising a brow in suspicion.

"Her boyfriend." I lie, effortlessly.

The nurse looks between Sylvie and me, as if waiting for her to protest. But the dumbass seems to realize she only speaks English and clears his throat and looks back at his screen to continue the questioning.

"When did it start?" He asks.

"About forty-five minutes ago," I respond, my hand going to the back of Sylvie's head again to massage her scalp.

"Any idea what could've caused it?"

"She tried shellfish for the first time and got an allergic reaction while eating it."

"Do you have any itching or swelling besides your face?" He finally asks Sylvie in English.

"Oh, um, yeah, my throat and ears are incredibly itchy, and my throat is starting to feel a little sore, enough for it to feel like it's closing, but it's been feeling like that for a while, and it hasn't closed, so I'm sure it's nothing." She mumbles shyly and shrugs.

And suddenly I have the urge to shake some sense into this woman.

"It's not nothing, Sylvie. You're having an allergic reaction. Every symptom you're feeling is important to know."

Sylvie rolls her eyes, then looks back at the nurse, who is clicking away on his mouse.

"Okay, I'm just going to take your vitals, and the Doctor will be in shortly to see you."

"You guys don't seem to have the right definition of shortly."

And I don't know how Sylvie knew what I had said, but she definitely got the gist of it because she whipped her head around and sent a death glare my way.

The minute Sylvie is done getting her vitals taken, she takes a seat back on the bed, and the doctor joins us immediately.

"Hello, how are you?" The Doctor asks, and I know Sylvie understands him because she responds with, "I've been better."

The Doctor tries his best with the English he knows, which isn't so bad. He lets us know he'll be injecting an antihistamine through her IV to help with the hives, itching, and swelling. And then they will also administer a corticosteroid to help reduce any airway swelling or prevent it from occurring.

"What do you mean, it can occur again?" I ask.

"Well, sometimes there can be what's called a biphasic allergic reaction. Which is like a second round of allergy symptoms. I'm sure in her case, we have nothing to worry about. And hopefully, if she's doing better within the next four to five hours, she can be released today."

The Doctor seems knowledgeable and calm about the whole situation, so I don't question him further and instead pull up my phone to read more about this biphasic allergic reaction. Just so that I know what to look out for.

The Doctor steps aside as the nurses enter, administering the medication through the IV inserted earlier during her vitals.

"What's got you so preoccupied over there?" Sylvie asks, lying back on the hospital bed.

"I'm just searching up what to expect if you get a second wave of allergy symptoms. I just want to make sure we're prepared." I say.

Sylvie lets out a giggle, and I look up from my phone to see the stunning woman that she is, even with a puffy, red, hive-infested face.

"What's so funny?" I ask.

"You." She taunts, scooting over to leave room on one side and patting it with her hand.

"Come lie with me."

I should say no, but I'm done saying no to the things I want. I stand up, walking over to the bed and lying beside Sylvie, bringing her into my arms.

We sit there for a while in silence with my arms around her body, and her head snuggled into the crook of my neck. It's not until she falls asleep that I hear her whisper a thank you.

And I want to tell her that she never has to thank me for caring for her and for wanting to make sure she's okay. But what would that even matter? Our fifth day had flown by, and we were spending it at the hospital. She only had two days left in Madrid, and then she'd be gone.

Sylvie was only ever meant to be a person I met along the way.

And it fucking sucked that I couldn't keep her as a person I could have forever.

But that seems to be my luck of the draw when it comes to love.

Day 6

CHAPTER THIRTY-SIX

Sylvie

"SYLVIE." Santi's deep voice wakes me from my sleep. I hear him, but I don't open my eyes right away. I'm not sure if it's the drugs or yesterday's chaos that makes me snuggle deeper into the mattress.

I slide my arms under my pillow and rub my cheek against the soft sheets, trying my best to fall back to sleep after the disturbance. But a gentle caress to my cheek stops me.

My eyes flutter open, and I take in Santi's appearance. He's already in his jeans and a dark blue shirt. His brows are furrowed in concern, but the minute they spot my eyes wide open, his lips curve into a grin and relax.

"How are you feeling?" He asks, his hand still following the motion of tucking a strand of hair behind my ear, and I'm sure he hasn't stopped because I find myself leaning into his touch.

"Better, how do I look?" I ask.

"You have some remnants of the hives lingering, but they seem to be fading. I'm not sure if your lips are still swollen or if they wake up that plump in the morning." Santi's thumb grazes the bottom of my lip, and there's a slight pause between us.

The moment isn't awkward, it's just still.

Almost as if a candid was being taken at this very moment, both of us still so as not to disrupt the image.

I clear my throat and raise myself up slightly from the bed, breaking the tension that seems to appear every time we are in a room alone, ever since that night at the rooftop.

"I feel better than yesterday, that's for sure." I shove away the sheets, and Santi's eyes shift down towards my bare thighs. I squeeze my thighs tightly, forgetting that I had completely chosen to wear pajama bottoms that barely covered any of my assets.

I clear my throat and slowly slide off the edge of the bed awkwardly. I'm sure he thinks that the antihistamines that were given to me have affected my brain cells somehow, but the last thing he needs is to see my goods.

"So, what's the plan for today?" I ask, standing opposite him with the mattress in between us.

"Well, I had something planned out for today, well, really it was planned out for yesterday, but my mother decided to take over that day, and then you decided to be dramatic and go into anaphylactic shock." He utters, inclining himself forward and pulling the sheets of my bed up and spreading them across it.

Was he making my bed?

"I-I didn't go into anaphylactic shock. I'm pretty sure I'd still be in the hospital or fucking dead." I snap back.

Santi doesn't seem to be listening, though. He grabs the pillows I stacked on his side of the bedroom and starts placing them on the bed like a neat freak, and for some reason, it's pissing me off.

"Stop that!" I finally growl, slapping his hands away from the pillows he's currently trying to fluff.

"You leave your bed unmade all the time... it bothers me." He admits with a shrug.

"You're such a freak. You've been peeking inside my bedroom?" I cross my arms over my shoulders.

"I can't help it, I usually make Javi's bed every day."

"You mean to tell me you mother your roommate?"

Santi finishes the placement of the pillows before looking up at me with a scowl.

"I don't mother anybody, Javi and I are like a symbiotic relationship."

I chuckle and grab my clothes from the drawers, throwing them on top of the bed as I decide what to wear today.

"Hm, so you play his mommy, and he does what exactly? Play, daddy?"

Santi smirks and grabs the clothes. I plop down on the bed, beginning to fold them like the neat freak he is.

"I usually play both roles, Americana."

Santi says it so nonchalantly, but the tone he uses tells me all I need to know about what he meant.

I shake off the image of calling Santi Daddy while on my knees and grab a pair of jeans, a top, and underwear before making my way to the bathroom.

"I shouldn't take too long," I shout on my way out.

"Good, because we have a train to take."

"Hurry, we are going to miss the train," Santi mutters, dragging me along past the people who are heading the opposite direction. Probably just having left the train, we are currently getting on.

"Where are we even going?" I mutter, trying to keep up with his quick pace.

Santi ignores my question like he has been doing since I got out of the shower. I hope it's not too far because I have to be back in time to pack for tomorrow.

My stomach tightens into a knot as I think about my last day here tomorrow. I had been ignoring the fact that the week was coming to an end, and so would Santi's and my friendship.

I had obviously grown to like the guy, and he also made traveling alone feel… Well, less alone.

I had a companion, and though he was grouchy most of the time, he was also quite fun to hang out with.

There would be no Santi in Paris, Berlin, or Rome.

Probably just a lot of annoying Emilio's.

But I guess he wasn't too bad either.

He just wasn't Santi.

"Alright, here we are." Santi huffs out a breath and pulls us into the train, dragging me along the aisle until we get to our seats.

"Now, can you tell me where we are going?" I ask again, this time trying to catch my breath from all the running.

"We are going to what was once known as Spain's capital, Toledo."

"What's in Toledo?"

"History."

"History that we can't find in Madrid?" I ask. I didn't mind going to Toledo, but it was my last day in Madrid, and I would've liked to see some last-minute places I hadn't gotten to see.

"Toledo has much more history than Madrid; it's known as the city of three cultures. Toledo is a great example of Spain's diversity. For years, the muslim, Christian, and Jewish communities lived together in the city. And we were surrounded by each other's faiths and cultures."

"How come not anymore?" I ask my walking textbook.

"Well, you know, same old, same old. Catholic ruling, who wants to rule amongst other catholics. So, they give people the ultimatum of conversion or death, and well, that's where harmonious living begins to decline." Santi shrugs off the statement like it's a well-known fact of sorts and adjusts himself on his seat to lie comfortably.

He leans his head against the glass window, and I use the moment to take in how much his hair has grown since the beginning of the week; he's even begun to grow a five o'clock shadow.

I didn't think that Santi could get hotter, but it seems I've been proven wrong.

"My dad used to take me here." He says, adjusting his head on the window to look back at me.

"We would go during May because that's when the poppy fields are in full bloom. It's mid June now, so I can't promise you the best of the fields, but I'm sure it's still worth our while."

"I'm sure Toledo will be beautiful," I murmur, lying back in my seat and turning my head to face him.

"If you're there, it will be," Santi says the words without a single hesitation before looking back at the window. And I'm so grateful that he's looking away because it means he can't see the blush that's currently creeping up my cheeks.

Santi, you're going to make it so hard to say goodbye.

CHAPTER THIRTY-SEVEN

Sylvie

"SANTI." I groan after him as he leads the way to some prehistoric mosque that he wants me to see.

Usually, I wouldn't be bothered by all the walking. I mean, we've been on actual runs together.

But Toledo's weather is at a whopping 93 degrees Fahrenheit, and according to my phone, it feels like 96, which, to a curvy body like mine that chafes and sweats in places a human mind couldn't even imagine, means it actually feels like 100 degrees.

"Am I killing you?" He finally stops and moves to the side of the road, leaning against one of the buildings, allowing people to pass by.

I lean right up against the wall and look up at him, and for the first time ever, it's me rolling my eyes at Santi, and that makes him smile like a giddy child.

"It's not you that's killing me, it's this damn sun," I mutter while lifting my hand up to block it.

Santi seems to acknowledge how irritating the heat makes me

and moves away from the wall to stand in front of me instead, blocking the sun from hitting my face.

"I didn't know the weather was going to get this hot; it usually doesn't even get this hot early on in the summer." Santi's voice sounds sweet and very apologetic, which quickly feels like a punch to the gut.

I get the grumpy boy excited about a vacation he's not even on, and in return, I turn into the grumpy one.

"It's alright, I didn't check the weather either. And I didn't exactly dress for it." I murmur, waving down towards my jeans that aren't the best material to have stuck to sweaty thighs.

"My dad would bring us here around Easter every year." Santi looks out the window as he tells his story, and I'm sure he's recalling the memory that brings him here every time.

"Not too far from home."

"Not at all." He chuckles.

"Growing up, we didn't go on many trips. And even though we'd come here every year, I never got sick of it. Because it was something different from our everyday lives." Santi admits, shuffling a little closer to me so a group of teenage kids can pass by.

"I get it," I murmur, making him turn back to face me.

"We traveled a lot because my parents were constantly moving. But we never really went on any sort of family vacations. So, I guess moving to a state that was farther away was our sort of vacation. Marlene and I would always have such a great time on the road trips. We'd guilt our parents into getting us a bunch of snacks and drinks from the rest stops, which they were never privy to because it always ended up with one of us throwing up in the back seat. But there was nothing they could say no to when they were moving us away from our home all over again." I sigh and give a shrug as I recall the many road trips that my family went through. Santi lets out a deep chuckle, breaking me away from the memories.

"And look at you now, traveling around Europe." He says, waving a hand across the air, insinuating all that I have yet to see.

I grab that same hand, push away from the wall, and pull Santi back toward where we were walking.

"And look at you now, reliving a bit of that family vacation with me, the bubbly American woman that turns into a grouch in the heat."

Santi walks beside me, not once pulling away from my hold, and just shrugs.

"I think it's good that I see all of your personalities." He teases, and I stick my tongue out at him.

"I will say, though, grouchy Sylvie is still just as nice to be around as bubbly Sylvie."

"I'm sure she is , Mr. Grumps." I giggle, poking fun at him.

Santi just sighs and looks forward, trying his best to hide that radiant smile I love seeing on him.

Santi ends up showing me not only the mosque, but also the cathedral and the Jewish quarter of Toledo. We spend our day walking to each location, then finding a shady spot to listen to him share historical facts.

He throws in some cute details about the memories he's made with his parents during his visits.

"Would you move here?" I finally ask him, as we sit outside a restaurant that Santi says is one of the best.

"No, I mean I love it, but I also love the city I live in now, I love my job. I love everything about it. I just enjoy the history of Toledo, and I love that I shared it with my dad." Santi leans back in his chair, takes the menu from the waiter, and asks for two bottles of water, which I'm very grateful for.

That was the thing about Santi, unlike me, he grew up calling a place home, and to tear someone away from that would be unfair. And I think that deep down Carol knew that too, which is why she had to go. Not because she didn't love Santi enough, but because she saw that he already called a place home, and she couldn't see that as her own home.

"I have to say, you coming to Madrid was something I needed." He admits, opening up the bottle of water and taking a sip.

I perk up in my seat and lean forward, placing my head on my hands and batting my lashes at him.

"Please, Santi, tell me more." I tease, and Santi chuckles and shakes his head at my teasing, but I know he's enjoying my playfulness.

"I think that I was stuck. I mean, I was planning to use my honeymoon week to just mope around my apartment and think about all the things I got wrong. But you came in and showed me how beautiful life still is and how right life is. I guess you can say your personality rubbed off a little bit."

I lean back in my chair, and I can't help but pout at his words.

"Don't cry." He sighs.

"I'm not going to cry." I clear my throat and take a sip of the water that the waiter had brought out to us, and look down at my menu that I can't even read in order to distract myself from Santi's cute speech.

"You definitely were."

Of course, he has to argue with me.

"Was not." I bite back, looking back up to catch him smiling at me.

"Were too, but that's okay. My grumpiness tends to bring a smile back on your face." He says with a pointed look.

I roll my eyes and look back at the menu, trying my best to hide the smile that would prove him right.

CHAPTER THIRTY-EIGHT
Santi

"**ARE** you sure we will make it in time to catch our train if we go see the field of poppies?" Sylvie asks, looking at the directions between the field of poppies and the train station.

"Sylvie, we will be just fine," I say, covering her phone with my hand so she stops staring down at it.

We had spent the day around Toledo, and just as we were catching a bite to eat before heading out back to Madrid, I remembered the poppy fields I wanted her to see.

Sylvie had said it wasn't important, but I knew it'd be something she'd appreciate.

"Why do you think that everyone loves a field of poppies so much?" She asks.

Knowing Sylvie, she was probably just trying to kill some time rather than actually being curious.

Or maybe it was just both.

"I'm not sure, it has a lot of historical connections. It could be due to its connection to World War I , the reference to them in poems or any sort of literature, and how often they've been portrayed in artwork by some of the most famous painters like Van Gogh, Monet, and Frida Kahlo."

I look back at Sylvie, whose brows are now furrowed.

"Of course you'd have an actual answer to that question." She giggles.

"You asked," I say as I nudge her slightly with my shoulder.

Sylvie's body moves to the side slightly, but it falls next to mine every so slightly, and she lets her head fall on my shoulder, and I move in closer for her to use me as she pleases.

"What's the plan for Paris?" I ask, even though I'm not sure if I even want to know.

The thought of Sylvie being anywhere but in Madrid makes a knot form in my chest, and I absolutely hate the feeling.

"Hm, I mean, what's there not to do in Paris? I want to see the Mona Lisa and the Eiffel Tower."

"A good reason to visit Paris."

Sylvie hums and watches the road ahead as the Uber driver approaches our destination.

"I'm super excited about this private tour that this Parisian man is taking me on under the catacombs of Paris. He's actually having me meet him in the middle of some street that has a secret entrance."

"You what?" I growl, shrugging my shoulder for her to lift herself up and look at me.

"You better be joking, Sylvie." Sylvie looks up and furrows her brows in concern as if trying to figure out what she said that was so wrong.

"No, his name is Pierre. He says I'll get the whole experience going in through that entrance anyway." She says it so nonchalantly that she must be telling the truth, and that pisses me off.

"Sylvie, you cannot meet up with strangers like this. And you should not be going into the catacombs alone with random people. I'd rather you not go down there at all, but if you must, it better be through the main entrance with actual tour guides." I'm practically fuming, and I'm tempted to ask her to give me her phone so I can message this guy to see what his intentions are.

"Calm down, of course I'm joking with you." She giggles in her seat, and I'm tempted to push her out of this car.

Instead, I let out a sigh of relief and lay my body back against the seat as Sylvie struggles to compose herself.

"Sylvie, that was not funny in the slightest," I growl.

"Yes, it was. I love seeing you all broody." She continues to say between giggles.

"I don't appreciate it."

"Don't worry, I'm sure you'll miss my teasing after I leave." She scoots a little closer this time and rests her head back onto my shoulder.

And I don't say anything, but I know damn well she's right.

It takes the Uber driver just a few minutes to drop us off at the main entrance of the field. Sylvie gets out and thanks the driver, and I follow her, sharing the same gratitude.

"Give me your phone," I say as we walk into the field.

"Why?" She asks, but pulls out her phone anyway and hands it to me.

"Don't you want your picture taken?" I ask.

"You're right." She shrugs and walks alongside me, walking towards the field of poppies you can see in the distance, thanks to their bright red color.

"Did you come here often with your mom and dad, too?" She asks.

"Yeah, my mom really liked it, and dad liked watching her like them."

Sylvie smiles and looks over at me. The sun is setting, so it lands on her just right, radiating a warm glow around her.

"And what about you? What do you like most about the poppies?" She asks.

I ponder on my answer just a bit before going with the truth.

"I think I'm about to find out."

Sylvie looks perplexed by my response, but turns her head away slowly to look back at the field of poppies before us. But I don't miss the way she tries to hide her blush with her hair.

"Go ahead and run through it. I'll take your picture." I encourage.

"Don't you want your picture taken?" She asks.

"I'll get it." I nod her over to the field, and Sylvie jumps excitedly into it. I open up the camera app on her phone and take a couple of pictures, some candid and some posed.

In both, she looks beautiful. The sun is setting behind her, so I try my best to toggle with the contrast and lighting so she doesn't come out as a silhouette.

"Come here with me." She shouts, and I walk through the field and make my way over to her, plucking a flower from its stem, and the minute I reach her, I place it right behind her ear.

"One last picture," I state, and I take my own phone out and snap some images up close, at the angle I am in, and I can even see the freckles that have appeared thanks to the sun today.

Sylvie gets a bit silly with the pics and gets up close to the camera, giving me all sorts of faces I wasn't even sure a person's face could contort into. But nonetheless, it's very her, and that's exactly what I want.

"Hand me your phone, I'll take some pictures for you." She says, showing me her palm to hand it over.

Instead, I fish her phone from my pocket and hand it over.

"I already did," I say, putting my own phone back into my pocket.

The corner of her brow lifts a bit as she puts the puzzle together. Sylvie opens her mouth to respond, but a crashing sound jolts her over to me.

We both look up and watch the clouds grow closer and darker, letting us know the day's sun is setting and a storm is coming.

"We should probably get going; it's going to start raining." Sylvie pouts, and I bring my phone out immediately, ordering us another Uber before we get caught in this rain.

"Santi."

I look over at Sylvie, who stands patiently beside me as we wait for the car to arrive.

"Yes?" I ask.

"Thank you." She says, and I'm not entirely sure how I should even respond to that.

"For everything." She adds, looking at the car getting closer to us.

I nod and open the car door for her, not entirely sure how to tell her that it's me who should be thanking her for everything she's done.

CHAPTER THIRTY-NINE
Sylvie

"WHAT'S TAKING SO LONG?" I ask the Uber driver as he stops once again due to the upcoming traffic. I know I'm being an asshole, but Sylvie's already anxious about missing this damn train back to the city. And I'm afraid to let her know that she might just be right.

"There's traffic." The driver says, his snarky tone not going unheard.

"Yeah, I know there's traffic, why?" I ask.

Obviously, this man has no idea why there would be traffic at this very moment, but damn it, I'm pissed off by the whole situation.

"Santi, relax. Give the man a break. You would not last long in Chicago traffic. We will get there on time, Santi." Sylvie pulls me back to my seat, and I begrudgingly let her.

I look down at my phone's time and see we have exactly 30 minutes to get on the last train of the day; if not, we are shit out of luck. I check if there are any Ubers available from the train station, and zero drivers pop up.

"Oh great."

"What is it?" Sylvie asks, craning her neck over to take a look.

"What are you so worried about? We'll just take the next train, or maybe even a bus if we have to."

I nod and relax, trying not to worry about it. We aren't even too far from the train station. We might be able to make it.

"No bus." The driver says, his eyes finding mine in the rear view mirror.

"What do you mean, no bus?" I ask.

"Flood warnings, there's no bus driving out to Madrid tonight. Maybe in the morning." He sighs, braking once again as the traffic continues to pile up.

Great.

We get to the train station with five minutes to spare. Sylvie and I run as fast as we can, trying not to slip on the station floor because of our wet shoes.

"I don't understand. It was hot all damn day, and then we suddenly got a storm out of nowhere." Sylvie mutters out of breath. We run towards the train doors when suddenly I hear a smack behind me, and Sylvie's on the fucking floor.

Damn it.

I run back over to her as she lies spattered on the floor.

"Sylvie, crap, are you alright?" I ask, helping her get back up.

"I did not bring the right shoes to run through the wet floors of this station." She answers, still winded from her fall.

"Fuck Sylvie, I'm so sorry."

"It's alright. At least we made it." She mutters.

And just as she says those words, the doors to the train close behind, and it's too late now to do anything but curse at our damn luck as the train pulls out of the station for the last time tonight.

"Damn it," Sylvie mutters next to me, and this time, my bubbly American is annoyed.

I'm not sure what's up with me, but I immediately console her. I grab Sylvie's face and force her to look up at me, her eyes brimming with tears. Probably from the stress and the fall.

"Hey, it's okay, your flight isn't until tomorrow night. We can find a place to sleep tonight, and then we can head out to Madrid tomorrow morning." Sylvie sniffles and nods her head in agreement, and I take her hand in mine as we walk back to the entrance of the station.

I pull out my phone and try my best to find an Uber that's willing to take us back to any hotel. But I am currently met with zero drivers.

"No luck with any drivers. Let's just find the nearest hotel, walk over, and hope they have a room for us tonight."

Sylvie doesn't say much; instead, she just gives me a nod, and we do just that. But instead of running, we speed walk over to the hotel, trying our best to seek cover from the rain when we can.

Sylvie and I rush into the hotel's lobby and let out a huff of air the minute we enter. I can't help but take a look at the wet fabric of her shirt as water rides down from her hair down to her luscious breasts.

And the way the rain has helped her jeans shape up against her curves should be illegal.

She looked absolutely gorgeous, even caught in the rain.

"Santi?"

Fuck, she was mesmerizing, and I probably looked like a fucking mess.

"Santi."

But still, I can't help but think what if she let me lick those droplets of water away from her creamy skin.

"Santi!" My eyes snap up to her, and she nudges her head over to the concierge who's staring over at us.

I clear my throat and walk over to the man who's obviously disturbed by our wet presence in the lobby of the hotel.

"Hi, I'm sorry for the late booking, but we've missed our train home and need a room for the night," I say.

The man types away at the computer, looks back up at me, then at Sylvie.

"Two or one bed?" He asks.

"Two," I reply, even though I'd damn well wish it could be one.

He hums and continues typing on his computer before looking back over to us.

"No two, just one bed available." He says.

"So then what was the point in asking me for a preference?" I ask, the annoyance in my tone completely noticeable.

"Sir—"

"I'm sorry, we are just so tired. But yes, the one bed is completely fine."

"Sylvie." I protest, but she moves a hand up to shush me instead.

"Anything will do for now, and it's just for one night."

The concierge nods and types away at the computer before asking for one of our IDs and a credit card. And no way in hell was I going to make Sylvie pay for any of this, so I handed the guy everything he needed.

It doesn't take too long for him to set everything up and give us the pass to our room. Sylvie and I thank him and move towards the elevator doors.

"You didn't have to sound so upset about having to share a bed, you know. I've been told by many that I am a fantastic bed partner." Sylvie moves her hair away from the front of her face and moves it towards the back, wiping away at any of the droplets still running down her chest.

God, this is torture.

"I don't doubt that you are." I manage to say, trying my best to keep my eyes focused on anything but her tits.

The elevator brings us up to our floor, and the minute the doors open, a tension seems to build up between us as I take the lead to the hotel room with Sylvie following right behind me.

"Then how come you were so insistent on the two beds?" She challenges as I hover the card over the reader, unlocking the door.

"Sylvie, I thought you wanted to be friends."

"Yes, and friends can share a bed for the night." She argues, obviously not seeing how different things are for me.

"Not friends like us." I sigh, dropping my wallet and keys on the desk of the hotel.

"What's that supposed to mean?" She bites back.

"Sylvie, be serious, you know how I feel about you," I utter the words like some sort of revelation that I need her to understand.

Sylvie looks at me with a puzzled look and nods.

"Sorry, you're right. I didn't think that it would bother you this much. I was just tired and wanted to be in bed by this point. I didn't really think things through." Sylvie removes her bag and leaves it on top of the desk and I take in every little detail of this woman, knowing this is our final night together.

Tomorrow she'll be gone.

"It's alright." I manage to say, and her brown eyes meet mine; the silence between us is not awkward but rather calming. And the tension grows as we take each other in.

"Tomorrow is goodbye." I manage to whisper.

"Tomorrow is goodbye." She parrots back, a grin spreading on her face, but never meeting her eyes,

My feet find themselves inching closer with every step until I'm hovering over her, and Sylvie doesn't make a move to push me back or move away.

Instead, her eyes continue to meet mine, and I know she's thinking everything through.

I know she's evaluating if this is worth it.

But the way her chest rises with each breath and the way her tongue grazes her lip, I can't help but utter those two little words in my mind that will change everything.

Fuck it.

CHAPTER FOURTY
Santi

I SHOULDN'T DO THIS, I really shouldn't do this.

Santi's lips hover over my own as our bodies remain dripping from the outside's weather, and the neat freak that he is doesn't seem to even care. His eyes continue to stare down at my lips, and I know what he's waiting for.

Something that I've come to learn about Santi is that he's a true gentleman. Even when he's upset about having to do something like save me from a wild peacock and row a boat, he doesn't even want to be on, so that I don't have to, he comes to a party late at night so that I don't go alone. Damn it, he even makes my bed in the morning for me.

So, this man won't make the first move; he's not willing to cross the line that I've drawn between us.

But fuck me if I'm not already gliding my foot across that imaginary line.

"Sylvie." He whispers, his hands gliding up my back, not yet tightening his hold, still awaiting my response.

"I'm leaving," I explain as if it weren't already obvious.

"I know."

"It's a one-time thing."

"And forever a memory to reminisce."

And just like that, the contract with the terms and conditions of accepting a brutal heartbreak is signed. My lips collide with Santi's, and his hands lower to my ass, bringing me closer.

We kiss feverishly, like long-time lovers who have been waiting forever to consummate their unwanted love. This moment feels yearnful, forbidden, and beautiful.

Beautiful.

I pull away from our kiss and look at Santi, his eyes scattered across my face, like he's trying to make sure he remembers every single detail. As if he'll recall this memory and have it instilled in his mind like a Polaroid hung up on a teenage girl's bulletin board.

"Make sure not to forget my mustache when you draw me, it took me a while to grow it out." I chuckle, not used to having someone's eyes on me the way he does. But, I guess I was doing the very same, just taking in every piece of him.

I wanted to remember the stubble that was slowly growing on his face, the buzz-cut that had started growing out enough for one to notice the hair growth, but not enough for his curl pattern to make its presence known. The freckles that had begun appearing on his nose were thanks to our days out in the sun. And those green eyes that were staring right through me.

Santi raises his right hand up to my face and caresses his thumb against my upper lip. "I would never forget to add the mustache that brought me warmth after being caught in the cold, wet rain."

A gasp escapes my lips as I slap his arm, "You fucking di—"

Santi stops me with a kiss that I can't help but turn into a giggle, but that doesn't stop him from kissing my smile, and then my jaw, cheek, all the way down to my neck, where he sucks and bites.

Moans and breathy words of encouragement slip my lips as I pull him closer to me.

Santi licks my neck and blows on the sensitive area, sending shivers down my spine and a wave of lust towards the center of my thighs.

He pulls back and presses his head onto my forehead, his hot breath teasing my lips.

"I want all of you." He whispers.

"I'm all yours."

Santi's eyes darken, and his hands slide up my ass, making their way underneath my wet shirt. I know he can feel my skin lifting by the smirk on his face.

"Nervous?" He asks.

"Excited."

And so fucking nervous.

"It's so weird to admit this, but with you, it almost feels like the first time." He says it without a single hint of embarrassment on his face. And I don't laugh or make a joke to shove down this awkward feeling that rises in my chest because I completely understand what he means.

And I also completely understand that, in this moment, the feeling in my chest isn't so much awkwardness or anxiety but rather something deeper, soulful. Something I'm going to validate as being present, but not give in to.

Because love like this has no business blooming in a limited encounter.

"I know." Is all I can manage to say.

And it seems to be enough for Santi because his hands grip the hem of my shirt and pull it off. And instead of dropping the sopping shirt on the floor, he walks over to the desk chair in the corner of the room and hangs it there to dry.

He removes his own and lays it on the desk as I admire the small tattoos scattered across his back. Tattoos I haven't really gotten to see, let alone admire.

Santi removes his pants and lays them beside his shirt. I move to unhook my own jeans, but Santi's voice stops me.

"Don't." He walks over to me and brings my face into his hands, forcing me to look up at him.

"I want to undress you, I want to praise you, and I want to make love to you. And I know you want to walk around eggshells on the topic. I know you will still have to leave tomorrow night. But I don't care. I want to pretend just for today that you are forever. Can you at least give me that, Sylvie? Please?"

I swallow the knot that forms in my throat and nod.

Santi pecks my lips and makes his way down my neck and towards my chest, and he stops to admire the way my breasts fall as he unclasps the bra that holds them elevated. The straps fall off my shoulders and down my arms as he pulls them off completely.

My pebbled nipples seem to be to his liking as he skims his thumb against the sensitive nub.

"How is everything about you so perfect?" He asks, bending down and leaving kisses down my chest, bringing a nipple into his mouth and sucking it, extracting a moan right out of me.

"Even that sound is perfect."

Santi kneels completely in front of me and kisses down my stomach, and I have to say that I'm a little self-conscious to have him so close to me like this. I know he doesn't care that I'm not skinny, and from the look of his boxers, I can tell he's turned on by my body.

But the thoughts of not being perfect enough still make their way into my mind as he begins to unzip my pants.

"Sylvie." He says to me in a hush that I almost don't hear it.

"Hm."

"Look at me." He demands.

I don't even realize that my eyes are closed and my body is stiff until I force them open and look down at him.

"You are perfect, every inch of you. I've imagined you in every angle that not even you have probably pictured yourself in, and let me tell you that I find every single one of them so fucking attractive." He growls the words, pulling down my pants, leaving me just as bare as him. Our underwear is the only thing standing in our way.

Santi helps me lift each foot out of my pants and then lifts himself up to bring them over to the chair to dry alongside the shirt.

He walks back slowly, his eyes taking their time to crawl up and down my body. He closes the gap between us and grabs hold of my hand.

He brings it over to his hardening member and grips it tightly.

"Do you see all that your perfection does to me?" He growls.

"This is all you, Sylvie. You drive me insane, you piss me off, and you turn me so fucking on. I want nothing but to be inside you and claim you for myself. Will you let me do that to you? Just tonight?" He asks even though he already has the answer.

"All yours means all yours."

Santi pushes me onto the bed, and I bounce up lightly. I lift myself up on the back of my arms and watch as Santi spreads my legs wide open and leaves kisses on my inner thighs, his eyes focused on my already wet panties. I'm sure he can see the wetness leaking right through the cloth, but he doesn't speed up the kissing process. He takes his time peppering my thighs with kisses, sucking and biting the sensitive skin.

I desperately inch myself closer to him, begging for him to lick up every inch of my arousal. I'm sure it excites him even more knowing how badly I want this, how badly I want him.

"Please, Santi." I finally utter the words, and Santi looks right at me as he inches closer to my panties and spreads his tongue over the wetness, sucking my lips over the cloth.

Fuck me.

I bring my hands down to my hips and try to pull down my panties, but Santi stops me.

"It's mine— you're mine… and I want to undress you."

He grips my panties and tugs them down.

"God, it's true. "

"What's true?" I ask, suddenly feeling like some sort of science experiment, and closing my legs in the process.

Santi chuckles and grabs my knees to open them back up.

"This was the only part of you I haven't seen, and fuck, Sylvie, it's just as perfect as the rest of you."

My heart stops as his eyes lock with mine as he says those words, and a teardrop of spit falls past his lips and lands perfectly on my bundle of nerves, and I'm sure that I've just experienced a mini-orgasm without him even touching me.

"Sylvie."

Santi runs his hands up the outside of my thighs, admiring them as he makes his way around the curves of my hips and back down to the inside of my thighs.

"Yes?" I squeak.

"I'm going to eat you out, and I need you to suffocate me with these beautiful thighs of yours. And by no means are you to let go of me until I've made you come all over my tongue."

I open my mouth to speak, but the only thing that comes out is a shaky breath.

"Okay?" His eyes flicker back up to mine, looking for a confirmation, and I give him a nod and manage to squeak out an "okay" from my lips.

Santi lowers himself down to my wet center and presses a gentle kiss on my mound. His tongue teases the outline of my pussy, gently gliding past my lips.

Santi teases the entrance with his tongue, sliding it slowly as if only to get a taste of what he's about to devour, and I shift my hips forward for him to fucking take all of me already.

He glides his tongue painfully slow up my folds and flicks it teasingly around my swollen clit. And I can't help but let out a frustrated growl.

I feel Santi's lips turn into a smile against my folds.

The grumpy fucker wants to smile now? When my pussy is in need of his— Oh fuck.

Santi's hands grab on tightly to my ass as he brings his lips around my clit and begins to suck.

My hands immediately shoot straight down to his head, holding him in between the heat of my legs.

His tongue goes back down to my entrance and curves into me impressively. His hand is now pressing down on my mound as he presses his thumb into my throbbing clit that's currently begging to have his lips around it again.

"Santi, more, I need more." He applies pressure to the clit and moves his thumb in a circular motion. His other hand reaches out to my breasts, where he takes one of the perky nipples and squeezes it between his fingers.

"Fuck me." I moan, arching my back further, needing him to speed up this process and get me dripping and ready to take him.

"I need you."

"And I need to be suffocating between your legs until they're shaking, Sylvie. So get to suffocating."

Santi's tongue grazes my clit and brings it between his lips and sucks. My legs instinctively close around his neck and tighten, bringing him closer to my core.

Santi moans into my clit, and I arch my back, practically begging for more. He seems to get what I'm asking for because he slides two of his fingers into my wetness and begins teasing my inside slowly.

It's like he's trying to get to know every part of my body.

I'm practically turning into putty in his hands as he curves his fingers into my sweet spot and begins to glide his fingers in and out of me at a quicker pace. His lips are still sucking around my clit with an occasional vibration from his moans, sending shivers down my body.

"Oh, God." I cry as I begin to feel the intense buildup.

My thighs tighten even more around him, and I'm sure Santi is in his own heaven right now. His thrusts suddenly stop, and suddenly he presses his fingers strictly to that sweet spot and rubs it like he would my clit and fuck me if I don't fucking see stars.

I scream out Santi's name as my legs shake and loosen their hold around him. He pushes himself up and hovers over me, his lips plump and wet and so fucking kissable.

Santi brings his wet fingers up to my lips, and I take them into my mouth, sucking my juices off of them. My eyes never leaving his.

"You taste so fucking good, Sylvie." His eyes trail down my body, and the way he looks at me makes my stomach flutter.

And as sad as it is to admit, I don't think that anyone has ever looked at me the way that Santi does.

"You are so beautiful, Sylvie. In and out. And it feels almost like some sort of joke of fate to have brought you into my life for such a short time, because you're someone that I'd want forever."

Fuck, why did he have to say that?

I feel my eyes watering, but I hold them back because the last thing that I need is for this to end in me sobbing into the crook of his neck.

Instead, I reach for the back of his neck and pull him down towards me, allowing our lips to collide. This moment is better said through action, rather than words. I know what he's trying to tell me, and that's more than enough. I don't need to hear the words to know how he feels. And it's better left unsaid anyway.

I moan into Santi's mouth and push my hips up towards his groin. I can feel his hardened dick through his briefs, and I want nothing more than to have him deep inside of me.

"Fuck me," I whisper.

Santi grins and removes the last of his clothes, and his cock shoots up, touching his lower abdomen. The tip of his cock glistens, and I am reminded of the importance of contraceptives.

"Um, Santi, do you have a condom?" I ask, almost feeling like I'm seventeen again, losing my virginity to my high school sweetheart.

Santi drags a hand over his face in mortification and groans aloud as he looks back down at his hardening dick and then flicks his eyes up at me again.

"Fuck, I don't, but it's okay. We don't have to do anything else." He grabs his briefs from the floor, but I reach out and grab hold of his wrist, stopping him from retrieving them.

"I'm clean, and I have an IUD placed in, if you're okay with that."

I don't normally agree to this, even with all my exes; I've always made them wear a condom, and that was just because it made me feel safer. But with Santi, it feels different, and in just a couple of days, he has shown me that he's more trustworthy than any of the other men I've dated, which is disappointing to admit, but nonetheless the truth.

"Are you sure?" He asks, his hand instinctively grasping his cock and stroking it right in front of me.

I spread my legs wider and lift my brow in question.

"Are you going to keep stroking your hand until you come all over it, or will you be taking me up on my offer?" I ask.

Santi's eyes look down at my pussy, and he immediately grasps my thighs and pulls me towards him like I'm weightless.

Santi slides the tip of his cock up and down my folds and inserts it slowly at the entrance. His eyes meet mine, and he lowers himself so that he's hovering over me.

"Sylvie." He moans as he slowly penetrates me, my pussy clenches around him, and it feels as if in this very moment we've connected a puzzle piece that's been missing.

Santi brings himself in and out of me and lets out breathy moans beside my ear. He picks up his speed with each thrust, slamming right into me and moving his hips at an angle that has him fucking that same spot that made me see stars.

He brings his face up to mine and pushes my dark strands of hair behind my ears and takes a look at me.

"Sylvie, I—"

I bring my fingers to his lips to stop him from uttering anything that will break me right now. Instead, I lift my hips to collide against his, and he grasps them and meets me with his long and quick strokes.

Colliding with me until he releases his final moan and releases into me.

Santi lays his head on the crevice of my neck and gives me a kiss before pushing himself off of me and lying right next to me. I turn and lay my head on his chest and wait for his heartbeat to relax underneath me.

No words are said between us; our small touches say enough. I glide my hand up and down his chest, and he glides his own up and down my arm.

For a moment, we both pretend that this is the first of many.

For a moment, we pretend that this …

was the beginning of forever.

Day 7

CHAPTER FOURTY-ONE
Sylvie

9 hours before sylvie's flight

WE REMAIN silent as Santi takes out his keys and unlocks the building's door. He waits for me to enter first before shutting the door behind us and leading us up the stairs slowly.

He had woken me up with what was barely a whisper to make sure we had enough time to get home for me to pack. My flight wasn't until later tonight, but it was fine. I would be leaving a little early anyway, out of fear that my father instilled in me during all our family vacations.

He swore up and down that we would be late if we didn't leave the house five hours earlier than our damn flight.

Our train ride back to Madrid had been silent, with a few words shared here and there.

Santi opens the apartment door, and we walk in silently. The day is a little gloomy today, which doesn't help our situation.

"Should we pack up first?" He asks, and I turn my head over quickly.

"We?"

Santi walks over to the counter, lays his keys down, and shrugs.

"Yeah, I thought I could help." Santi shrugs and looks over towards Javi's door, and I don't know why I get the feeling that he's only looking that way to ignore my eyes.

And damn it, that hurts.

"Yeah, sure, but only if you promise not to pocket any of my underwear."

Santi chuckles and looks back over to me.

"What, I can't have a little memento?" Santi bites his lip, which seems to be unintentional, and then nudges his head over to Javi's room.

I follow him inside, and really, all that I can think about is those damn lips of his.

Was that it last night?

Was that all that there was of us?

And damn it, why did it even matter?

Why was I so fucking hung up on this?

"What should we start with?" He asks, opening one of the drawers I had stuffed with my clothes.

"I guess we'll start with folding first." He sighs, answering his own question and pulling out the crumbled clothes from the draw-ers, and tossing them onto the bed.

I chuckle, and Santi raises his eyes to look at me and gives me a sly grin.

"Hey." The word slips my lips before I can think straight, and Santi quirks up a brow.

"Yes?"

"You can always text me or follow me on Instagram. You can at least follow along on my adventures." I don't know why I even bring that up, but I just need a way to clear this awkwardness between us. I need to feel like this isn't exactly a goodbye before we even said a hello.

This is the reason why I shouldn't have let yesterday go as far as it did. It wouldn't be fair to either one of us.

Santi doesn't say anything right away; instead, he continues to fold my clothes like nothing was said. And I swallow the lump forming in my throat.

It shouldn't matter, Sylvie.

You wanted this.

The whole point was not to fall for him or anyone else, for that matter. You were supposed to be here to find yourself, not to find someone else. And now you're all caught up in your feelings because he's a grumpy, caring, and amazing head-giver.

"You don't have to, you know. It's just a suggestion, obviously there's nothing going on between us, but you know our time wasn't nothing. It was special in its way. And it's not like I don't care about you, of course I do. It's just that it wouldn't work and we wouldn't be able to make it a thing, not that you're even asking that of me. I just—"

"Sylvie." Santi's voice breaks me from my thoughts, and when I look up, I realize he's right beside me. I turn to face him, and I know that my face is flushed from the embarrassment.

Why the hell did I go on a tangent?

"I would love to text you, but I just think it will take me a while to do so."

His voice is steady, but his eyes hold all the emotional validation I need. This isn't easy for him. Santi caught feelings just as much as I did. And now he was just maneuvering them the way he knew how, which was through silence and grumpiness.

He didn't want to speak about last night, not because he regretted it but because it actually meant something to him. And that was even worse.

"We have time until your flight leaves." He says, clearing his throat in the process.

"Yes, we do." I inch a little closer, needing to be near him, wanting to be touched by him. And Santi seems to need the same thing because he brings his hands up to my arms and holds them gently, pulling me closer to him.

"This will only make it hurt more." He says, but I'm not sure if this is a reminder to him or to me.

"Pain isn't always a bad thing."

You're such a fucking liar, Sylvie.

"Are you a masochist, Americana?" Santi whispers as he inches closer to my lips.

"No, I'm just addicted," I reply smoothly, closing the space between us, our lips moving in unison again, just like last night.

Santi pushes me onto the bed, and a giggle escapes my lips. I can't remember the last time a giggle like that escaped my lips with a man. I can't really remember a time when being with one made me this happy, and that's sad to even admit because I've been in so many committed relationships and not one of them has made me feel the way Santi does.

"What are you thinking so deeply about?" He asks, his hot breath on my lips and his hands trailing under my shirt and up towards my breasts.

"You," I admit.

"You don't have to keep thinking so hard about it. I'm right here."

Santi presses our lips back together, and my head falls against the mattress as his hands trail up to gather my breasts, and I allow myself to fall into this man once again.

"I don't want to get up," I murmur, my cheek pressed against Santi's bare chest. I liked outlining all his tattoos scattered around his body. Tattoos that no one would ever see unless they were lucky enough to be in my position. But just the thought of anyone being in this same position was gut-wrenching.

"We have a few hours left. There are some things I want to do before you leave."

Santi pulls the covers off of us, and I groan as he slides down from under me to get dressed, but even though he's left the comfort and safe zone of the bed, he doesn't feel distant like this morning.

In fact, there's a pearly white smile that teases me as he ushers his head over to my suitcase for me to get dressed.

"Ugh, but I just want to rot and ignore everything right now." I groan and sprawl my body across the white sheets, looking up at the ceiling, trying my best to control the anxiety that's rising in my chest every time I think of having to leave tonight.

Santi grabs my face and tilts it to the side so that I'm looking at him.

"Please." That's all he says and all he needs to say for me to strip my naked body from the sheets and get up and dressed.

Santi and I quickly finish packing, and we decide to do it my way, which means just shoving everything back into a suitcase without folding it or putting it in a particular order.

I know my hecticness is killing Santi, but he validates it the moment I tell him it's so we can spend more time together.

"What exactly are we up to?" I ask Santi as we walk around the city.

I didn't mind taking one last stroll around the city, but if I could lie naked in a bed with him for the rest of the time, rather than walking around a city I had already seen.

"Can I get your phone?" He asks, turning abruptly into a narrow street in the city that doesn't feel walkable, let alone drivable, but alas, there's a car coming from the opposite direction.

Santi pulls me to the side instinctively, and I'm not even sure he realizes he does, but it's cute.

I take my phone out of my purse and hand it over to him.

"Why is it you need my phone?" I ask.

"I'm going to print the pictures, so you can take them with you, or better yet, add some of them to your scrapbook." Santi slides the lock screen and turns the screen over to me so that I can enter my pin.

My heart practically bursts out of my chest, and I have to calm myself down as I enter my password and open the photo album app.

He's printing out our pictures for my scrapbook?

That's the cutest thing someone has ever done, correction, it's the most loving thing someone has ever done.

Be still, my beating heart, because this is not the right time to fall in love. Not nine hours before I'm due to be on your flight to another country.

We stop by a small shop, and Santi turns to me with a smile.

"It'll just be a quick second, I'll have them download all the pictures into their system, and while they print, we can grab something to eat." Santi gives me a quick kiss to the top of the head and enters the shop, immediately speaking to the man behind the counter, and my heart has yet to be still because Santi just gave me a fucking forehead kiss.

I'm freaking out over a damn forehead kiss.

It only takes Santi a couple of minutes to come back out with my phone in hand.

"He's downloaded all the pictures so we can go grab something to eat and pick them up after. I'm not sure if you—"

I shut Santi up with a kiss, not because I didn't want to listen to him, but because I didn't want to waste any time not being as close to him as I could.

Santi grins into the kiss before pulling away, and I have to say it's quite odd but successfully satisfying to not only see the grumpy man smile but to also be the reason for his smile.

"As much as I would love to stay here and kiss you all day. I am hungry from all the strenuous activities we've been up to." I giggle into his lips and nudge my head for him to lead the way.

Santi grabs my hand in his and pulls me a couple of blocks down towards an iron-like structure with multiple food markets inside.

Talk about giving an indecisive girl options.

"Okay, anything you want we'll get," Santi says, bringing his arm around my shoulder and pulling me close.

And even with so many options from seafood, meat, pastries, fried goods, and drinks, I was somehow sick to my stomach.

"How about a water to start?" I suggest, and Santi chuckles and nods his head, bringing us to the nearest vendor.

We walk around for a few minutes, and we try some of the food. I nibble on some choices here and there, but I've completely lost my appetite.

And as we walk around the market, a sudden thought comes to me that I haven't felt this way about leaving a place since I was a kid.

The last time I felt like this, I must've been around eight years old. Old enough to have made and remember my best friend in Minnesota. Her name was Mia, and for the first time since jumping around with my family from state to state and school to school, I felt like I had met someone who made me happy to have moved.

And I remembered the last day of the school year, when my parents sat both Marlene and me down in the kitchen and told us we'd be moving again this summer.

None of us complained because this was our normal. But I had felt that pit in my stomach that anchored me to Minnesota. That same anchor that had me crying for days after we left, and when my parents had asked me what was wrong, I blamed it all on a stomach ache that just wouldn't go away.

It wasn't until a couple of days later that Marlene had crawled into bed with me and talked about how she didn't mind moving as long as I was always with her because I was her best friend.

And from there on out, Marlene had been my only friend. I even moved to Chicago because that's where Marlene was, and she was all I truly needed.

And throughout school, I never made any real connections with people; I didn't understand what the point was when I'd be leaving again anyway.

And now here I was with a man in Madrid, someone I knew I had a limited time with, and I still chose to let my guard down and fall for him enough to make me physically sick at the thought of leaving him.

"The photos should be ready by now if you want to head over there now." Santi sighs, throwing a wrapper from our pastries out in the trash.

He must feel my distance, and it bothers me enough to grab his hand and interlock our fingers together.

"Sure." I put on a grin and let Santi pull me along with him towards the shop.

"You want to wait out here again?" He asks as we near the store.

"Sure." I shrug.

Santi enters the store, and I lean against the stone building, watching him through the glass window as he stops to speak to the man behind the counter.

"Sylvie?" A man's voice pulls me away from the window, and I look over to see Emilio dressed in his suit and tie as usual.

"Emilio." I suck my teeth and give him a wave, unsure of how to greet a man who, the last time I saw him, had a whole argument with me over whether I should pursue anything with Santi.

"How have you been?"

"I'm on vacation, so I can't say my life has been too bad."

I'm currently dying, Emilio. I'm about to get on a fucking plane to another country that I was very excited to visit, but the truth is that now I'm already feeling homesick over a place that's not even my home but rather has someone who feels just like one.

Emilio nods, and for some reason, something in the way he looks at me tells me that he knows I'm not being one hundred percent with him.

"You never did come by the cafe again." He says, breaking the moment of silence between us. I shrug and cross my arms over my chest.

"I wasn't sure if I was even wanted there, let alone my guest." I nod my head over to the window, and Emilio takes a glance over at Santi and gives me a nod.

"Well, I guess it's not like it really matters because you're leaving, right?"

I rock back and forth on my feet and give him a nod.

"That's kind of the whole point of a vacation. At some point, you either have to go back home or get to your next destination."

Emilio forces out a chuckle and nods his head. He stands there for a minute, not saying anything, looking at anything but me, and then finally his eyes find my own.

"Can I say something?" He asks as if my saying no would stop him anyway.

Regardless, I give him a nod and choose to hear out the words that come out of his lips next.

"That whole bullshit about setting something free and if it comes back to you, it's meant to be is inaccurate. If you let someone go, they just think they aren't worthy enough to want to be kept around. So I suggest admitting what you want because if you leave and don't say a single thing, there will always be that what-if scenario plaguing the back of your mind."

Emilio speaks as if it's from experience, and I want to tell him to mind his business because just a couple of days ago, he was being a real fucking dick.

But I don't say that.

Instead, I give Emilio a short nod and murmur, "goodbye, Emilio."

And he waves a goodbye as he walks past me towards wherever he was going.

Santi comes out with a bag and a large frame in hand, and I raise my eyebrows at him in amusement.

"What did he want?" He asks, nudging his head over to Emilio.

"Just wanted to say goodbye."

It's not exactly a lie, so I don't feel too bad about not admitting word-for-word what Emilio had said.

"What's up with the picture frame?" I ask, trying to pivot the conversation.

"It's for the puzzle that we are going to finish and frame in the apartment."

I squeal and grab the frame from him, picturing how nice the puzzle will look on his bedroom wall. There wasn't much left of the puzzle because both Santi and I would fill in a couple of pieces here and there. And in fact, I think Santi was starting to come around to liking the hobby.

"Come on, we should get going if we want to finish this puzzle."

I hand the frame back to Santi, who already has his hand out to take it, and he hands me the bag with the photos.

We walk beside one another back to the apartment. I take out the photos and look through them one by one, showing them to Santi and reminiscing about memories that were just made this week but already feel eons away.

CHAPTER FOURTY-TWO
Santi

6 hours before sylvie's flight

"I CAN'T BELIEVE we are almost done with this puzzle." Sylvie squeals as she adds the last of the puzzle pieces to the rest of the frame.

"I can't believe I got you to complete a whole puzzle." Her grin spreads from ear to ear as she peers over at me.

"I can't believe you got me to do half the stuff that we did this whole week." Sylvie leans back in her chair, and I can tell her mind is roaming through the memories we've made this whole week.

"Thank you for doing it." She finally says, breaking the silence and stretching over to put my hand in hers.

"I know it was annoying, and you probably had better things to do. But I appreciate you giving me a tour of your city. I appreciate the history lessons and the adventures." Sylvie opens her mouth to say something else, but I cut her off with a kiss.

A tender, achingly slow, and emotionally painful kiss.

We pull away slowly, and I can see so much emotion behind her brown eyes, but she's good at holding herself back.

I know she feels exactly what I feel, I know she wants this as desperately as I do. But it just doesn't make sense. I live here, and she lives across the fucking Atlantic. And it would be unfair to alter either one of our lives.

Especially after just meeting. I mean, this is probably just some deep infatuation we have for one another.

Fuck, and as much as I want to believe that, I know what this is, and I especially know what last night was.

But there's nothing to be done with this feeling.

Fate had made this out to be a love that just passes you by in life.

A love that got away.

"I think we may have lost that final piece." She says, breaking the silence and shifting her eyes down to the table with a missing puzzle piece.

I dig into my pocket and pull out the last piece.

"It's for your scrapbook… that way the missing piece in my frame will always have some sort of story. And who knows, maybe it'll be a famous part of history. And when someone finds that last missing piece tucked away in one of your leather journals all the way across the Atlantic… maybe then they can put a name to what we are."

I inch the piece closer to her and watch as her eyes hold back a river from dispersing out of them. Sylvie clears her throat and takes the piece in her hand. She looks down at the piece with such mesmerization. As if it were more than just an oddly shaped cardboard piece.

"You're making it hard." She whispers.

"You never made it easy."

Sylvie's eyes shift back to my eyes, and just like that, she's back in my arms, her lips on mine. And unlike last night or this morning, I take her in like it's the last time I'll ever see her again.

Which is probably more accurate than the fantasy we had last night because the likelihood of us ever meeting again or talking is almost nonexistent. But still a fantasy I've been daring to entertain in the back of my mind.

Sylvie pulls me closer to her, this time taking the lead. She walks us towards the couch, her lips never once stopping their movement with mine.

I pull away quickly to remove my clothes, and Sylvie does the same. I push her onto the couch, and she spreads her legs wide for me. Her pink folds glisten for me, and I want to get to my knees and lap my tongue around those folds, taking in her sweet taste. But I know it isn't what she needs right now, and my hardening cock is telling me that it needs this more.

I bend down and align the tip of my cock at her entrance, and Sylvie arches her back to give me more space, and by the look on her face when I thrust into her, I'm sure the position has allowed me to hit the best spot.

"Oh fuck, yes right there, Santi. Fuck me."

I bring my hand to the back of her head and fist her hair as I ram my cock deep into her. The sound of her wetness coating my cock turns me on even more as I thrust deeper and quicker into her, listening to her moans turn into a melody that's only meant for my ears.

"Sylvie, what the fuck are you doing to me?" I groan, pulling out of her and grabbing her hips to turn her so that her ass faces me.

I look down at her voluptuous ass and watch my cock disappear behind those gorgeous globes.

"Santi, this all feels like a joke." She moans into the couch's cushion as I thrust into her, making sure I'm deep enough for her to feel all of me. Her walls tighten around me, and I moan into her as I hover over her.

"Fate is cruel, but I think I'm crueler because I still want to take all of you, Americana."

Sylvie pushes her ass back and moves herself to match up with my thrusts, and I drop my head back and groan as her walls tighten around me. Our moans dance around the room as we collide into each other.

I bring my hand around her hips and lower belly and press my fingers against her clit, rubbing it in circles and watching as Sylvie falls apart right in front of me.

And I crumble right beside her.

Spilling my seed deep within her.

We stay still for a moment, catching our breath.

My cock softens inside her as it completely empties, and I watch as her body relaxes under me.

I pull out slowly and watch her breasts jump as she turns around to face me.

"Well, I guess there's only one last thing to do."

I arch a brow and turn to lie right next to her.

"What's that?"

Sylvie turns her head so she's looking at me and smiles.

"We'll have to scrapbook that last puzzle piece."

CHAPTER FORTY-THREE

Sylvie

5 hours before sylvie's flight

"WHY DO YOU SCRAPBOOK?" Santi asks, as he presses his lips onto my shoulder, while his hand brushes through my hair.

I'm in a pair of his underwear and in one of my t-shirts, and he's barely dressed with just his briefs on.

"I started doing it around the age of eight. I was really upset about the constant moves, and my mother brought up the idea to both Marlene and me. It was kind of a way to make the constant moving feel like an adventure. And since we were always there for a brief moment, it was crucial that we gather as many things to fill up our scrapbook with memories."

As I give my answer, I continue to fold a small piece of paper into an envelope. It's the perfect size to pocket the puzzle piece that Santi gave me.

"And now you continue to scrapbook when you go on vacations?" He asks.

"Hm, think of it more like a diary. I like to scrapbook when I have something I want to remember, or sometimes I scrapbook in order to forget and take my mind away from whatever's bothering me." I glue the envelope onto the journal's page and wait a few seconds before inserting the puzzle piece within it.

Afterward, I grab one of the pictures Santi had printed of us and cut around the image so it's mostly a cutout of us.

"And what's the reason for the scrapbooking now?" He asks.

I smile and shrug before looking over at him.

"A bit of both, I guess."

Santi hums in understanding and watches me continue to decorate my final pages for the Madrid section of my journal.

"Would you um— follow me?" He asks once I've finally finished and closed the journal.

I turn and watch as Santi hands my phone over to me.

I look at my home screen and see an Instagram notification with a new follower. I unlock the phone and look down at Santi's name and profile picture staring back at me.

"I thought you didn't do social media?" I ask.

Santi shrugs and runs a hand through his hair, probably unsure of what to do or say.

"I guess I never had a real reason to keep up with anyone online."

"I'm not sure if I'm worthy of being that reason. I'm quite boring outside of the vacationing." I tease, accept his request, and follow him back.

"Impossible, even if you post about paint drying. I'd like to have seen a glimpse of what your day was like."

"You've got jokes now?" I tease.

"It's not a joke, Sylvie." His tone is serious, and I know it's not because he's angry but because he's being genuine.

He'd rather have some of me than none.

A complete difference from where we started at the beginning of the week. I look over at the clock and know I'll have to be out in an hour or two.

But not before doing one last thing.

"Santi?"

"What is it?"

"Will you just take me to one last place again?"

"Anywhere, just say it, and we'll go."

I grin and pull him into a kiss before walking over to my bedroom to get changed and grab my Polaroid.

CHAPTER FOURTY-FOUR
Santi

"ARE you sure you're heading in the right direction?" Sylvie asks, once again fighting me on how to get to a location I've been to more times than I can count.

"How is it that you ask me to take you somewhere we've already been to, and you still have the nerve to ask if I know if I'm going the right way?"

Sylvie shrugs and giggles as she walks down the trail beside me.

"Men don't have the best sense of direction."

"Says the woman who not only got lost the last time she was here but also got attacked by a peacock."

"Hey! This place is huge, I don't know how someone can remember how to get around here."

"It's fairly simple when you've grown up around here," I grumble, turning down towards the path that'll lead us to the palace.

"And those peacocks are vicious, Santi. I didn't even do anything to him. I was sitting there enjoying my time when he decided to attack me."

"Maybe he was just attracted to you; he did have his feathers out." I tease, knowing that'd creep her out even more.

"Listen, all I know is that I'll be leaving Madrid with Pavophobia. Which is not something I'd ever thought I'd have." She grumbles beside me, and it's kind of cute to see Sylvie actually furrow her brows for once.

"Pavophobia? I know that's not even a phobia you knew existed until after your interaction with the bird."

"You're damn right I didn't, and I wouldn't have ever had to discover it if they hadn't tried to kill me."

I pull Sylvie under my arm and press a kiss on top of her head, and she looks up at me with those warm brown eyes that I've grown to find comfort in.

"Don't worry, I'm sure you'll find very few peacocks along the way in life."

"I guess Madrid will always have a special place in my heart, then," Sylvie says in a whisper, and we come to a halt right in front of the palace.

"I'm sure your trip will always have a special place in my heart, too," I murmur as I grasp her face in my hands.

I lean down to press my lips against hers, but Sylvie pushes back lightly and takes her Polaroid out.

Sylvie sets up the camera and passes it over to me.

"Take a picture, please."

I take the camera away from her hands and hold it up at an angle for it to face us, and press my lips against hers. I kiss her delicately and continue doing so after the light flashes and the Polaroid printer starts printing.

I use these last few moments to take in Sylvie completely.

Sylvie pulls away gently and lets the tip of our noses linger with the remnants of the kiss for a moment before pulling back and swiping away the printed polaroid to look at.

"Come, I want to take more pictures of us here."

"Why here?"

"Because it's where it all began."

Sylvie doesn't have to explain much further than that because I am completely aware that her world shifted that day we first spent time together. And I can so confidently say that because I was spinning on an entirely new axis, and I was sure the moment she left, I would go back to spinning on an axis where the sun never seemed to touch the land that I was on.

CHAPTER FOURTY-FIVE
Sylvie

SANTI HAD SURPRISINGLY ALLOWED me to take a bunch of pictures of us. And when I had run out of Polaroids, he allowed me to take a few pictures on my phone.

Pictures that I had immediately organized into a Madrid album. I even got him to smile a couple of times when I had him take pictures of me for my Instagram.

It was a redo of the day we were first here, but without his constant furrowed brows.

But the joy of our redo leaves our system as quickly as it came, the minute our feet come back to the entrance of the apartment complex.

"This is it, huh?" Santi says as he opens the door for me to enter.

"I guess so." I sigh as we go up the stairs towards what feels like doom. But it's not doom at all; it's just my luggage sitting in Javi's bedroom.

We enter the apartment slowly, as if moving slower would slow time itself.

"I'll order you an Uber to the airport." Santi clears his throat and pulls out his phone.

"Oh, you don't have to—"

"Sylvie." Santi clears his throat again but doesn't look away from the phone.

"Just let me do this."

I nod even though he's not even looking at me and walk over to Javi's room to grab my luggage.

I roll the suitcase out of the bedroom and towards the living room, where Santi just stands there, waiting.

Small hues of orange and pink begin to dance around the room as the sun sets outside, and it feels like a cinematic goodbye before the screen were to fade to black in the movie.

"Um, the Uber will be here in like five minutes. Do you want to wait here or would you rather bring everything down now and wait?"

I rub my suddenly clammy hands against my jeans and give Santi a shrug.

"I guess we can bring everything down now."

Sant gives me a short nod and grabs the suitcase from my hand, tugging it out the door with him and down the steps.

We don't say anything when we make it outside.

Instead, we just stand there staring into one another, and as much as one would assume that it would be awkward, it isn't.

It's bittersweet.

The gray Honda pulls up beside us, and the driver gets out to help me with my suitcase. Santi brings it over to the trunk and says something to the man, who gives him a nod in agreement and enters his car and waits patiently.

Santi comes back over to me, and this time I'm actually holding back tears.

"Sylvie."

"You said you wouldn't say anything." I croak.

"Vale, pues mejor te lo digo en un idioma que no conoces. Estos siete días contigo han sido caóticos, molestosos y exasperantes. Y sabes qué? Lo haría todo de nuevo porque, sinceramente, Sylvie, has sido una de las mejores cosas que me han pasado en la vida. Una persona que brilla como el sol se merece el mundo, Sylvie. Te amo."[*]

I don't need to understand the language to know exactly what he says, and the final kiss he presses to my lips finishes it off. Yanking my heart away with him. And though this torturous feeling in my chest is so very painful. It almost feels worth it, because as crazy as it seems, in only seven days, Santi made my heart belong to him.

He pulls away, but I keep my eyes closed, lingering in the moment before having to say goodbye.

His lips find my forehead, and finally, Santi whispers his goodbye.

"Safe travels, Americana."

---

[*] "Okay, then I'll just say it in a language you don't know. These past seven days with you have been chaotic, annoying, and exasperating. And you know what? I'd do it all over again because, honestly, Sylvie, you've been one of the best things that's ever happened to me. Someone who shines like the sun deserves the world, Sylvie. I love you."

After

CHAPTER FOURTY-SIX
Santi

I **ENTER** my apartment and don't bother with turning on the lights, and instead walk straight into my bedroom and let myself fall onto the bed.

The day seems to be so gloomy, despite the beautiful weather.

This is fucking stupid; there's no reason for me to be feeling this way. Not after only knowing Sylvie for a week.

But fuck, in one week, she had met my friend, my mom, and my uncle. She even met my fucking ex and still managed to make everyone like her.

Despite Carol's jealousy, she had actually liked Sylvie. And of course she did, Sylvie was hard not to like, even for an asshole like me.

And just like that, she was gone.

I let out a frustrated groan and sit back up to sit at the side of my bed and run my hands through my hair.

This feels wrong.

It all feels so fucking wrong.

She shouldn't be getting on a plane right now.

She should be sitting at the kitchen table, adding more paper and tape to her scrapbook while I make her something to eat, and later bring her straight back into my bed.

I don't even know what to do.

Fuck, I can barely think with all that crunching.

Wait… crunching?

I spin around and spot Javi, munching on some ham-flavored chips that I keep hidden in my room for him not to steal.

"Javi?! What the hell are you doing here?"

Javi munches on his chips and shrugs before walking over and taking a seat on the bed.

"We had a break in the tour, so I thought what better way to enjoy some time off than coming home and spending it with my best friend."

Javi munches on his chips, nonchalantly, as if he weren't standing in the corner like some freak watching me have what currently feels like the biggest crisis in my life. And that's saying a lot because I had my fiancé leave me at the altar without a word.

"When did you get here? How come I didn't see you?"

"Well, I was here when you came back from whatever date you were on with our guest. But, it was kind of awkward, and you guys were kind of just staring at each other, so I just stayed hidden in here."

Javi walks over to the bed and sits right down on the edge of it, continuing his munching as he looks at me for some answers.

"It's nothing."

"You seemed to be in distress a couple of seconds ago."

"Well, I wasn't."

"So she wasn't anything?"

"No—" I bite back my tongue to stop myself from saying anything that I'd regret because Sylvie was everything.

"So, you like-like her. Like you fell in love with her? In seven days? Wow, that's quick."

"Says the guy who was texting me all about some girl in Paris he was willing to marry in twenty-four hours, if she hadn't said no." I bark back.

"Yes, but that's because I'm me and you're you." Javi reasons as if what he's just said is enough of an explanation.

"And what's the difference between you and me when it comes to love?"

Javi sighs and licks his salty fingers dry before rolling up the bag and tossing it onto my bed, rather than placing them back in the drawer where he's found them.

"You don't just fall in love, Santi. You're calculative. You find the woman who would bring you stability and less of a headache. That's why you chose Carolina." Javier says with no second thought.

"You don't choose someone, you love them," I argue.

"Oh, really? So, what made you fall in love with Carol?"

His question catches me so off guard that I actually stutter when answering him, but the truth was, I couldn't exactly tell you what had made me fall in love with Carol, not like I could tell you what made me fall in love with Sylvie.

"I-I don't know, she was pretty, and she was there."

"She was there, huh?" Javier looks almost disappointed in my response, but I'm unsure what it is that he wants from me.

"What's up your ass?" I finally bark.

"Nothing, I'm just saying that if someone ever asked me to marry them and their response to why they fell in love with me was because I was just there, then I'd definitely leave you at the altar."

I hope it's noted that, in our many years of friendship, I have never hit my best friend—until now.

Javi falls back on the bed, holding his face, which I totally regret punching. But one minute my hand was fisted on my side, and the next it's like it took on a mind of its own and swung.

"Fuck, Santi."

"Fuck, I'm sorry. I don't even know why I did that." I grab Javi by his shoulders and bring him back up to face me, his face now beginning to redden and purple.

"Yes, you do." Javi sighs.

I finally sit beside him, and Javi looks over at me.

"Santi, why did you fall in love with her?" He doesn't have to specify who he is talking about because he's not dumb enough to ask the same question twice.

"She's so fucking annoying, Javi, but she's her own person. She doesn't care about what anyone has to say. She's messy but creative in her own way. And she loves puzzles and pictures, even though they're so annoying. She just does what makes her happy, and she's so fucking happy, Javi—"

"And she makes *you* happy?" Javi asks, already knowing the damn answer.

I just give him a slow nod, and Javi's eyes soften like they usually do when he feels sorry for me.

"So then why are you here?" He finally asks.

"What do you mean?"

"You didn't run after Carol when she left, which is self-explanatory based on the admission of your feelings. But this girl had you wallowing in sadness a couple of minutes ago. So why the hell are you not chasing her down if you love her?" Javi asks the question as if it has a simple response.

"Javi, she lives across the Atlantic."

Javi lifts himself up from the bed and paces around the room before looking at me with a disbelieving look splattered across his face.

"And? People make long-distance relationships work until they're sure that this is what they want. Once that part of the relationship is figured out, then one of you moves across the Atlantic to be with the other."

I groan and get up to face him this time, hoping to get through his head and have him drop the topic.

"Javi, I am not moving across the country. My life will always be here, and that's it. There's no reason for us to even entertain the idea."

"What about when she becomes your life?" Javi asks, obviously not willing to drop this nonsense.

"What are you talking about?" I groan at this point, driving myself completely insane with this conversation.

"Santi, please. Don't be an idiot. If you love this woman now, imagine after a year or two of being with her and trying to make it work across the Atlantic. Don't you think you'd be willing to start a life across the ocean just to be with her? Just to see her smile, just to see her happy?"

The room is silent as I take everything in, and for the first time in our friendship, I can't believe I can say that Javi is absolutely right.

And I'm a dumbass.

"I have to go," I say.

"Your Uber is waiting downstairs, and he's annoyed cause he's *been* waiting," Javi says nonchalantly.

"You ordered me an Uber?" I ask, running out of the room to put on my shoes.

"You're welcome!" Javi shouts as I make my way out of the apartment and down the stairs.

I open the door, and right there is the Uber driver who immediately rolls his eyes once he takes a look at me.

I get into the car and confirm the destination.

I couldn't believe that I was doing this, but it would be worth it.

Sylvie would be worth it all.

I reach for my pocket to pull out my phone to text Sylvie immediately, in hopes of stopping her from getting on that flight, but I freeze the minute I realize they're empty.

"Hey, what time does it say that we will arrive?" I ask him.

"It's looking like there's traffic, so twenty minutes."

Fuck.

I'd be cutting it short for her boarding time.

But I could run.

CHAPTER FOURTY-SEVEN
Santi

"COULD YOU GO A BIT FASTER?" I mutter as the Uber takes its sweet time sliding into the exit that leads to the terminal.

"I'm driving the speed limit." He argues, obviously annoyed by my insistence.

"The speed limit? I could open the door and walk out of here without a scratch while the car remains moving." I remark, knowing damn well this man is driving below the speed limit.

"Then walk right out if I'm going so slow." He argues, unaware of how unhinged an American girl has made me.

And the guy doesn't even see it coming when I unbuckle my seat belt and open the door to the moving car and jump out, which has me tumbling onto the floor and the Uber breaking instantly.

"What the fuck!" We both scream simultaneously, but for two very different reasons.

"Are you fucking crazy?" He roars, walking right out of the car to come and help me up. But by the time he gets to me, I'm already brushing off any debris.

"No, not crazy, just in love," I respond before beginning my run.

We aren't too far from the entrance, which tells me I'm very fucking impatient and probably just wasted time by jumping out of a moving car, but right now I still have time.

I run into the airport and head straight for the Air France counter. A tall, thin blonde woman stands there talking to her coworker. Both with their hair tightly combed back and held into a ponytail by a hair-tie that looks like it's been wrapped around the said ponytail about twenty times.

"Hello, I need to buy a ticket urgently. I've left my phone—"

"You must buy the ticket online, sir." She murmurs and continues on with her conversation with her coworker.

"As I was saying, I can't make it online because I've left my phone—"

"Sir, there is nothing we can do, we don't us—"

This time, I cut the woman off myself, hoping to get her to listen, because I can't take no for an answer.

"Ma'am, I'm in love."

The women both look at me, stunned, but wait for me to continue.

"And the woman that I love is about to get on a flight to Paris. And maybe she doesn't love me enough to want to stay for the remainder of her trip, but that's okay. I have to at least be honest with her and try. I have to tell her that I love her and that—"

"Okay, okay, that's enough. We really don't care. Just give me your information." The coworker responds, extending her hand out for me to give her what she needs.

I slide my wallet out of my pocket, hand over all my information, and wait for her to type. She was going a bit slow for my liking, but I wasn't going to be snarky now when she was getting me a ticket.

The lady tells me the total, and I hand over my credit card for the transaction.

Immediately after, she prints the boarding pass and hands it over to me.

"Safe travels." She murmurs.

And I give her a quick thanks.

I start to speed off, but turn quickly when I realize that they didn't want to give me the ticket in the first place, and turn back to them, interrupting their conversation once again.

"Fuck you."

With that, I run towards the security lines.

"No me jodas." I mutter the minute I see the length of the line.

I instinctively reach for my phone in my pocket to distract myself, or text Javi to say I'm not going to make it in time, but I remember I left my damn phone at home.

Fuck me.

I practically pace in line as much as I can pace when I'm between two people. And time seems to go even slower.

At some point, I end up asking the girl next to me for the time, and I know I have less than 15 minutes to get to my gate on time.

I wasn't going to make it; this had all been for nothing.

Why hadn't I brought my phone?

"Next!" A voice calls, and finally, the man stands there waiting for me to give him my information. I walk over and give him my European Identification and boarding pass.

The middle-aged man seems to take his time looking at the card and back at me.

"This is you?" He asks, lifting his brow as if analyzing me.

Give me a fucking break.

"Yes, it's me," I mutter through my teeth, trying to be as polite as possible.

"Hm, you've got curly hair in this." He leans back in his chair and stares right at me, my card still in his hand.

"Right, because I hadn't buzzcut it, as I have now." I probably sound exasperated, and that's because I really fucking am.

"Hm, you're telling me your hair is curly?" He asks.

"Are you fucking with me, sir?" I finally ask, not giving a fuck that he could probably give me an even harder time getting through this airport.

"Excuse me?" He asks, pushing himself forward again so that he's up close to the glass.

"I'm sorry, listen, I have to get to my flight as soon as possible. You see, the love of my life is going to get on that plane, and I need to stop her."

The man looks at me like I've grown a head and slides my boarding pass against the scanner.

"Why didn't you just call her?" He asks.

I don't fucking know.

"It was a spur-of-the-moment thing, and I forgot my phone," I admit.

Screw me for wanting to be romantic.

"I'm just messing with you anyway, you have the same big nose in the picture, anyone could tell it's you."

"Thanks," I say, the sarcasm thick in my voice as I collect my items from him. The man only laughs and nods for me to continue.

I walk over to the security line and run right through it, thanks to the lack of items to hold. And the minute I grab my wallet back from the scan, I begin to sprint.

And no fucking early run through Madrid has ever prepared me for this moment. Maybe it's because I'm running towards something real for the first time in my life.

I know what I want, I know I need Sylvie in my life.

I run as quickly as I can and finally make it to the gate. But as I look out the window, I see the plane is closed, and the gate is pulled back.

I'm too late.

CHAPTER FOURTY-EIGHT

Sylvie

I HAD CRIED the whole way to the airport and ended up sobbing at the security line.

And note to self, Spaniards aren't the most comforting.

But which security officer is?

The man just told me to keep it moving and then rambled on in Spanish to his coworkers. He was definitely talking shit about me, but I didn't care.

I was too upset over leaving.

And I shouldn't be because this was the plan all along, and whatever I feel for Santi is just some fluke.

I was just so used to catching feelings with everyone that my mind is just having a hard time getting over this bad habit of mine.

Even if I continued to stay here and try something out with Santi, not that he'd even be interested in that. It would be too complicated. It wouldn't work out, not with an enormous body of water between us and a time difference.

My phone buzzes, and a text from Marlene pops up.

. . .

MARLENE

Paris, the city of love! And of rats, so please stay
safe and don't try to domesticate any of them.

SYLVIE

City of love, huh? I think Madrid is trying to give
Paris a run for its money.

You mean to tell me that I can't befriend Remy
the rat?

MARLENE

Is Madrid the new city of love, or is there someone
that you love in that city?

And I'm serious, Sylvie, no fucking domesticating
the rats, I can't have another NYC incident.

I tuck my phone away and ignore Marlene's question, not feeling entirely ready to answer truthfully.

Besides, if just the question alone was making my eyes brim with tears, then I didn't want to turn into a sobbing mess when I'd respond.

It doesn't take long for the plane to start boarding, and I'm dumb enough to look around and see if Santi is here.

But why would he even be here?

It wouldn't make any sense.

I board the plane behind everyone else, and something that should feel exciting feels tremendously terrible, like I'm making the wrong decision.

To make it worse, I'm stuck sitting in the middle of a middle-aged man who's watching Facebook reels loudly on his phone and a teenage boy who thinks he's discreetly picking at his nose.

Great.

I rest my head against the seat and watch as everyone moves

through the aisle, the couples, the families, and the happy solo travelers.

All of them are excited to be traveling.

God, Sylvie, this isn't some romantic film.

This isn't Leap Year. You have set plans and a life.

This world isn't fictional; it's real.

And this, too, will pass like every other relationship.

Santi is just like the rest.

Time with him was short and sweet, but ultimately it all comes to an end anyway.

CHAPTER FOURTY-NINE
Santi

"NO, no, no , no, I need to be on that plane." I groan, running my hands through my hair and looking at the attendant, who looks displeased.

"Sir, I'm afraid there's nothing I can do. You're too late." She shrugs, and I let out an aggravated sigh.

All this for nothing.

But it hadn't really been for nothing, had it?

I mean, I was still here; all I needed was to see Sylvie. And if that wasn't here, then it would have to be in Paris.

"When's the next flight to Paris?" I ask the lady, and as she types away at her computer to find the response, I hear her beautiful voice from behind me.

"Santi?"

I turn around, and there she is.

Sylvie is there, staring right at me.

This couldn't be real.

I look at her and back at the plane already making its way out of the gate.

"Sylvie?" I ask, looking back at her.

"You're not on the plane? You're here? How—" With every question, I take a step closer, and before I can utter anything else, Sylvie practically slams into me, her arms wrapping around my neck and her lips meeting mine.

I don't care that people are probably staring and that the attendant is probably annoyed by this whole fiasco.

I don't care because Sylvie is here, she is in my arms, and her lips are on mine.

I pull away and look down at her, and I immediately bring my hands up to her cheeks, touching them to assure myself that I haven't gone mad.

"Sylvie, what are you doing here?" I finally ask.

"I should be asking you that." She giggles.

"Isn't it obvious?" I ask her, her dark eyes filling with emotion as she waits for me to answer.

"Declan shouldn't have let her leave Ireland."

A single tear drops from her cheek, and I'm quick to wipe it away for her.

"Now, Sylvie." I clear my throat, trying my best to control my own emotions as my own eyes water.

"You going to tell me why you're not on that plane?" I ask.

Sylvie smiles and presses a brief kiss to the inside of my wrist before leaning her head into my touch.

"I did get on the plane. And as I sat there, I waited for everyone to get in their seats. I realized I wasn't as happy as I should be to go to the city of love. And that's because here in Madrid is where I found my love. The love you only see in movies. And I decided that I want to keep living in that type of love. I realized that I want to be here with you, Santi."

Sylvie swallows and grips my wrist tightly before bringing her hand up to cup my own face.

"I love you, Santi."

"I love you, Sylvie," I say, as I bring her closer into me.

Her lips press against mine once again with passion and hunger.

Our lips move towards one another, never getting enough, but Sylvie makes the first move to pull away and looks up at me.

"Santi?"

"Yes?" I chuckle against her lips.

"Not that this isn't romantic, but why didn't you just call me?" She asks.

A sigh leaves me, and I groan as I press my forehead against hers.

"It's a long story," I admit.

"I have time, plus I think we might be going to the same destination." She teases.

"And where's that?" I ask.

"Home," Sylvie says, giving me one of those annoyingly radiant smiles of hers.

"That sounds perfect, Americana."

EPILOGUE
Sylvie

SOMETIMES RELATIONSHIPS DON'T WORK out. And the breakups can sometimes be brutal. It feels like all the time and effort given to a person were for nothing but a broken heart and a multitude of questions swirling in your brain, one of the biggest being: *What* now?

As much as I'd love to say that I have the answer to that because of the multitude of breakups I've gone through, I don't. Because every experience was different and every breakup hurt in a different way.

And honestly, I got lucky enough to say that the one true love that would've destroyed me if we were to separate has decided to stick around with me forever, or at least that's what the engagement ring on my finger says.

And after a little over a year of flying back and forth to be with one another and all those dramatic, but real, heart-wrenching good-byes at airports, I can finally call Madrid home.

Better yet, I can finally call Santi home.

As much as I wanted to jump on the first flight to Madrid every day and move in with Santi, I fought it and made sure we had enough time to find ourselves in the relationship.

Marlene hadn't understood how difficult it really was for me until Santi and I were six months into our relationship, and she caught me crying during one of our hangouts because I missed him terribly.

"That was the first time you ever showed any real emotion towards one of your partners. And you guys haven't even broken up." She had said, patting me on the back with at least two feet of distance between us.

I did end up squashing that distance between us by bringing her into an embrace and sobbing into the crook of her neck.

"Oh my god, you're in love." She murmured, continuing to rub my back.

I had sat and cried for what seemed like hours before I received a call from Santi, who at the time should've been asleep due to the time difference but had been missing me too much to prioritize his sleep schedule.

But now it was all over.

Now, I was making my way off a plane and practically running to the exit, just to be able to jump into Santi's arms.

I rush outside and look around for his car, but don't see Santi anywhere.

Oh, crap, had he forgotten?

I pull my phone out and click on Santi's number. I listen to the rings until I'm jolted out of my concentration when two arms hug me at my center.

"I can't believe you're finally here." His voice soothes the panic that had arisen from inside, and I fall back into him before turning around and wrapping my arms around him.

"I've missed you so much," I murmur into his chest and try to hold back the happy tears from spilling.

"I've missed you, too." We pull back enough for our faces to meet, and Santi's lips press against mine deeply. We move in sync, and I'm so in tune with the moment of finally having him here with me that I cancel out all the noise surrounding us.

Santi pulls away and pecks my face with dozens of kisses.

"I can't wait for you to be home, in our bed," Santi whispers into my ear as he trails kisses down my neck and jawline.

"I can't—" My words are cut off by an obnoxious beeping coming from a black Peugeot.

The driver lowers the passenger side window and extends himself forward so it's easier to see his face. And there is Javi waving his hand outside the window.

"Hurry up, I'm starving! You two can fuck later." I give Javi a tight-lipped smile and wave before looking back at Santi.

"I thought you said he was moving out to Paris to be with that French girl he fell in love with while on tour."

Santi sighs and tightens his grip on my shoulders.

"Yeah, about that—"

"No way."

"Just until he figures out what to do."

"We are not having sex; those walls are paper-thin, remember last time? He kept mimicking our moans the whole remainder of the week that I was here."

"That's funny." Santi chuckles.

"What's funny?"

"I actually don't know what's funnier, the fact that you think we won't be having sex or that you don't think that I haven't come up with millions of ways to keep you quiet while I'm fucking you," Santi says the words so nonchalantly as he pulls the strand of hair from my face and behind my ear.

I practically melt into a puddle as he looks at me with those dark eyes, and I'm reminded of how long it's been since we've had actual sex that didn't include a screen and internet connection.

"Fine." I chirp, while shoving my luggage between us for him to take.

"I like Javi anyway, he builds puzzles with me, and the last time I visited, he even let me paint his nails. I'm sure he'll let me give him a perm this time around, too."

"I wouldn't hold your breath on that last one." Santi chuckles and grabs my suitcase in one hand, and interlocks our fingers with his other.

This all feels so surreal, almost like a dream. But it's not, it's all very much real.

And it's crazy to think that none of this would have ever happened if it weren't for those seven days in Madrid.

BONUS EPILOGUE

Sylvie

"**TIGHTER.**" I proclaim as my sister tries her best to pump the strings of my corset.

"Damn it, Sylvie. It's not going." Marlene looks aggravated with me but also concerned.

I have to admit that I have become somewhat of a bridezilla these last upcoming days and that's never the type of person anyone wants to be around.

"What's the problem anyway? You look beautiful Sylvie." Marlene tries to assure me.

But, the truth was that she hadn't seen the slight changes that had been happening in my body, slight changes that not even Santi had noticed yet.

Truth be told I might have not noticed them if it hadn't been for the symptoms that came with it.

And the little positive sign that told me I was right.

"You look beautiful, honey. Why are you so strung up about this corset?" My mother chimes in from across the room, where she had been standing beside Lourdes ranting about how she had gotten her dress at a flea market for only ten dollars.

I'm not even sure Lourdes gathered any of what my mother said, but she was sweet to even nod her head at any of her bizarre stories.

"Nothing." I sigh, instinctively placing my hand on the slight bump of my stomach that was just beginning to protrude.

I stand still for a bit just picturing what it will look like in just a few months. I'll be round and full, and Santi will probably be over thinking every little thing when it comes to this peanut.

I hadn't told him anything yet.

I had found out about two weeks ago and he had so much on his plate between work and this wedding. He hasn't said anything but I can tell that the whole idea of a big wedding freaks him out after his first time at the altar.

I didn't want him overthinking anything and getting even more nervous. I thought it best to get the wedding over with and then surprise him about the new chapter in our life that we would be heading into.

My eyes wander up to look at myself in the mirror and Marlene stares back at me. Her eyes wide, mouth opened, and cheeks flushed.

And I'm not sure if it's the anxiety of it all or the baby but a wave of nausea hits me and I run past Marlene, straight into the bathroom.

Where my knees hit the cold floor and I vomit what feels like my entire soul into the porcelain bowl.

Marlene runs right behind me and shuts the bathroom door locking us in.

"You're pregnant?" She whisper—yells.

My head is within the porcelain tub and my stomach is still contracting with every wave that comes my way. I'm not sure what to say because I can barely form a coherent sentence at the moment so I give her a thumbs up.

"Holy shit, congratulations! Does Santi know?"

I manage to shake my head before vomiting what little is left in my stomach.

"Great, so I have a vomiting pregnant bride and an overly anxious groom to deal with."

I raise my head away from the toilet and peer up to look at Marlene, "he's anxious?" I ask.

Marlene groans, knowing she's allowed something to slip that wasn't supposed to be said to me.

"No, yes, maybe. Just a bit. But nothing crazy."

I hold back the next round of vomit that's threatening to burst out of me and try my best to gain control before facing Marlene again.

"What do you mean nothing crazy?"

Marlene just looks at me with concern in her eyes and I'm sure she feels somewhat guilty having to reveal to me exactly what's happening.

But that didn't matter. This was my wedding day and I needed to have some sort of control.

Besides, what could Santi possibly be doing right now?

Santi

"All this vomiting can't be good for you." Javi says, his body leaning against the bathroom's vanity as I vomit into the toilet bowl.

"Fuck off." I groan, not able to lift myself up from the bathroom floor without having to vomit again.

I don't really know what's gotten into me. I was fine until I started picturing myself up on that altar waiting for Sylvie to make her way over to me.

But then the thought of Sylvie never coming down that aisle wrecked me.

"Do you think I should've done another whitening strip on my teeth?" Javi turns back over to me and gives me a malformed smile to show me his top and bottom teeth.

"Javi, fuck off."

"Relax you grouch, Luisa is on her way back with some tea." He mumbles walking over to help me up.

But as soon as I finally get the energy to bring myself off of my knees Javi's phone rings, and the asshole drops me back onto the bowl.

"Fuck, Javi, what the hell?"

"This is Javi." He says answering his phone.

"Oh, no." He murmurs.

I turn my head to look over at him and immediately feel my spine go rigid and my skin pale from the reality I'm about to hear.

She's leaving me.

"Javi, what's going on?" I ask.

Javi puts the phone close to his chest and whispers down at me, "the harp player is down, seems like she must've gotten whatever you and Sylvie have."

I could kill the guy or kiss him.

But at least it's just the harp player— wait did he say Sylvie is sick?

"Javi, what do you mean Sylvie is throwing up? What's wrong?" I ask, finding the energy to pull myself up.

Javi shrugs and steps back over to the vanity to look at his damn teeth again.

"Javi, focus!"

A sigh escapes his lips as he looks back over to me, and it's obvious whoever is on the other side of the line is still talking to him.

"Marlene says Sylvie wants to see you."

I tug on my suit and make sure I'm put together before walking to the bathroom door.

"Okay, so let's go."

Javi pulls me back and nudges his head toward the sink.

"Brush your teeth first." He states as he undoes his tie.

"And then we tie this around your head." He says, holding the tie up in front of me.

Of fucking course.

* * *

"Ouch, you keep stepping on my foot." Javi mumbles as he pulls me around the corner of the hall.

"You're the one leading me!"

It feels like we've been walking for an eternity and for some reason Javi is leading me down the hall with him, holding my hands and walking backwards in front of me.

"We are finally here." He says, as he pushes what sounds like a door opening and stepping inside with me in hand.

"Sylvie you here?" He asks, and I can't help but tighten my hold on Javi's hands waiting for a response.

"Let go, you're hurting me." Javi groans, shaking off my hand.

"Javi, are you there?" Sylvie shouts from further into the room, probably forced to cover her own eyes too.

"Yes, we're here." He says, grabbing my arm and bringing me closer to the sound of her voice.

"Santi?" She asks. I can tell by her voice that she's getting closer.

"Not any closer you too! You're lucky I've allowed this." Javi remarks.

"You're lucky I allowed you to be a part of this wedding at all." I mutter.

"Trust me when I say that now is not the time for your remarks, Javi." Sylvie mutters beside me and that seems to shut Javi right up because he doesn't reply.

"Sylvie, baby, are you okay?" I ask, reaching out and feeling her arm. I use that as a way to lead me up her body so I can finally caress her cheek.

"I'm fine." She sighs.

"Javi told me you were vomiting."

"Funny, Marlene said the same about you."

That's true, but then again I was throwing up because I was nervous about Sylvie changing her mind about this whole thing. And I feel that's only right, based on my past. But, why would Sylvie be throwing up? Was she overthinking this wedding? Did she want to end things now?

If she did, I wouldn't accept it.

I couldn't.

Sylvie is everything.

I needed her in my life.

"Javi, would you mind giving us a moment?" Sylvie asks.

"Okay, fine, but no tearing off the blindfolds." Javi states sternly before walking away, and closing the door behind him.

"Just give it a few." Sylvie whispers.

And I can't help but smile at the thought of her knowing my best friend as well as me.

"Those blindfolds better still be on." Javi shouts from across the room.

"Out!" Both Sylvie and I shout in unison.

The minute the door shuts once more, I pull my blindfold off and watch as Sylvie does the same with hers.

I watch an awe as I take in her ethereal appearance.

She looks absolutely breathtaking.

"I'm glad you like it." She murmurs, pushing her veil back as if it were a random strand of hair.

"Sylvie, what's going on?" I ask, stepping closer and bringing my arms around her waist.

"You tell me, I have an excuse for my vomiting, but you on the other hand don't." She teases.

"My anxiety is excuse enough."

Sylvie's hands reach to cup my face and she's looking at me with the wide doe eyes of hers.

So unbelievably gorgeous.

"Santi, anxious of what?"

"I'm not sure."

Yes I am.

I'm scared of her leaving me, of her getting tired of me. I'm afraid of her leaving me up in that altar all alone with a broken heart and tainted memories of our past.

"Santi, I'm all yours. I'm not going anywhere." Sylvie assures me.

Of course she knows why I feel like this.

"I've moved to a foreign country for you, I've been taking Spanish classes, and I'm pregnant with your child. There's no going back now." She whispers to me.

I smile down at her just at the thought of all those accomplishments we've done together. From her moving here to helping her find a j— did she just say she's pregnant?

"I'm sorry, I think I've misinterpreted something you've said." I say, obviously having not heard her correctly.

"I'm sure you heard right." She grins up at me and I practically choke on my own breath of air.

"Pregnant?" I ask, and Sylvie gives me a nod, her happiness radiating.

She was pregnant?

Oh my god, I was going to be a dad.

This is why she had been sick, she wasn't thinking of leaving me. She was just helping create our child.

I tug her in close and press my lips to her. And I can't help but chuckle midway through the kiss. I part and bend down on my knees.

"Why didn't you tell me sooner?" I ask, pressing my hand on her stomach and looking up at her.

"I didn't want to make you even more nervous before the wedding, but since you seem to be taking my shine away with your own morning sickness I thought it was best to tell you that you wouldn't be leaving my life so easily."

I chuckle and grab ahold of her hips with my hands, bringing her closer to me.

My lips press a kiss against her stomach and her fingers find my scalp, as she combs them through my short hair.

My eyes rise once again to meet Sylvie's and I know I'm safe here with her.

I know our life together will be infinite.

A scream from behind breaks us apart and Santi is standing there shocked.

"Where are your blindfolds?" He asks, stomping over and grabbing me by the arm like a petulant child and pulling me up.

"I told you to keep your blind fold on." He scolds.

I want to be annoyed with him, but right now I can't even do that because I'm going to be a dad.

"What were you doing down there? Trying to get a sneak peek of what forever was going to taste like. Well I've got news for you buddy, my Sylvie is an honorable woman." He mutters walking over and bringing his arm around Sylvie to hold her close.

"Was he harassing you?" He asks, but Sylvie doesn't even look at him. She looks straight at me, waiting for me to break the news.

Javi seems to get the hint when he looks between Sylvie and I.

"What is it?" He finally asks.

"Javi." I say, the silence in the room is heavy and I know he's the one who's anxious now.

"Come on, say—"

"I'm going to be a dad." I say and Javi freezes in his spot as he looks between us.

"You're going to be parents?" He asks, looking between Sylvie and I.

We nod and Javi brings Sylvie into a crushing hug immediately.

"I'm going to be an uncle!" He cheers, unwrapping his arms around Sylvie and turning over to me, suffocating me with one of his embraces.

"You're going to be a dad!"

I embrace Javi back and watch as Sylvie's smile radiates, looking at Javi and I.

"Hey." Javi says, pulling back. "Do you think the harpist is also pregnant?"

I roll my eyes and shove him lightly.

"I'm sure it's just food poisoning, don't start any rumors."

Javi shrugs, "she's my cousin, I'm allowed to start drama."

I roll my eyes and look back at Sylvie who stands there taking our interaction in.

"I'll meet you at the aisle?" I ask.

"Front and center."

"I love you. " I say, as Javi begins pulling me out the door.

"We love you more." She says, placing her hand on her lower abdomen.

And I swear any nerves I've had dissipate and all that's left is the excitement of what our forever will be like.

284

Continue on and read chapter one of the
First book in the Fated Lovers Series

The Muse

Eliana Vazquez

chapter one

Jasmine

It's a waste of time to stop and think about the past. We're better off sticking the old memories in the back of our minds and refusing to look back at them. It's easier said than done when your mind keeps replaying intimate memories of someone that, after a while, only feels like some kind of dream. But reliving the heartbreak only reminds you of how real it all was.

They were so close within your arms, and then suddenly, they shattered into pieces, never to be contacted, seen, or loved again– or at least not by you.

But sometimes, life has a funny way of throwing it all back at your face even when you want nothing to do with it, like coincidentally coming across your ex-fiancé on Instagram once again engaged, but this time with a prestige heiress who seems to worry more about her photoshoots in front of her Ivy League school than about studying.

Well, maybe I'm just stretching it. I judge her only by her aesthetically pleasing social media profile. And I would be lying if I didn't say I was quite jealous that my ex moved on to someone younger and prettier than me.

Additionally, she's intelligent or well-off because the woman goes to Columbia. Here I am, working at a bookstore that pays me enough to get by with rent and groceries but too little to keep up with my social life. But somehow, I'm still stuck in the same place, rather than taking a chance and beginning to write my novel or owning the book café of my dreams.

Well, that had been a dream that was once ours, but he seemed to focus on another aspiration that didn't involve me. Regardless of my late-night Instagram searches, you can blame fate for having my ex-fiancé, Will, and his soon-to-be wife, Eloise, sitting across from me at a restaurant tonight.

"Can you stop hiding behind the menu?" my best friend Oren asks as he takes the menu out of my hands. I quickly pull it back, shielding myself from the enamors across our table.

"Oren, I am on a mission right now; I am trying my best not to be seen by my ex-fiancé and his fiancée. The last thing I need is for them to come over and pity me for still being in the same position I was in when he left me a year ago." I move the menu back up to cover my face, and though I can't see him, I can imagine Oren shaking his head as he chuckles.

"First of all, who the fuck cares? Second, how the fuck would he know if anything has changed in the last year? It's called lying. Tell him your book is about to be published and that he is currently looking at the new owner of *"Jaz's Book Café."* I roll my eyes and bring the menu down again, making sure that Oren gets a look at me, cringing at the made-up name for my dream café.

"I would never call it that," I remark. Oren only smirked as he looked back down at his menu.

Oren's vernacular has always been vulgar for as long as I can remember. His parents and little sister Phoebe had moved next door from New York into my little suburban town in New Jersey.

His parents were Greek immigrants who spoke little English but always showed so much love through embraces and meals. Of course, our friendship was tested when our mothers decided they wanted to play Cupid and tried to get us to date. But it had never been that way between Oren and me.

We became great friends, and nothing would ever come between us—not even when he left for Boston to pursue his education in the arts.

"Oren, you know I am not going to lie. Lies only lead to more lies, and I can't keep up. I can barely keep up with my rent, let alone entertain Will and his lover." Oren doesn't hesitate to show his distaste on his face.

"I told you to move in with me; we could turn my office into your room. You don't even need to worry about rent; just focus on writing your novel and looking at different locations you'd be interested in having your book café instead of continuing to work for that dickhead, Marvin."

Marvin Scott was, in fact,t a dickhead, but he did pay me enough to be able to afford rent. Of course, that meant that there wasn't much money to spare. I didn't have any other close friends besides Oren, who I live with, but I wouldn't intrude in his personal space even if he asked. I knew he liked his office and wouldn't take that away from him.

"You could also always share the bed with me; you know I don't mind sharing, Jaz," Oren smirks as he arches his eyebrow up.

I blush in embarrassment, reaching across the table to slap his arm with the menu. "Shut up, you idiot. Don't even mention that again." Oren only laughs at my discomfort. You'd think that after years of meaningless flirting and teasing, I wouldn't get so flustered by his comments.

"Am I so disgusting that you can't even fathom sharing a bed with me? You know we used to cuddle all the time as kids, right?" Oren teases.

Truthfully, I wasn't disgusted at all. Oren was an attractive man. His beautiful Greek attributes would have landed him a role in any Hollywood film about a Greek god. He was tall with a dark head of curls and light green eyes that stood out against his olive-toned skin. What made him even more attractive was that he was an artist of many sorts. The man could draw, paint, and sculpt and was a god behind the camera.

But we had never seen each other as more than friends and wouldn't have wanted to, either.

"You know I don't," I say, sipping my water. "You're very hand-some. But I would never want to intervene in your private life like that. Everyone needs their privacy, Oren. I know you love your office space; you keep all your work there. Where would you put all of that? You're a freelance artist; you need an office."

Oren shrugs and looks down at the menu. "Don't worry about it, Jaz. You know I'd do anything for you. Plus, it gets lonely alone in my New York City apartment."

Living in Jersey could get expensive, and if you were like Oren, living in New York, you would pay an arm and a leg. But that wasn't a problem for Oren. Despite coming from a lower-income household, he had become very successful in his career, which allowed him to enjoy the perks of living luxuriously.

Often, he's hired as a freelance photographer or videographer in another state or country. Sometimes, paying for a couple of months a year becomes silly.

"Oren, I said no already. Just drop it and pick out what you want to order. I'm starving." I mutter.

"Ugh, fine, just promise me you'll at least think about it, Jaz. I could use a roommate, and I plan on getting a cat and some plants, so I would need someone to take care of both when I'm away for work. That would just be a great advantage of having you around."

I knew Oren was bluffing, or at least about getting a cat, not so much about the plants. He was trying to throw anything that would make me say yes.

I rolled my eyes and finally set the menu down, only to have my eyes land on a tall, well-dressed William hovering over our table with his fiancé.

"Jasmine, I can't believe it. I knew it was you. You have not changed one bit."

Ouch.

I mean, I cut my hair; he could at least notice that.

William and I had been together for four years, during which time I maintained my long bundle of curls. During our relationship, we dedicated our weekends solely to ourselves. We'd lay in bed for hours after our intimate endeavors, and he'd brush his hands through my dark curls, which had made their way down my back. That was until I decided to chop them off after our breakup.

And as much as people liked to view it as some form of lashing out or trying something new after a breakup. I had just done it because he loved it. He would spend his weekends brushing his hands through my curls, and after he left, I wanted the length gone, too.

"Hello, Oren. It's good to see you, too. How's the art going?" William asks, facing Oren, who shows nothing but a blank expression, declaring his disinterest in my ex-fiancé.

William stood over Oren, but even if Oren had been standing up, William would still be a few inches taller than him. He was very well put together in his polo and black slacks, and his dark hair was slicked back, a strand falling over his face. But regardless of the loose strand, it didn't look out of place. But then again, William was never the type to look disheveled. It was one of the few reasons I felt we wouldn't work out right from the beginning.

William came from a wealthy family. His father owned a multi-millionaire tech company, and William was following in his footsteps. Meanwhile, I was just a girl still working at a bookstore, hoping to get by until I found the time to write my novel and hopefully get it picked up.

Even when I met his parents, they did very little to acknowledge me in William's life, even after he had proposed. I guess they had seen the breakup coming from a mile away.

"Great, as always, William," Oren states, setting down his menu, this time looking annoyed at William's presence.

By the whitening of her knuckles, I was guessing that Eloise seemed to be tightening her grip around William's arm to get his attention. But despite her strong grip, William didn't seem to be aware until the clearing of her throat reminded him of her presence.

"Oh, sorry," William says, turning to face Eloise. "Jasmine, Oren, this is my fiancé, Eloise Richardson." William states, bringing his arm around her waist and pulling her closer. It would be a lie if I said that Eloise was all photoshopped on her social media, but the woman looked just as beautiful.

She was tall and slender, to the point where you could confuse her for a model with her sleek blonde hair and the blue eyes that matched William's so perfectly. The blue silk dress she was wearing complimented them even more.

"Hello, it's very nice to meet you—especially you, Jasmine. William has told me so much about you. It's finally nice to meet the first woman who had my Will ready to tie the knot before meeting me." Eloise giggles.

I wasn't sure if I should be ecstatic that Will had me on his mind enough to speak about me to his gorgeous fiancé or annoyed that her voice seemed to somewhat taunt my past with William.

There was never a doubt in my mind that William wouldn't have ended up with someone like Eloise. She had been the heiress his parents had wanted him with initially.

"What brings you here?" Will asks.

"We are famished, William; why else is anyone at a restaurant?" Oren responds with an aggressive tone, which only insinuates the desire to have him away from our table.

"I know that, Oren, but Jasmine isn't a big fan of Thai," William states.

"No, she isn't a fan of Pad Thai, but she loves everything else on the menu, especially pho." Oren remarks.

"Did I hear you say fiancé before, William? Congratulations to both of you. You must be excited." I cut in to diminish any argument between the two men.

Oren was never a big fan of William, but he tolerated him because I had asked him to. That was until he decided to break up with me a couple of months after our engagement. Since Oren made it his duty to be William's biggest hater, the fact that he hadn't thrown himself out of his chair to attack William showed a lot of self-restraint. "Yes, look at the ring; isn't it so precious?" Eloise asks, extending her hand towards my eyes to show the enormous rock sitting delicately on her finger. It was larger than my own, but not that size mattered at all; it was just enormous. I had seen them in the pictures, but I assumed Photoshop had made them stand out even more than usual. Obviously, I stood corrected.

"It's very gorgeous, Eloise. Again, congratulations." I say, looking down at my own finger, which William's engagement ring had once hugged. Oren brings his hand over to my own and grips it gently. I look up and see his little menacing smile, which means he has something up his sleeve.

"Honestly, where are my manners? Congratulations to both of you. It seems like both you two and Jaz and I have new doors opening up for us." Oren states, tightening his hold on my hand.

"You two are engaged as well?!" Eloise exclaims in excitement while William's face pales right before me.

"God, no, well, at least not yet, but we are currently moving in together. We want to test the waters before committing to living together for life." Oren says nonchalantly.

If there was ever a moment in which I wanted to strangle Oren, this would be that very moment. Oren always liked making up little white lies or pranks, but this was stupid and too big of a lie.

"Since when– how long, wait, you guys are dating?" William asked, a shocked expression on his face. As terrible as it might be to admit, it brought me some pleasure knowing that William seemed to care.

"William, you always knew that Jaz and I had a connection. I mean, we've been friends for sixteen years. I guess when you left, everything seemed to come together, and one thing led to another, and now, we are madly in love." Oren gives him a sly grin. I swear I could see William's jaw tighten at the smug look on Oren's face.

Oren was enjoying this too much, and it was time to end this conversation.

"Well, congratulations to both of you! Will you be having a housewarming party?" Eloise asks cheerfully. Now that Oren and I are madly in love, there is no need to be so nasty towards us anymore.

But the answer was going to be no. The last thing I needed was for this to become a theatrical play.

"We are. This upcoming Saturday. You two are welcome to come. William, you have the same number, don't you? We will just send you our address, and you two are welcome to come if you'd like." Oren says.

I kicked his shin from under the table, causing him to jolt slightly. He looked at me and rolled his eyes as if I were being dramatic. He was taking this lie out of hand and needed to stop.

William opens his mouth to respond, but Eloise quickly beats him to it.

"We would love to be there, right, William?" Eloise asks, focusing her gaze on William.

"Yeah, why not? Jasmine, you can send me the address and time, and we will definitely make it there," William says, but his jaw tightens, indicating his irritation with the whole situation.

Eloise squeals in excitement before clapping her hands. "Yay! This is so exciting. I cannot wait to see you guys this Saturday. It was so nice meeting you two. But we should be returning to our table and leaving you so you can enjoy your dinner."

"Yes, it was great meeting you, Eloise, and it was great seeing you, William." Oren murmurs before they both turn around and walk back to their table. I nudged Oren again from under the table to have him look back at me.

"What the fuck was that, Oren?" I yell in a whispered tone.

"Whatever do you mean, my love?" He teases.

"You know what the fuck I mean. Why would you even say that? Why would you let your lie go that far?" I fall back onto my seat, crossing my arms over my chest, glancing around the entire restaurant, too annoyed with Oren to look back over at him.

"Jaz, there isn't much of a lie. You were already going to move in with me. I only added in a little spice by saying we were lovers." I turn my head back towards Oren and glare at him.

"But that's the thing; I am not moving in with you. I already have an apartment." I reiterate.

It was always typical of Oren to try to help me however he could, but I didn't need his help. I am doing just fine on my own.

"Well, we'll have to let your landlord know as soon as possible that you are leaving, so we should also start inviting a couple more people to the housewarming party. If it's just us four, it'll be awkward." Oren rambles as he calls the waiter to take our order.

"Oren, I am not moving in with you," I utter, hoping that he will listen and stop this nonsense this time.

"Fine, then you can text William and tell him that it was all a lie and that we were just trying to make him jealous." Oren's stare battles my own from across the table, and even though there's chatter among us, I can only hear the silence between us. I clench my hands around the table's cloth before letting go and letting out a sigh of frustration.

Oren knew I would rather play this game with him than admit to William that I had only agreed to this lie. I enjoyed seeing William's blank expression when he discovered I was with Oren.

"Fine, but I am paying half the rent, and you're paying for the moving company." I snap.

"Yes, love, don't you worry about anything. I've got this under control."

I hope he did because something told me we would get into a bigger mess than we were already in.

acknowledgments

Thank you to my chicas, Lila and Katya, who, when I told them I would be putting this book on hold, encouraged me to write it instead.

To my now fiancé, Farhan, thank you for a lovely few days in Madrid. You make every city feel like the city of love.

Jenny — Thank you for loving Javi as much as I do and for being my Marlene. You are my biggest cheerleader, and like Miley Cyrus once said when introducing her little sister Noah Cyrus on stage, "I want to be her when I grow up."

A big Thanks to Yenthe, who did a phenomenal job bringing my book cover to life. When I first came to her with the watercolor idea, she let me know that it might not be exactly what I wanted, and I have to say she was right. It surpassed my expectations. Thank you for putting so much time into a book cover that means so much to me and these characters.

Of course, I can't forget to thank the Ink and Velvet Designs team. Specifically, Samantha, who was in communication with me throughout the process, and Mel, the artist who brought my characters to life.

And lastly, to all my readers. Thank you so much for choosing this book and reading it until the end. I hope I've captivated you enough to keep reading my books. There's so much more to come, and I am just getting started, so feel free to stick around so you can gloat and say that you were there from the start.

about the author

Eliana Vazquez is a self-published author from Kearny, New Jersey. She graduated from the University of New Haven, where she majored in communications with a concentration in Film and Media Production. When she's not at her desk writing, you can find her enabling her coffee addiction and buying more books than she could ever read.

www.ingramcontent.com/pod-product-compliance
Lightning Source LLC
Chambersburg PA
CBHW031140160726
47991CB00004B/1509